Favorite Camper

Copyright © 2009 Jenifer Brady
All rights reserved.
ISBN: 1-4392-2750-0
ISBN-13: 978-1439227503

Visit www.booksurge.com to order additional copies.

Favorite Camper
Abby's Camp Days

Jenifer Brady

2009

Favorite Camper

For Alan and Nancy,
who gave me camp

Thank you to Andy Larsen for the back cover photo.

But seek first his kingdom and his righteousness, and all these things will be given to you as well.
Matthew 6: 33

CHAPTER ONE

The Saddest Day at Church Ever

I had never gone to a funeral until this summer. I didn't even really know what they were. The only time I'd seen a funeral was on my best friend Carin's mom's soap opera, and I don't think it was very realistic because in the middle of it, the guy who was supposed to be dead walked in and three women fainted. Then, after the commercial, the guy said he was some long-lost twin brother of the man who had died.

Since that was the only funeral I'd ever seen, I didn't really know what to expect when I went to a real one. My dad was the one who had to go up front and talk about the person who had died. That's because he's a minister. I'm used to seeing him behind the pulpit at church, but usually it's for normal stuff like Sunday sermons.

I had never felt so rotten at church before.

It's a good thing I don't think church is boring because I'm a PK, so I have to do church things a lot. PK means preacher's kid. We go to two churches every week, which is what happens when a minister has a two-point charge. That might sound incredibly dull, but it's not too bad. The people are different at each church, and so are the churches. One was built in 1896 and looks like a stone castle. The other is newer and white inside and smells like paint. Lots of old people go to the castle church, and people with little kids go to the new one. The castle church has a choir that sings "How Great Thou Art" and "Amazing Grace" to the hum of an organ, and the new church has a praise band with a loud acoustic guitar and drums.

We go to Sunday school at one church and Wednesday night Bible study at the other. We also have potlucks and Vacation Bible School and other things.

The one thing I'd never done in church before was cry. That funeral took care of that. I cried so much that I ran out of tissues and had to use my hand towards the end of the service, which, for the record, is pretty gross.

Before this, the only person I ever knew who died was Puffy, and she doesn't count because she was actually a cat. She was my sister's cat, but we loved her so much, she was like a person.

Scott was the first person who I actually knew who died. I met him last summer at camp where he was a counselor and I was a camper. He died because he hit a tree with his car when he swerved for a deer in the road.

It's weird to know someone who died. I never knew anybody who died before.

The whole two days before the funeral, my dad walked around our house muttering things about how Scott was too young to die. I had always thought of him as old. He was twenty-one, and compared to ten, twenty-one is pretty old. He had finished high school and was in college. And he had a girlfriend.

My dad is forty-three years old, so compared to that, twenty-one must seem young.

We had to drive a long way to get to the church because it wasn't one of our regular churches. It was in the U.P. (Upper Peninsula of Michigan) kind of by where Camp Spirit is (but not close enough that we actually got to go to camp). We sat in a pew like it was a regular day at church, only it wasn't. Lots of people wore black, but not everybody. And nobody wore a hat with a black thing that covered their face like all the women on Mrs. Morgan's soap opera.

I thought that we were going to stand in the cemetery and throw flowers into a big hole while somebody lowered the casket into the ground like they did on that television funeral, but we didn't do that. My dad and Scott's family went to the cemetery later, but nobody else got to go there.

Dad stood up front and talked about some things, and Scott's brother read a Bible verse. Some people I didn't know sang. The bulletin had a picture of a cabin in the woods on it. In the corner it said that Scott had drawn it. Scott was a great artist. Last year at camp, he helped me with my craft project, and I helped him with his window-painting project.

Those parts of the funeral weren't utterly heartbreaking, only sad. At the end, my dad said that other people could say something about Scott if they wished. That was when we got to the utterly heartbreaking part. Scott's cousin, Ben, went right up to the microphone and talked for a long time. I know Ben from camp because he's one of the lifeguards. I didn't know they were cousins until the funeral because they aren't the kind of cousins who have the same last name.

Then some people I didn't know stood up in their pews and said things about Scott. One was his third grade teacher, one was his neighbor, and one was his girlfriend's mother. Those talks only made a few tears drip down my face.

Somebody stood up behind me, and I turned around as he spoke.

"My name is Mark Chandler, and I knew Scott from Camp Spirit," the guy said. "He was one of the best counselors I've ever known. He had a kind spirit and a gentle heart. He was the person who knew exactly which campers needed a friend."

That was when I really started to cry, and my big sister Angela put her arm around me. Last summer, I was one of those campers who had needed a friend. My whole life, I've been used to going to camp as a dean's kid. My dad isn't just a minister; he's a camp dean, too. He and his friend Rick are in charge during the junior high camp week. They find counselors and plan activities for the campers. When you're a dean, your family gets to go to camp with you and hang out and do whatever they want.

Then I went to elementary camp as a camper. My dad was not the dean. A minister named Dean Ron and another guy named Dean Jamie were. It was very different being a camper than it was being a dean's kid. There were all kinds of rules, and I had to stay with the same people all day long, and I wasn't allowed to swim outside of the buoys, and I didn't know anyone except for Carin, and the cook yelled at me, and I had to use the boys' bathroom (That is a very long story and actually not as horrible as it sounds, just weird.)

I had pretty much decided not to come back to elementary camp when Scott and I had a long talk. He also helped me with my craft project. It was a Noah's Ark model, and my animals looked messed up. But Scott helped me fix them, and he convinced me that elementary camp was okay. After that, I had a fantastic time at camp.

I even gave Scott one of the animals he had helped me make. So far, my sister has not asked me why the Noah's Ark model I gave her only has one elephant in it but two of every other animal. I wonder what will happen to the elephant now. Did he give it away to someone in his will?

Once this old lady died, and our church got a bunch of money. Mom told me that in her will, she had said that she wanted church to get the money. I wonder if Scott had a will. I don't have one, but I'm only ten.

I think I would give most of my stuff to my sister or to my parents. Except for my pink stretch pants. I'd give those to my best friend Carin because she really likes them, although I don't know if they would fit her too well because she's several inches taller than me.

I wanted to be one of those people who stood up and said things about Scott. I wanted to say, "My name is Abby, and I knew Scott from camp. He wasn't my group's counselor, but he helped me when I was feeling sad, and if I hadn't met him, I probably would have had a very bad week and would not be going back to camp later this summer."

Talking in front of people I don't know freaks me out though, so I didn't say anything. I prayed it instead, so God could know what I felt. Maybe I could write a letter and send it to Scott's parents and his brother. That would be easier than standing up in front of everybody.

After the funeral, six people wearing suits picked up the casket and walked out of the church. One was my dad, and one was Scott's dad. I know that because he was sitting next to a lady who I think was Scott's mom and the guy I know was his brother Steve. Steve and Ben also carried the casket. Ben waved at me just a little without taking his hand entirely off of the casket as he passed our pew. I didn't know the other two people carrying it, but they sort of looked like Ben, so I bet they were more cousins.

Then we went downstairs and had a potluck. It wasn't like any potluck I'd ever seen though. Some old ladies set out all of the food, but I think they made the food there at church instead of bringing it from home. Nobody ran around or hid under the tables. There weren't very many kids there. A couple with a baby and two girls about my age sat with Ben. I think they were related to him. There was one boy who seemed a little bit older than me with another group of people, and three really little kids at another table. That was it. Everybody else there was an adult.

People talked, but they were a lot calmer and quieter than the people at my church are during potlucks, and nobody said anything about making a quilt for the bazaar or about what they had learned in Sunday school. I ate one cookie and half of a brownie. The other desserts looked good, and I thought about trying one of everything like my sister and I usually do at potlucks, but I didn't think I was supposed to do that at a funeral.

They had a big collage set on a table that had lots of pictures of Scott and some of the people who were at the funeral on it. After we ate, Mom, Angela, and I looked at it. Those pictures made me want to cry again. I wanted to look at the real Scott, not just pictures, but when we had arrived at the church that morning, the casket was shut and had a big thing of flowers on top of it, and nobody opened it the entire time. So all I got to see of him was a bunch of pictures taped to a blue board.

***

I took this little, cream-colored card that had Scott's name on it from a pile by the picture collage. I studied it in the car on the way home. It said "Scott Demas Koski" on the top and had his birthday and the day he died underneath. Then it said the name of the church where we had the funeral, the name of the cemetery where he was buried, and "Rev. Robert Riley, officiating." On the other side of the card, it said, "God grant me the serenity to accept the things I cannot change, courage to change the things I can, and wisdom to know the difference."

I looked at the card until my eyes got tears in them and dried three different times. I read the words and studied the faint pattern in the cream color until it got so dark outside that I couldn't see the writing very well anymore. I planned to put it in my Bible for a bookmark so I'd see it every day. Well, probably not every day. I *should* read my Bible every day, but I don't. Maybe I'd try harder to remember now that I knew I'd see Scott's card every time I opened my Bible.

I looked out the window into darkness and the faint outline of trees, and I felt tired and more depressed than I had on the ride to the church. The ride home to Wisconsin felt longer and lonelier. I started thinking about another long car ride to the U.P.—the drive to camp.

I hadn't felt nervous all spring about going to my second year of elementary camp until my dad told me what happened to Scott. What if I had a bad time at camp again? Who would help me? I knew there were lots of other counselors, but nobody helped me last year except Scott.

I felt bad for all of the new campers. They didn't get to know him.

How could I be thinking about campers I didn't even know? I had enough to feel bad about after losing a friend. Out of everyone there at that funeral today, I think I felt the saddest. I think it's because of the gift of compassion. At least, that's what my dad calls it.

When I had called Carin to tell her what had happened, she had said in a quiet voice, "That's awful. He was going to teach me how to make a gimp cross." Then there was this big pause and she asked, "What are you wearing to the funeral?"

That's a normal response, to feel sad or "awful" as she put it, to think about what you have personally lost, and then move on. I don't know that most people would jump right to funeral fashions, but hey, that's Car.

What did I do after I hung up the phone? I lay there on my bed and looked up at the ceiling and thought. I thought about Scott and replayed every memory I had of him in my mind, every time I talked to him or saw him kicking a soccer ball or laughing with a friend. I thought about how much I would miss him, and I wondered about the car accident and if he had died right away or if he had had a lot of pain, and that made me feel even worse, the thought of him lying hurt in the hospital.

Then I thought about Steve. I didn't know Steve that well because he hadn't been my group's counselor, but he was my counselor's friend and Scott's brother, so I got to know him well enough to know that he was nice and the sort of person who would be crushed that his brother had died. That made me think about Scott's parents, who I didn't know at all. I made up what they looked like in my head, which I knew now wasn't even close after seeing the real people.

I thought about what it would feel like if my sister Angela died.

I wondered if Steve and Scott were like Angela and me or Carin and Joey. Joey is Car's seven-year-old brother, but just about the only things they do together are eat breakfast and dinner and ride the bus to school. They don't even sit by each other on the bus. Mostly Carin complains about what a pest Joey is, and Joey whines about Car not letting him play with her.

Angela is my best friend in a way. Carin is my real best friend when I talk about who I do the most things with and the person I would pick first if I were a captain in gym class. I don't see Angela as much as I see Car because she's busy with swim team and high school homework and going out with her friends. I don't think she knows stuff like what my favorite movie is and what playground equipment I run to first at recess, but I tell her other things. Carin knows most of my secrets, but the important secrets that I don't want anybody else ever to know are the kinds of secrets I tell Angela instead of Car. My sister and I always double-pinky-swear on every secret. She tells me secrets, too, like what boy she likes and who on her swim team annoys her.

Carin tries to keep secrets, but sometimes she can and sometimes she can't. I know that Angela will never ever, ever tell one of my secrets to anybody, not even if she got a boyfriend who she told everything else to. You know that feeling you get when you tell somebody something and then you realize about five seconds later what a mess you would be in if that person ever mentioned it to somebody else? Sometimes I get that feeling when I tell Carin a secret, but I never think twice about it when I tell my sister.

Angela and I are friends, not just people who happen to share the same parents. I know it's mean, but I kind of hoped that Scott and Steve were more like Carin and Joey. It would be easier for Steve that way. I think that if Joey died, Car would, of course, be sad, but it's not like her whole life would change. There would be one less seat at dinner, and she wouldn't climb the school bus steps in front of him. If Angela died, I don't know who I would tell my really important secrets to anymore.

I lay on my bed and felt horrible until someone knocked on my door. I couldn't even muster up the energy to say, "Come in," even when the knock got louder. Finally Angela just walked in. She sat next to me for a while and rubbed my back as I cried, but I didn't start to feel better until she showed me the reason she had come to my room. She had bought these glow-in-the-dark star stickers to put on her ceiling, and she wanted to give me the leftovers.

We decorated my whole ceiling and even looked on the chart on the back of the package that showed you how to arrange the stars in the shapes of real constellations. I felt better for a while until it was time to go to sleep and I lay there staring at the ceiling and the stars.

I know that heaven isn't really in space, like hiding behind a star or something, but it's hard to imagine where it really is, so I think of God when I look at the stars. Every night since I put those up, I've thought about Scott and how he's up in the stars somewhere.

I wish I were brave like Carin. I wish I didn't cry so much and think about so many awful things like how Scott's parents must feel. Whenever I cry about something that happens to somebody else, my dad pats my shoulder and says with a smile, "You have the gift of compassion, Abby Leah." He says it like it's a good thing, but sometimes I don't see what's so good about it. It just makes me feel extra miserable.

CHAPTER TWO

Back at Camp

My dad and Carin's mom drove us to camp in the Morgans' car. Carin's dad had to do an emergency root canal (that's an operation on someone's teeth that sounds very, very painful), and my mom was in charge of church instead of Dad because it was United Methodist Women's Sunday when the women ran church, so Dad and Mrs. Morgan ended up bringing us. Car's little brother Joey complained the entire way because he had to sit between us in the back seat. We couldn't take our mini-van because it was at the shop getting an oil leak fixed.

Angela waved at us when Mrs. Morgan backed the car out of our driveway. I waved back at her and tried successfully not to cry. I miss my sister when I have to be at camp without her. Junior high camp is the best because Angela and I go with Mom and Dad, and we get to hang out and do whatever we want. Elementary camp is fun, but it's kind of a bummer because I don't get to do things with my sister.

We didn't get to camp early this year. Last year, my mom made us leave way too early, and we were almost the first people there. Carin wasn't thrilled with that because she likes to make cool entrances.

Car and I have been best friends since first grade. We used to look pretty similar when we were younger. We were the same height, and we both had long hair. I've stayed the same though, and Carin has changed. She cut her red hair a couple of years ago and has kept the shoulder-length style. My brown hair is still long. Carin has grown a lot the last couple of years, so she's now much taller than I am.

We've never been alike in personality. I'm loud and outgoing with my friends and family, but with strangers or even people I don't know that well, I am very, very shy. Nobody has ever called Carin shy. She could go into a room full of one thousand people she's never met before and come out with fifty new friends in ten minutes. She is very dramatic and wants to be an actress when she grows up. I don't know what I want to be quite yet, but I know it will not involve a job where I have to stand up in front of a crowd of people.

I was just as excited as Carin was as her mom pulled the car into camp, but I didn't wiggle around as much as she did. There were cars, trucks, mini-vans, campers, and even a motorcycle parked all over the place. Campers, family members, and counselors went into and came out of the dining hall and headed for cabins on all sides of camp.

Last year, I got to elementary camp and found out that none of the people I knew from junior high camp were there. They were all strangers except for a few camp staff members who work at camp all summer. What if that happened again? Maybe I should have stayed at home this year. I had gotten to go to junior high camp already, after all. One week of camp was enough for one summer, right?

"Abby, look over by the canteen!" Carin said. It was more of a squeal than a sentence.

I unbuckled my seatbelt so I could turn around and check out the canteen, and there, three cars behind us in the circle of drivers waiting for the line of cars to move, was Dane, one of our counselors from last year. Carin waved at him wildly and almost jabbed Joey in the eye with her elbow. Dane waved back a two-fingered salute, taking one hand off the steering wheel, and I saw that his sister Rachel was in the passenger's seat. She was in our cabin last year, and she's fun to hang out with, especially when she eats chocolate before bedtime and tells hilarious stories about people in her family who annoy her.

"Maybe Rachel will be in our cabin again," I said as Mrs. Morgan inched the car towards the dining hall.

"Maybe Dane will be our counselor again," Carin said, running her fingers through her hair.

Car had been so irritating last year. She had a big crush on Dane, and she actually thought that he would want to go out with her, even though he was seventeen and she was nine. All week long, she sat by him at every meal and hung out with him more than she hung out with me, her best friend (who brought her to camp in the first place).

I hope she doesn't repeat that nonsense this year. She's entirely too boy-crazy...and getting worse! At school this year she made fourteen valentines for this guy named Jay Matthews. He was the guy she had a crush on in February.

I don't know why she likes boys so much. I sure don't like them yet. I don't think they're gross or anything, but I don't want to make valentines for them. I only made valentines for the ten boys in our class because we were supposed to make one for everybody.

I liked Dane a lot, too, but not as a boy. I liked him as a counselor and a friend. Last year, he had this girlfriend named Stacey. Hopefully Stacey will be at camp again this week and she will still be his girlfriend. Then maybe Carin will spend her time with me instead of with him. Car did not like Stacey much, mostly because of Dane but also because of a battle over eating peanut butter crackers at game night. We might have a problem if Stacey ends up being our counselor this year.

We all got out of the car and walked into the dining hall. As we crunched our way over pebbles to the door, a kid with messy brown hair and a missing tooth ran out of the dining hall screaming and waving his arms around. He wasn't screaming like there was something wrong; it seemed like the hyper kid was yelling just for the fun of making noise.

Dad opened the door, and we walked up to the registration table. The kid ran back inside, pushed me into Carin, and made a beeline for something under the table. "Hey, a marble!" He immediately popped it into his mouth, and the man who was with him grabbed his arm and dragged him out from underneath the table, pleading with him to spit the marble out.

That kid's counselor was going to have an interesting week.

This time I knew the man sitting at the registration table. His name was Dean Ron. He's a minister, and he was one of the deans last year. I did not know the other two people helping him with registration. Last year, we met Dane and our other counselor Eva during registration.

A boy and girl who looked like they were in college were helping Dean Ron with everyone's paperwork. The girl had jet-black hair and wore a lot of makeup. The guy had brown hair and smiled a lot more than the girl.

"Hi," Carin was saying to the guy. "My name is Carin Alexandra Morgan. What's yours?"

I bet she thought he was cute. Last year, Carin got her crush on Dane as soon as she met him in the registration line. Hopefully she did not have a crush on this other guy, too. I really did not want to put up with that again this year.

"My name's Bruce," he said.

"Hello, girls," Dean Ron said. "I'm glad you're back this year." Wow! The dean remembered us. Usually, the dean only remembered you if he really liked you or if you got in a lot of trouble the year before. I bet Dean Ron will remember Crazy Marble Eater next summer.

"What cabin are we in?" Carin asked.

She leaned over the table and almost bumped heads with Bruce. Bruce leaned back and gave her a funny look.

"I think that Noelle has that list. I have the list of who wants a camp picture."

"Ooh, what cabin are we in?" Car asked the girl counselor, inching closer until she was hovering over her. "Is it Bunny Cabin again?"

"Hold your horses," the counselor snapped. "I have to find it."

She looked at her list for a minute, and I could tell that Car was getting antsier and antsier by the way she bounced up and down.

"Chipmunk Cabin," the counselor finally announced.

Yea! We were no longer in Bunny Cabin, the cabin for the younger kids. That's the closest cabin to the bathroom so the little kids can make it in time. We were not the youngest campers this week. We were fifth graders now.

Last year, I was very shy during registration. I pretty much said three words, and Dane, Eva, and Dean Ron probably thought I was a big dork before they got to know me better. I had decided in the car (during the long drive, sometime after we had eaten fast food lunch and before I saw the sign to Nature Mountain, the camp across the lake) that I would not be shy this year. I wanted to be more outgoing like Carin and funny like Rachel and cool like my sister. Not just nice and boring anymore.

So, even though talking to people I don't know is usually about the last thing I want to do, I opened my mouth and asked, "Is Eva our counselor again?"

"Who's Eva?" Noelle asked.

How could she not know who Eva was? Didn't the counselors have orientation for this camp the day before camp started like my dad and his co-dean have for junior high camp?

"Is Dane our day group counselor?" Carin asked.

"No," Noelle said. I hoped she wasn't our counselor because the way she glared at Car from behind her black eyelinered eyes every time Car asked a question made me think she probably wasn't much fun.

Carin looked at Bruce and smiled. "Are *you* our other counselor?"

"I don't think so," he said. Bruce should feel very lucky that we weren't his campers. If we were, Car would probably bug him all week like she did with Dane last year.

"Your cabin counselors are Katherine and Brenda," Dean Ron said, looking over Noelle's shoulder at the list.

Oh, good. I knew Brenda from last year. I didn't know her well, but I knew who she was at least. That was better than not knowing somebody at all. I did not know Katherine.

"And your day group counselor is Steve," Noelle said.

Another person I knew. This was going to be a lot easier than last year. Nothing to worry about.

Then I walked to the next table...

The Scary Nurse! She's this old lady who wears black and has a cauldron in her cabin. Well, the cauldron is probably just a bucket of laundry soap, but you never know. My friend R.J. used to think she was a witch because she has a wart on the end of her nose and smells funny. Last summer at junior high camp, I finally got R.J. to admit that he didn't think she was a witch anymore after I told him she took communion just like all the other Christians at this camp.

"Why, hello Abigail and Karen," she said.

Abigail and Karen were not our names, but Car and I didn't correct her. We just handed her our medical forms and got out of line as quickly as we could.

My dad stood there and talked to her. He knows The Scary Nurse from junior high camp because she's the nurse there, too, sometimes. He put his hands on the table and leaned over as they talked about how many campers had signed up for the week.

"Dad, hurry up," I said, unable to stand the fact that we were finally at camp but still stuck in the registration line. "We want to go to the cabin and unpack."

"Yeah, Pastor Bob," Carin helped. "I want to get a top bunk before they're all taken."

Dad said goodbye to The Scary Nurse, and we walked out to the car. Carin's mom drove us up the hill to Chipmunk Cabin. I meant to help Dad with the luggage, but as soon as we were in front of the cabin, I got really excited. I was at camp!

I grabbed my duffle bag out of the trunk and ran up the porch and into the cabin. Carin followed me, carrying her backpack and pillow. There were four people in our cabin already, and I only knew one of them, the counselor Brenda. A girl who had long brown hair like mine sat on a bottom bunk, and a tall girl with a blond ponytail was setting up her sleeping bag on a top bunk.

"Guess what?" Carin yelled. I don't know why she was yelling. The cabin wasn't very big. We could all hear her just fine. "Dane Cunningham is here. I saw him at the canteen! He was our counselor last year, and he is really cute."

I don't know why she would say something like that to a bunch of people we didn't know. I would never, ever, ever tell anybody who I had a crush on, unless the person I was telling was a very good friend, like Car.

Car threw her stuff on a top bunk. "Abby, you can share with me."

I agreed and put the duffle bag on the bed underneath Car's. A girl who looked about the same age as my sister (seventeen) was sitting on the bunk next to mine. She must've been Katherine, the other counselor.

The door opened, and my dad and Mrs. Morgan walked in followed by Joey, who looked a little intimidated about entering a girls-only zone. Dad was carrying the rest of our stuff and looked like a sleeping bag and pillow monster. You couldn't even see his face until he put all of the suitcases and bedding down.

"Thanks for the help, girls," he teased.

"Sorry, Dad," I said. "I was too excited to wait."

"Thanks for bringing my things in, Pastor Bob," Carin said.

"Hello, Bob," Brenda said, crossing the cabin to us.

My dad smiled and hugged her. "Brenda! I haven't seen you for years."

"I haven't counseled junior high camp for a while. I'd like to get back into it, but there just aren't enough weeks in the summer."

"Tell me about it," Dad said.

We said goodbye to Dad, Mrs. Morgan, and Joey. When I hugged my dad, I realized that I didn't want him to leave. I was excited to be at camp, but it's a little scary watching your dad walk down the steps of your cabin to the car, knowing that you won't see him again for a whole week.

Last year, I felt homesick, but I didn't admit that to anybody in my cabin, not even Carin. I told Scott. I talked with him about how I wasn't having a good week and told him everything I didn't like about elementary camp.

Who would I talk to this year if I got homesick? Maybe I would tell Carin or Dane.

CHAPTER THREE

Freezing Cold Swim Test

Our counselor wasn't Eva, but she sure looked like her. She *was* the girl I guessed was the other counselor in our cabin. She was about the same height as Eva, and she was pretty and had blond hair almost the exact same shade as Eva's. She was younger than Eva, though. She was sixteen and in high school. She also did not have bright white teeth like Eva. She had normal teeth.

I don't think she knew much about being a counselor because during cabin introductions, she made us tell everyone how many brothers and sisters we had and *three* interesting things about ourselves. It's hard enough to think about two interesting things about myself (like Eva made us do last year), much less three. And I was planning on using the fact that I had an older sister for one of the things about me.

I had to think pretty fast to come up with something. I said that I had been going to camp since I was a baby, I was in gymnastics classes, and that swimming was my favorite part of camp. Carin said that her favorite colors were hot pink and purple, she wanted to be a famous singer or a movie star when she grew up, and that if she could go anywhere in the world she would go to Paris.

I wish I could think of good stuff like that.

The other girl in our group was named Teresa, and she was an only child. Her three things about herself were that she had never been to camp before, her favorite food was spaghetti, and she liked sports. We had a very small group this year. Brenda told us that there were a lot less campers signed up for camp this week than usual for some reason.

Our counselor said that her name was Katherine, or we could call her Kate if we wanted to because that was her nickname at camp. She said that she had an older brother named Mark who used to be a counselor here. She was going to be a junior in high school, liked to read and watch movies, and had a pet dog named Woofie, which I thought was not a very creative name for a dog.

The three girls in Brenda's group were named Lindsay, Jennie, and Autumn. I was way excited that Lindsay was in the cabin with us. She was in our cabin last year, and we got to be pretty good friends. We even wrote to each other a couple of times throughout the year. Lindsay is very cool, and she's shy, just like me. Something you would never guess about Lindsay is that she plays hockey. I don't know how such a shy person plays an aggressive sport like that, but she does. She even sent me a picture of herself dressed in her hockey uniform.

The bad thing was that she was in our cabin but *not* in our day group. The two counselors in the cabin would split up into two groups during the day. Carin, Teresa, and I were going to do all of our activities like swimming and going on hikes with Kate. Brenda would have the other girls in her group during the day. I wished Lindsay was in our group. At least she was in the same cabin as we were. Rachel, Cindy, and Samantha from last summer weren't even in our cabin. We'd never get to see them probably.

I didn't want a new counselor; I wanted Eva. Kate seemed okay, but Eva was really, really nice. She had helped me when I fell and scraped up my hands and knees. I was very embarrassed, but Eva told me a story about how when she was an elementary camper, the lifeguard had to rescue her during swim time and she hadn't put her buddy tag on the board, so she got in trouble by both the lifeguard and her counselor. Her story had made me feel much less embarrassed.

I like when things stay the same. It's a lot easier that way.

***

I stood waist-deep in the lake, shivering. I knew it wasn't the weather's fault because weather didn't have a brain and couldn't know that it was swim test afternoon, but it could have been a little more cooperative for us. Swimming at camp in the sunshine is great, but it stinks when it's cold and windy.

It was nice to be able to do something with Lindsay and the rest of Brenda's campers, but I wished it were something better than freezing while swimming out to the buoys and back. I don't know how the temperature had gone from sweaty to chilly in two hours, but it had. That's the Upper Peninsula for you. They have even weirder weather here than we do in Wisconsin.

"Why do we have to take a swim test?" Carin asked. She had her arms wrapped around herself and shivered even harder than I did. "It's freezing."

"Can't they look at the paper from last year and see that we already passed?" I agreed. "You can't really forget how to swim."

"That would be better than freezing to death," Lindsay said. She bounced up and down in the water, and her blond curls bounced with her.

Taking a swim test in this lake was pretty pointless because the tiny area we're allowed to swim in is so low that it doesn't even come up to my neck in the very deepest part.

"Ready?" one of the lifeguards yelled from the dock.

The six of us campers nodded as we shivered. I didn't know this lifeguard. He was tall and had dark hair. Eva's husband Jason and my friend Ben were the lifeguards last year. I wondered where they were.

"All you have to do is swim to the far buoys and back," the lifeguard said. "Cord is out on the raft if you need any help." Like we'd need help in this shallow lake.

I looked at the raft. Cord, the other lifeguard, waved at us. He had been the maintenance guy last summer. Cord looked so far away on that raft. Usually, the swimming area seems small, but the thought of having to make it all the way to the end in order to swim in the "deep" area all week in such freezing cold water made the buoy lines suddenly seem three miles apart.

"Ready, set, go!"

We started moving, walking at first, then dropping under to our shoulders and swimming. I'm a decent swimmer, but my arms didn't move as well as they usually do because they were so cold. On the way to the buoys, my arms felt icy every time I pushed them under the water, but by the time we were swimming back, my body was used to the water and it didn't seem cold...until I got out.

When I got out of the water, I ran for my towel and wrapped it around myself tightly. One other group had arrived at the beach already. I was glad that they were the only ones who saw us swim. Last year, a whole bunch of people watched us, and it's not fun to have to do your swim test with everyone staring at you.

I put my sandals on right away, even though my feet were full of sand. It was too cold to worry about washing my feet off. Cord jumped off the raft and swam to shore. The other lifeguard walked down the dock to the sand. We dried off as best as we could and met the lifeguards at the buddy board. Cord had big goose bumps on his arms from having to swim, like the rest of us, but the other lifeguard looked warm in his navy blue sweatshirt.

The buddy board is this big wooden thing with hooks on it. On one side, probably a hundred of those metal washer things with numbers on them hang on hooks. The other side says "swimmers," "non-swimmers," and "boaters." When we're at the beach, we have to take our buddy tag (the metal washer) from the one side and put it on the other side next to our buddy's so the lifeguards know where we are at all times.

When all six shivering girls from my cabin had gathered around the lifeguards, Cord told us the beach rules like no dunking people under and how it was important to put your buddy tag on the board and know who your buddy is. That's easy; Carin is always my buddy.

"My name is Cord, and I'm the head lifeguard this year. This is Tony." The other lifeguard looked up from his clipboard and raised one of his hands in a wave. "He's the aquatic observer. You all passed the swim test, so Tony's going to tell you what number you are."

Cord went around to the other side of the buddy board. We followed him.

"What cabin are you?"

"Chipmunk," Carin said.

"Okay, then when Tony tells you your number, take it from this section."

He pointed at a group of washers under the red-stenciled words, "Chipmunk Cabin." Each washer had the letter "C" before its number.

Tony read our numbers off of his clipboard. I was number five. Carin was number three, and Lindsay was number six. I think it went alphabetically. That would make sense because Morgan would come before Riley and Spencer.

"And for passing the swim test, I have a sticker for everybody," Cord said.

He took the clipboard from Tony, flipped to the last page, and pulled a package of stickers out from under the metal clip. He passed them around, and we each got to take one. The stickers were funny shapes with lots of colors on them.

"What are those supposed to be?" Tony asked.

"They're just cool-looking stickers," Cord said.

"But they don't have pictures of swimmers on them or anything," Tony pointed out.

"Aren't they cool though?" Cord asked.

I looked at my sticker. It was a green and blue speckled wavy circle. It didn't really look like anything in particular.

"Leave it to you to get artsy stickers," Tony said. "You couldn't have gotten the kind that said, 'Great job!' or 'Superstar!' on them, could you?"

Cord smiled and shrugged.

That was the end of the swim test, but even though it was cold and we wanted to go to the cabins to change, we had to wait for everybody else to go through the swim test because the counselors had to do some kind of swim test of their own, and they weren't allowed to let us go back to the cabins alone.

"But it's cold," Carin whined to Kate and Brenda as we stood there wrapped up in our towels. She didn't even try to meet any of the boys who would be in our group—that's how cold and miserable she was.

"Here," Kate said. She took a handful of my wet, dark hair and pulled it into a high ponytail on top of my head. "Put your hair up, so it doesn't make your shoulders cold. Dry off as best as you can, put your clothes on over your swimsuits, and play a game where you have to run around so you warm up."

When she was done with my hair, Kate undid Teresa's ponytail, which had fallen out a little during the swim test. She wrapped Teresa's hair into a bun on the top of her head and fastened it there. Then she pulled Carin's shorter, shoulder-length hair into a tiny ponytail at the back of her head. Kate took her own hair clip out of her hair to fasten Carin's ponytail.

If Ben were here, he would not have made us take the swim test in such freezing water. I wondered where he was. He's been the lifeguard at camp for as long as I can remember. He lets Angela and me go outside of the buoy border at junior high camp, but at elementary camp, he makes me follow the rules like the other campers. I guess that's fair.

He knows everything about camp and the lake, and if he were here, I bet he would have said, "It's much too cold out to swim today. Everyone back to the cabins, and let's have a party!" Ben was not here, though, and we were freezing! I hadn't seen his big, black truck when Mrs. Morgan drove past his cabin this afternoon, just a little red car under a tree on one side of the cabin. The red car did not have rust around the wheels the way Ben's truck did. I hoped that didn't mean he wasn't going to be at camp this year.

We dried off as much as we could and stood in the cold breeze as long as we could stand it. Then we put our shorts and T-shirts on over slightly damp suits (yuck). Some of the kids were playing freeze tag. *Freeze* tag had another meaning that afternoon. Our cabin joined in, and after some running around it didn't seem all that cold out.

We found Rachel. She told us that she was in Blue Jay Cabin this year. Darn. I was hoping that she'd be with us again and that she just hadn't gotten to the cabin yet for some reason. It's so much easier to be with old friends than it is to make new ones.

"Hey, look!" a kid named Chad yelled in the middle of our game. He had been in our group last year, and he was really okay as far as boys go. "The counselors have to take a swimming test!"

We watched as the counselors lined up on the beach in their swimsuits. Their test was different than ours. They had to walk to the end of the buoys and back, and they held hands. Thank goodness we didn't have to hold hands with the boys and walk in the water. That would be the worst swim test ever.

"That's really weird," Carin commented.

"Yeah," I agreed. "They're not even swimming."

"It's a walking test!" yelled a tall boy I didn't know. "I asked the lifeguards if we could take a walking test because the lake is so low, but they said no. And now they're letting the counselors have a walking test."

"No fair," Rachel said.

The counselors got less wet than we did, but after their weird walking test, they were cold, and we finally got to go back to the cabin to change.

CHAPTER FOUR

Dinner Surprise

One thing about camp stays the same year after year after year: spaghetti is *always* the first dinner. We have this camp cook who has been here forever. Her name is Aunt May, and she's very crabby, but she cooks great food. The only thing that Aunt May has ever made that wasn't delicious was this gross bread pudding she made for dessert last year. She kept giving it to us (even though nobody ate it) until we hid it in the milk cartons and threw it away. Then we got good desserts like chocolate chip cookies and cake.

This night's dinner ended up being the weirdest dinner I've ever eaten at camp. It started out normally enough. Carin and I sat next to each other. I ate my spaghetti and garlic bread like usual. Nothing strange or unusual about that. When I had eaten enough so I wasn't very hungry anymore, I looked around the table.

Chad was in our group again. I knew a little bit about him from last year. During the summer, he lives in the cottage on the beach right next to camp property. The rest of the year, he lives in Chicago. Last year, he had medication, and The Scary Nurse came to our table every day at dinnertime. I hoped he didn't have medication again this year.

I didn't know the other two boys. They seemed okay, except one of them, a small kid with dark hair, found an ant crawling on the napkin dispenser, picked it up, held it between his thumb and index finger, squinted to study it better, then ate it, which I thought was pretty disgusting. What is it about boys eating weird things? First there was Crazy Marble Eater from earlier and now a kid in my own group was eating an ant. I mean, who in their right mind would want to eat either of those things? Do ants and marbles secretly taste good? I guess I will never find out because I'm not going to put either one of those things in my mouth.

Just as I was thinking about how I'm not grossed out by most boys anymore but I don't really like them either, I looked across the table at our counselor, Steve.

That's when the weird thing happened.

I kept looking at him. I knew him from last year and from the funeral and all, but there was something different about him now. I don't know what it was, but something made me want to keep peeking up at him between bites of my spaghetti. I never noticed what nice eyes he had. They weren't just plain eyes; they had a pattern to them, mostly blue but with a few brown lines. He smiled at me, and my heart did this weird, quick beating thing like it had when my gymnastics coach made me demonstrate a back walkover in front of a bunch of people on Parents' Night.

I think Steve's hairstyle was new this year, too. His brown hair was wavy and looked like Carin's favorite movie star's. In fact, now that I thought about it, that movie star and one of the singers in the boy band she liked were pretty cute, too.

"Hey, Abby," Steve said, catching me looking at him. "That's cool that we're in the same group this year."

I opened my mouth. I wanted to say, "Yeah, I bet we'll have fun." Instead, I said, "Uh, um, yeah." I don't know why I said that. For once, I didn't feel shy. At least, I didn't *think* I felt shy. I knew Steve.

But something about him made me act stupid.

Something about him made me want to sit next to him. It reminded me of how last year Carin tried to sit by Dane at every activity.

Oh, no.

It couldn't be.

Did I *like* Steve? The way Carin likes boys? Like having a crush on my counselor? A *boy*? No, way!

I looked at Steve again. Yep, I thought he was cute. Great. Now I was going to be annoying just like Carin. Why did I have to get my first crush on a boy at camp when my sister wasn't here for me to talk to about it?

Kate was saying something about the boys in our group being named Chad, Mason, and Wade, but I didn't listen to her much. I was distracted...just like when I'm talking to Carin, but I know she's not listening because there's a cute boy near us.

***

One thing that brought me out of my crush stare was Mr. Newman, one of the camp staff members. At home he's our school guidance counselor, but at camp he's a regular counselor and staff worker.

Mr. Newman stood in front of everyone and announced who the staff members this year were. When he announced their names, they ran out of the kitchen and stood in a line in front of the counter.

The counselors and deans usually only go to camp for one week. Sometimes the counselors are there for more than one week, but most of them aren't, and they don't get paid or anything like the staff members. The staff members get paid to stay at camp all summer long and do things like cook food and work at the beach. Last year, Mr. Newman was a counselor at junior high camp and the assistant manager during the other camps.

Aunt May wasn't the cook this year. The food had tasted like her cooking, but the cooks were this big guy named Randy and a lady named Rose. Maybe they had all of Aunt May's recipes so they could make the spaghetti taste just like it had last year and all the years before that.

For about half a second, I was kind of sad that Aunt May wasn't here because she had been the cook at camp for as long as I'd been coming here...my whole life at junior high camp. But then I remembered how crabby she was and how she yelled at me last year just for putting a plate that didn't have the food scraped off it in the dish window, and I wasn't sad anymore.

The lifeguards were Cord and Tony, but I already knew that because of the swim tests. I had known Cord for a long time. He's Mr. Newman's brother, and he has been a staff member and counselor for a while. Tony did a flip when Mr. Newman introduced him. I'm learning how to flip in gymnastics classes. They're actually called handsprings, but most people call them flips. Any lifeguard who could do a front handspring must be cool, even if I didn't know him.

After everyone settled down from clapping for the lifeguards and cheering Tony's flip, Mr. Newman said, "In his seventh year as a Camp Spirit staff member..." He paused to make it dramatic. I wondered who had been there that long. I could only think of one person, and that was Ben, the lifeguard. But he wasn't here. If he was, we would have seen him at the beach. Tony and his red car were here this year instead.

"Your assistant manager..." Mr. Newman went on, getting louder. "The one and only...Benjamin McAllery!"

Yea! I jumped up and clapped as Ben ran out of the kitchen. He *was* here. But he was now the assistant manager instead of the lifeguard. That was good. Very good. Eva and her husband Jason and Scott weren't here. I was glad that Ben was. I had been worried that he wasn't going to be here this year when I didn't see him at the beach during swim tests.

Mr. Newman announced that Elissa LaBoyer was a staff member this year, too. I know Vanessa, Elissa's older sister, a lot better than I know Elissa because Vanessa counsels at junior high camp for my dad but Elissa doesn't. Elissa usually just hangs out at camp because Mr. LaBoyer is her dad and all, kind of like I do at junior high camp.

When Mr. Newman said Mr. LaBoyer's name, everybody clapped and cheered very loudly for him like we were at a football game instead of eating dinner at church camp. Everybody loves Mr. LaBoyer. He's one of the nicest people I've ever met. He knows my parents and has been the manager for a bazillion years. I've never been at camp without him. He's like Ben and Mr. Newman—always there.

Mr. Newman finished by introducing himself as Christian Newman, the maintenance assistant. I thought that "maintenance assistant" was a very fancy way of saying "toilet cleaner and heater fixer." Then he went back into the kitchen, and Ben gave us a hopper speech about how to set the tables and clean up afterwards. He started out by saying, "Good day, mates!" Then, he spoke with an Australian accent the whole time. It was pretty funny. Last year, he did an impression of a famous cartoon character for the whole hopper speech. He started talking about computer printers and nail guns in the middle of it. I don't know what that has to do with hopping, but it was funny. I think Ben does goofy stuff during the hopper speech to make us pay attention because, otherwise, nobody would listen to a five-minute talk about cleaning up a table.

CHAPTER FIVE

Beach Bonfire

When Dean Ron first announced that we were going back down to the beach after dinner, I wondered if it was for the water Olympics or another swim test or something new. It was way too cold for any of that, and as I walked with my group down the wooden steps, I wondered what the deans were thinking. Since Car walked in front of me and I couldn't see much around my taller friend, I felt it before I saw it: a huge, blazing campfire right on the beach.

Mr. Newman and Ben stood next to the fire, moving the kindling around with big sticks.

It was a little scary during the swim tests when I didn't know if Ben was going to be at camp this year or not. It wouldn't be right if he and Mr. Newman weren't there. It would be like showing up at school on a Wednesday and finding out your teacher and the principal were gone, except I like Mr. Newman and Ben better than any of the teachers at school because they're my camp friends. Although, when he's the guidance counselor at school, Mr. Newman can be as strict as the teachers, especially about running in the halls and chewing gum.

"What are we going to do?" I asked Kate, as we got so close to the fire that I could hear the sticks crackling.

"We get to hang out by the fire tonight," she said. "I think they're going to have s'mores and juice for snack."

So far, camp was even better this year than it was last year. I'd never had a bonfire at the beach before, not even at junior high camp.

"Maybe we can play volleyball," Teresa said, eyeing the beach volleyball court.

"Or nuke 'em," Carin suggested. Most elementary campers prefer nuke 'em to volleyball because you just have to catch the ball and throw it back over instead of hit the ball like in volleyball.

"Yep," Kate said. "I'm sure that would be fine. Hey, there's Steve over there." She pointed to where he stood by the dock. "I'm going to go talk with him. You guys can come with me or hang out with the other campers."

"I'm going to the volleyball court," Teresa said. She hadn't taken her eyes off the campers who had found a ball and were hitting it over the net since we got there.

I watched the other campers for a minute as Teresa ran over to the court and thought about following her, but there were probably a dozen kids playing already. I didn't know any of them except for Teresa. I stink at volleyball anyway (something about my growth spurt refusing to happen), and I hate playing it with people I don't know.

"I'll go with you," I said to Kate.

"Carin?" Kate asked.

"I want to play nuke 'em."

"Okay."

Kate and I started walking toward Steve. He stood on the end of the dock closest to the beach. He wasn't looking at what was going on at camp though. He faced the houses across the lake.

We walked around the big bench by the buddy board. Dane ran along the beach, leapt onto the dock next to Steve, and pushed him down the dock further away from us.

"I have a funny story to tell you!"

We couldn't hear the rest of Dane's story because after yelling that he had something to tell Steve, he told the story very quietly like it was a secret. Even as Kate and I got closer, we couldn't hear what he was saying. I did hear Steve laughing a little. I wished I knew what the story was. Steve and Dane did that a lot last year.

"Hi, guys," Kate said.

"Hey, Kate," Dane said. He looked at me and smiled his usual half-smile. "Did you know that you have two of the best campers ever in your group?"

"I think they're going to be great," she said.

"Want to switch?" He put his arm around her shoulders and leaned on her.

Kate laughed and shook her head. "No way. We have perfect campers, right Steve?"

Steve turned around more so he was facing us. The dock wiggled underneath our feet.

"I have a camper who eat bugs," he said. I giggled thinking about that kid who ate that ant at dinner. "He's a good kid, though. I think we lucked out on the camper draw."

"I had good campers last year," Dane said, winking at me. "Apparently, once you have the good campers, you get the weird and difficult ones the next year. You should see the yahoos in our group. It's not going to be a boring week, I can tell you that."

"Last year, I had that kid who used to hide out in the woods," Steve said. "And the girl who threw a temper tantrum every time we did something she didn't want to do. It's my turn for the good campers this year."

"I got my sister," Dane grumbled. "Why would the deans do that? Who would want to hang out at camp all week with their annoying—" He stopped talking and looked at his feet and the dock. "Uh, I guess, uh..."

Steve turned around and looked at the houses again.

"I guess it's not that bad," Dane finished. "But you guys got Abby and Carin and Chad. You got my kids from last year." He gave Steve a fake punch on the arm. "I'm their favorite counselor, so don't go being all great and changing their minds."

"Let's go to the bonfire," Kate said. She pointed back at the fire, which was even bigger now. "I see s'more stuff."

"How many s'mores are you going to eat?" I asked Dane.

"I don't know. I thought I'd start with a dozen."

That was a joke, but Dane really does eat a lot. Last year, he ate eighty-six potato chips at a picnic and ten tacos for lunch another day. I'd like to see him eat eighty-six potato chips *and* ten tacos at the same lunch.

Dane, Kate, and I walked down the dock to the beach. When we stepped onto the sand, Kate turned around.

"You coming, too?" she called.

"In a minute," Steve said, still looking at the houses across the lake.

We went to the fire. Dean Jamie handed out marshmallows, and Dean Ron had a bunch of graham crackers and chocolate pieces spread out on a plate. It's good to know the deans already because they decide stuff like who wins the clean cabin award and how many pieces of trash you have to pick up on Thursday when the volleyball court area becomes littered with everyone's canteen garbage from the week.

Kate took a roasting stick off the pile on the bench. "Want me to make one for you, or do you want to make your own?" she asked me.

"I can make my own," I said, taking the stick from her. Did she really think that we were such babies that we couldn't roast our own marshmallows? The deans should tell the counselors not to treat their campers like babies. I know they have a counselor meeting the day before camp starts, so there's no excuse for them not to know this.

Kate took marshmallows out of one of the bags next to Dean Jamie and stuck one on my stick and another on a stick she found leaning against the bench.

I hadn't had a s'more since junior high camp last year. My parents don't make them at home. One time, my sister Angela and I asked if we could make s'mores in the microwave for a snack, and my dad said that would be a sin. He was joking, but he did have a good point. S'mores are the best at camp. They are a once-a-year thing (twice-a-year for me now).

"Will you make one for me?" Dane asked, giving her his dimple smile. Last year, Rachel said that Dane gets things by looking cute, like once he got out of a speeding ticket by smiling at the policewoman.

"You're a big, experienced counselor," Kate teased him, apparently not falling for it. "Make your own."

"But they always end up burned."

"It's true," I said, holding my stick so the marshmallow hovered over the fire just far enough so it wouldn't catch a flame. "Last year, he made a s'more for me, and it was pretty burned."

"See?" Dane said, looking at her with a begging face.

"Oh, all right," Kate said. "But you owe me."

"That's cool."

"Dane!" yelled a tall kid wearing glasses as he ran over to us. Dane didn't yell at him for running, the way some counselors do. "T-Camp is killing ants with a flaming marshmallow."

Dane rolled his eyes. "Aw, man," he muttered. "Save that s'more for me. I'll be back."

I watched him walk over to a crowd of kids. When he pushed his way to the center, I saw a grinning kid in the middle, poking at the ground with a stick that had a still-burning marshmallow on the end of it. The kid was missing a tooth and had dirt caked on his face everywhere except the middle of his forehead, where he had stuck his swim test sticker from

Cord. I think his hair was dark brown, but that could have been more dirt. He was the same marble-eating kid who had been screaming in the dining hall earlier.

I wondered how he had gotten the name T-Camp. Hopefully, it was a nickname and not what his parents really named him.

Kate made Dane's s'more and held out the graham cracker and chocolate for me to put my marshmallow on. Then she rounded up Car and Teresa so they could make theirs. My s'more turned out less burned than the one Dane made for me last year but not as perfect as the ones my dad can make.

Steve came over after a while and got the boys in our group to join us. He didn't smile very much, not even when Mason (the bug eater) burped really loud and announced that the burp tasted like chocolate and made everybody else laugh.

I didn't see Steve much last year, but what I remember most about him is that he and Dane used to whisper things to each other, and then they would both crack up laughing, just like they had tonight on the dock only with much louder laughter. They went to camp together when they were kids. When you go to camp with somebody, you do things like tell secrets and laugh a lot, even if you only see them for one or two weeks out of the year. I had not seen either one of them crack up yet, but it was only the first night of camp.

"We have to come up with a group name," Steve said. "Anybody got any ideas?"

Nobody said anything except for Carin who said, "Not really."

"What kinds of things do you want to do this week?" Kate asked. She licked the marshmallow goo that was dripping down her graham cracker.

"Did you ask Dane about the ghost stories?" Chad asked. His mouth and nose were covered with marshmallow and chocolate.

"No," Kate said. "I forgot. But I'll ask him tonight."

"Can we play sports?" Teresa asked.

"Sure," Steve said. "What sports do you like?"

She shrugged. "Any kind, I guess."

I tugged on Carin's sweatshirt sleeve. "Ask if we can go to Mount Spirit," I whispered.

"Can we go to Mount Spirit?" she spoke up.

"That would be fun," Kate said.

More kids and counselors had wandered over to be by the fire, so Steve suggested moving our meeting over to a grassy area by the now-abandoned beach volleyball court. We all sat down and talked about what we wanted to do that week. Kate and Steve let us pick everything. I thought that was very nice of them. I don't remember getting to choose what we did last year when Eva and Dane were our counselors. They decided what we were going to do and then told us.

Carin came up with a name for our group: The Totally Awesome Coolest Campers Ever To Set Foot On Camp. Everybody agreed that it was a good name, but we kept messing it up and calling it things like The Really Cool Campers.

CHAPTER SIX

The Big Promise

When it was time for bed, Carin, Teresa, and I followed Kate back up the hill to our cabin. I got my bathroom bag out of my suitcase and walked down to the bathrooms with everybody else.

There's something lonely about being at camp at night even when you're surrounded by friends. All afternoon, I had had fun, but now that it was time for bed, I started thinking about things that don't matter when you're in the middle of fun things like swimming and eating s'mores. I missed my mom and dad and sister. I had forgotten how much I don't like sleeping in a cabin with a bunch of other people.

Last year, there was somebody who snored really loudly and kept me awake half the night. That person snored almost as loudly as Carin's old dog Zack. Something sad had happened just a few days ago to Zack. He died. He didn't have a car accident. He died in his sleep. He was probably snoring right before he died. The Morgans even had a funeral for Zack. It was kind of like Scott's funeral, only not as heartbreaking because Zack was a dog and not a person.

Carin's parents had that dog since before she was born, and I could tell that Car was in tears when she called to let me know what happened. I've only seen Car cry five or six times in all the years we've been best friends. That's just one of the ways we're different. I cry all the time, even when I try really hard to hold it in.

Not this year though, and especially not at camp. I had cried too much last year. I didn't want to be known as the kid who always cries at camp.

Thinking about Zack and Scott took away a lot of the cheeriness I had from the bonfire. I wanted to go home, just a little bit. I wanted to stare at my glow-in-the-dark stars until I fell asleep. The only thing I had to stare at in my bunk was the lump from Car's mattress above me.

I wanted Hoppity, my blue stuffed rabbit. I always sleep with Hoppity, but I didn't want to bring him to camp and have the other campers think I was a baby. Nobody else had a stuffed animal last summer, so Hoppity had to stay crammed in my dark suitcase alone all week. He's probably much happier sitting on my bed at home with the rest of my stuffed animals.

The good thing about stuffed animals is that they can never, ever die, no matter how old they get or how hard you ram into a tree with your car.

As we walked down to the bathroom, I could barely see Carin in front of me on the path. Why did it seem like everything at camp was darker than it was at home at night?

If Eva were there, I would have told her I was homesick. Kate was really nice. I mean, she helped me get the graham crackers around my chocolate and marshmallow during s'more time and everything. But I didn't really know her yet. I didn't want to tell some stranger that I was homesick.

I wanted to tell Eva or Scott, but Eva and Scott weren't here. Why can't stuff just stay the same?

It was chaos inside the bathroom, with a bazillion people trying to use the sinks, toilets, and showers all at the same time. Laughs and shouts and shrieks bounced off the tiled walls. Kids pushed each other to get to the mirrors. One girl danced around singing very loudly and off-key into her toothbrush holder. The bathroom was way too packed and loud for me. It wasn't like my nice, quiet bathroom at home.

I turned around and went back outside. I could always try the boys' side of the bathroom. At night and in the early morning, the girls are allowed to use both sides of the bathroom that is closest to our cabins. Carin and I learned all about the boys' bathroom last year, including the fact that boys use urinals, which are these things on the wall that look like a mix between a sink and a toilet.

I don't like the boys' bathroom though, so I stood there, wishing my sister was a counselor this week, but Angela had her job as a swimming instructor at the community center again, and she had already taken a week off for junior high camp, so she couldn't get another one.

I needed a break from all the craziness. The path down to the canteen area seemed pretty lit up. There's a huge light above the canteen and another one near the nurse's cabin. Maybe I could take a little walk down that way for some peace and quiet.

***

Since everyone was busy getting ready for bed and the bathrooms were crazy, it was easy to slip away without any counselors noticing. I only planned on walking to the nurse's cabin and back. I certainly wasn't going to go *in* the nurse's cabin knowing that The Scary Nurse was inside.

I needed to be by myself for two minutes. When you're from a small family, it's hard to spend every second with a bunch of noisy people breathing down your neck. I would be back in the cabin before Kate or Brenda noticed.

That plan changed when I got to the nurse's cabin and saw Dane sitting alone across the path in the canteen. I went over to the porch, opened the screen door, and sat down next to him. I set my bathroom bag on my lap.

"Hey, Squirt," he said. "What's up?"

"I needed to get away from all the noise."

"Yeah, me, too. T-Camp just glued another kid's toothbrush to our cabin wall."

"Who's T-Camp?"

"One of my campers."

I remembered the wild kid at the beach.

"Is that his real name?"

"No, it's a nickname I gave him. I should have named him Glue Stick though because he really stuck that toothbrush on the wall good."

"That doesn't sound too good," I said.

"The nurse had extra toothbrushes." He held up his hand and a blue toothbrush with a cartoon dinosaur on it. I couldn't believe he had gone into the nurse's cabin alone. "I'm not ready to go back to my cabin though."

"I can understand why," I said, thinking about T-Camp and the whole flaming marshmallows and marble-eating stuff.

Dane set the toothbrush on top of my bag.

"So, how's your first day going?"

"Okay, I guess," I said. "The swim tests were easy."

"You're kidding," he said, sarcastically. That lopsided grin was the same as last year, and that made me feel a little better. "The water is so high and dangerous."

I cracked a smile at that. The water in the swimming area at camp is pretty much the opposite of high and dangerous.

"Cord gave me a sticker and everything," I reported.

"Cool."

"But I'm not too sure about camp this summer."

"Why not?" Dane asked. "I'm having a blast already."

"I was, too. But then I got to thinking…and I don't like it when things are different."

I don't know why, but it was easy to talk to Dane. Maybe it was because he had been my counselor last year, or maybe it was because he was only eighteen, and eighteen didn't seem too much like an old grown-up yet. Usually, I don't like telling adults about all my problems. I feel silly. Most adults talk about work and bills and stuff like that. Talking about kid stuff to a grown-up seems funny.

"I miss Eva," I said. "And I wish you were my counselor again."

It's not that I didn't like having Steve be my counselor, but I felt kinda nervous around him. I didn't tell Dane that, though, because then he would want to know why Steve made me nervous and I would have to tell him about having a crush…on a *boy*.

"Aw, Squirt. That's sweet of you to say, but nobody gets the same counselors every year."

Then I remembered the worst thing of all, the saddest change from last year. "And I wish Scott was here."

"We all wish Scott were here," Dane said, his smile falling. "But you have great counselors this summer. Better than last year."

"But *you* were my counselor last year," I reminded him.

"Yeah, but Kate and Steve are better at hanging out with little kids than I am. They're good at that bandage stuff."

"What's bandage stuff?" I asked. "You mean like going to the nurse?"

"No, like chapel stuff," Dane said. "God stuff. Talking about your parents getting a divorce or your grandpa dying or having low self-esteem."

"I don't need to talk about God or any problems."

"Let me tell you a secret," he said, and I leaned in closer. "Between you and me, I don't really care who likes who and who is sad because someone in their cabin won't share their cookies. I like being here with my friends a lot more than I like taking kids to the bathroom and singing stupid songs after meals."

"Oh," I said, breaking his gaze and looking down at the toothbrush that lay on top of my bathroom bag. Dane always seemed like he was having a good time last year. Apparently, he was just playing along so he could hang out here at camp with his friends. I thought he had liked us campers.

"Hey," Dane said. I looked up at him. "I told you I like being here with my friends. Are you and I buddies or not?"

I smiled a little. "Yeah, we're buddies."

"All right then. Get rid of that sad, insulted face." He ruffled my hair with his hand. Usually, I hate when people do that, but I didn't mind Dane doing it.

I smiled even more. Then I remembered that Eva and Allie wouldn't be waiting for me at the cabin like they had last year.

"Why didn't Eva come back?"

"Jason is at law school downstate, and he had an internship this summer. Eva had to stay with him and work since law school costs a lot of money. But don't worry about Eva. You'll have an even more fun week with Kate."

"Don't you think Eva was a good counselor?"

"Sure, but she's strict, remember?"

I nodded. It's funny how when camp is over, you only remember the good things. Eva had yelled at me a couple of times. Once, during dinner, I had left the table for three minutes, and when I came back, she gave us all a really long lecture about telling the counselors whenever we went places. It was so embarrassing. Dane had finally told her to give it a rest and saved me from further humiliation.

"Kate is awesome. You'll like her."

"I know." I sighed. "I do like her. She's just not Eva. Plus, she's new."

"I was new last year," Dane said. "You didn't hold that against me."

"But I was new, too, so I didn't know who the new counselors were."

"I'm sure Eva wishes she could be here."

"Are you going to quit going to camp someday?" I asked.

"Nah, never."

"Promise?"

He just looked at me for a while. "I'll tell you what. I'll keep going to camp as long as it's fun."

"But camp's always fun," I said.

"Then I'll always go to camp."

"Promise?" I asked again.

"Promise."

And suddenly I felt a lot better about camp this week.

"You know what?" I asked.

"What?"

"You're not really bad at talking to campers. You're good at the bandage stuff, too."

He put a finger to his lips. "Shh. That's not part of the image."

I smiled at him and whispered back, "I won't tell."

I heard the crunching of pebbles and looked up. Kate was walking towards us. She opened the squeaky door.

"Abby, I've been looking all over for you."

I looked at Dane. Uh, oh. She was going to start lecturing me. Why do I always get in trouble for being in the wrong place on the first day of camp? At least Dane was there to get me out of it.

Kate held out her hand. "Come on, hon, you'll miss devotions."

I stood up and took her hand. That was it. No yelling, no frantic lecture. I turned around and shared my surprised look with Dane. He raised his eyebrows as if to say, "See?"

"Oh," he said. "I need Sam's new toothbrush."

I handed him the dinosaur toothbrush. He stood up, brushed the dirt off of his shorts, and moved towards the door with us.

"I'll walk you back to your cabin," he offered.

"I'm sure we'll be fine," Kate said. Besides the bathroom, our cabin was probably the closest building to the nurse's cabin on the girls' side. "I know you need to get back to your own cabin."

I stifled a giggle at the thought of T-Camp gluing more stuff to the cabin wall.

Dane leaned next to Kate and opened the door. We walked out, and he stayed with us as we went up the path.

"Are you going out tonight?" he asked her.

"Out where?"

"To the dining hall...or anywhere. We could go swimming. Or to Tony and Cord's cabin for a movie."

Oh, brother. Wasn't it enough that I had to spend most of my time with Carin and her boy-crazy talk and dealing with the fact that I, Abby Leah Riley, might be starting to like boys? Now I had to hang out with flirting counselors, too.

"I'll have to ask Brenda," Kate said.

"Stop for a sec."

We both stopped. Dane reached his hand out and tangled his fingers in some of her blond hair.

"You had a leaf in your hair."

He started walking again, right with us. It was dark and all, but I sure hadn't seen a leaf anywhere.

When we got to our porch, Kate said, "Well, here we are."

"Yeah," Dane said. "See you tomorrow, Squirt."

"Bye," I said.

"I'll see you later, right?" He was looking at Kate. She stood on the second step of our porch. He was on the ground right next to the porch, so they ended up about eye level with each other. If a boy stood that close to me, I'd jump away and yell, "Cooties!" Well, maybe not. It would depend on what boy it was.

"I have to ask Brenda."

He smiled at her and leaned even closer and put his hands on her waist. "You have to come see me later."

Kate smiled back at him. "I have to ask Brenda."

"You have to come see me," Dane insisted.

"Maybe," Kate said. But the way she said it, I could tell she was going to go unless Brenda said she couldn't.

I rolled my eyes and went into the cabin. I had had enough of that teenage stuff. I don't ever want to be a teenager. You have to talk to boys and let them do silly things to you like pretend to find leaves in your hair.

I looked out the window and watched them though. Even though flirting was icky, there was something interesting about it. They stood there talking for a couple more minutes.

"What are you looking at?" Car asked.

"Kate and Dane."

"Dane?" She ran across the cabin and pushed me away from the window. As soon as she saw him, she started patting down her hair. "Maybe he's here to see me."

"I think he's here to see Kate," I said. "I think he likes her."

Car wrinkled her nose. "He's probably talking to her about the schedule for tomorrow." Dane threw his head back and laughed at that moment. I didn't think the schedule would be that funny.

"Yes," Carin went on. "He's saying, 'What time do you have swimming tomorrow?' And she is saying, 'Three o'clock.' And he's saying, 'Oh, that's great. I have swimming then, too. I'd just die if I didn't have swim hour with that glamorous, wonderful, gorgeous Carin Alexandra Morgan.'"

The way Dane looked at Kate, I thought it was more likely he was saying something like, "Do you want to go to the movies with me after camp?" But I didn't tell Carin that because of the whole Stacey situation from last year.

Kate finally came back into the cabin when Autumn and Jennie got back from the bathroom. She went right over to Brenda, and they started talking in low voices.

"See," I whispered. "She's probably asking Brenda if she can go out tonight to meet him."

I hoped Dane and Kate would have a camp romance this week. The sooner Carin realized that he didn't like her and was never going to date her, the better. Even though I think I might have a crush on Steve, I don't go on and on about it and announce it to the world. That would be very embarrassing.

"She's not going to meet him tonight because he *likes* her. He likes *me*. He just doesn't know what to do about it. Everyone knows Dane likes redheads over blondes."

"It doesn't matter what color Kate's hair is." I had to whisper now because Kate had walked over near us to sit on her bed and open her Bible. "She's his age. You're not."

Car skipped over to her bed. I followed her. "She's going to meet him tonight, and he will say, 'I'm in love with a girl from your cabin.' And she'll say, 'Which one?' And Dane'll say, 'Carin of course. She's so lovely.' And Kate'll say, 'Yes, and mature for her age, too.' And then, Dane will give Kate a secret note for me that will say, 'My dearest Carin, I love you more than anyone at this camp. Even more than Stacey from last summer. Will you go to the beach with me tomorrow after lights out?' And I will sneak out, and—"

"Okay, girls," Brenda said, loudly. She clapped her hands. "Everyone get in bed. It's time for devotions."

The other campers scurried for their bunks. I sat down on mine. Car pulled herself onto the top bunk with a dreamy sigh.

Brenda read out of the Bible. When she finished, Kate prayed, thanking God for us and asking Him to watch over all of the campers this week. Then she turned the light off on her way outside.

"I'm going to wait up for my note," Carin whispered.

She ended up falling asleep about five minutes later though. I could tell because she started snoring. Not as loud as that person in our cabin last year or Zack the dog, but I could hear it because she was my bunkmate.

CHAPTER SEVEN

Clean Cabin "Bribe"

When the bell rang to wake us up in the morning, I didn't want to get out of bed. I always have trouble falling asleep the first night of camp. I don't know if it's because the bunks are squishy and squeaky or because there's always someone who snores, but I can never get to sleep easily after lights out until Tuesday or so.

I pulled myself out of bed anyway because I didn't want to have to use the boys' bathroom. I had a nice, cozy cocoon of sleeping bag and wanted to crawl back into bed as soon as I felt the cool air on my arms. I put my feet on the wooden floor, knowing it would feel like the ice pops we get from canteen.

Carin already had her flip-flops on and was digging through her suitcase for something, probably a towel. I opened my own suitcase, annoyed with myself for not setting everything out the night before so I could grab my bathroom bag and towel and run for the bathroom to be first in the shower line.

"Car, wake Teresa up." I didn't want Teresa to have to use the boys' bathroom just because she didn't know how fast the girls' side fills up in the morning. It was not fun to be a new camper last year and not know everything about camp.

The stomping sound of somebody coming up the cabin porch steps shook the floor, and Brenda opened the door. She was dressed in pants and a sweatshirt.

"Good morning, girls," she said, flipping on the light and making me squint my eyes shut. "It's time to rise and shine."

Most of us were working on the rising part. It was the shining that made it tough.

Kate let out a tired groan from her bed and lifted up her head. "It's six in the morning."

"Actually, it's five after seven," Brenda said, rubbing her still-wet hair with a towel.

"Not at my house," Kate mumbled.

"Mine either," I said, knowing how she felt.

She sat up on her bed, pushed her sleeping bag down, and shivered. She looked as tired as I felt, and her hair was a mess. Maybe some year camp can be on Central time, instead of Eastern, and we won't have to feel like we're getting up at the crack of dawn.

Car woke Teresa up, and it only took Kate a minute to get ready because she had her things set out on her dresser, like smart people do. We all walked down to the bathroom together, and I was ready for the worst. We hadn't made good time from the bell to the bathroom.

There must have been lots of tired people from the Central Time Zone that week because the bathroom wasn't as crowded as I expected. The showers were full, but the line was only two people long, which meant Carin and I would get in as soon as the campers who were finishing up were done, and Teresa would have plenty of time if she left her bathroom kit in line for her and brushed her teeth first.

Kate went over to the sinks and stood next to another counselor, a tall girl with brown hair that looked kind of reddish on top. I watched them while I waited for my turn in the shower. I wasn't trying to be nosy. There just wasn't anything better to do. There's a lot of graffiti to read in the cabins but not in the bathrooms.

"You look tired," the brown-haired counselor said.

Kate nodded and looked at her friend. "So do you."

"I am. But I'm not the one who stayed up after the potato chips were gone. Isn't he cute? What did you guys do?"

"Isn't who cute?"

"My co-counselor," the girl said, brushing her brown hair into a ponytail.

"Absolutely."

They started giggling. I could see their smiles in the mirror.

I wanted to know who this other counselor was and who her co-counselor was so I could see if I thought he was cute, too. That was weird because I have never cared before about boys being cute.

This was just the kind of conversation that Carin would love to eavesdrop on if she wasn't so busy looking in the mirror on the wall next to us and poking her cheeks every place she saw a freckle. I swear Car thinks that if she touches her freckles enough, they will eventually rub off.

A girl came out of the shower and I nudged Carin so she could take her turn. If she went fast enough, one of the other kids in line behind us might get a turn. I wouldn't count on that though because Car takes her time when getting ready is involved.

"Are you girls okay by yourself?" Kate asked.

"Yeah," I answered for all three of us.

I could totally tell that Kate was new at counseling and afraid that if she looked away for three seconds, one of us campers would get lost in the woods or fall off Mount Spirit and break a leg.

"I'm going to the other side of the bathroom to take a shower then," she said, pointing at the door.

I felt less scared about the possibility of having to see The Scary Nurse if I got sick or hurt. Our counselor was brave—brave enough to take on the grimy boys' side of the bathroom with its curtainless showers. I had a feeling that she could handle that scary nurse no problem.

Another camper emerged from behind the shower curtain that led to the individual shower stalls, and I went in. The open shower happened to be the one with decent water pressure. Not bad for the first morning of camp.

***

We tried really, really, really hard during cabin clean up that morning. Brenda said that the easiest day to win the clean cabin award was Monday if you were very careful and did an extra-tidy job because the new campers didn't know all the clean cabin rules, and even returning campers had forgotten some of them. It was our plan to clean as if it were Friday and we had heard the reasons other cabins had lost all week long.

"What makes a cabin lose?" Carin asked, as she smoothed out her sleeping bag.

Lindsay and I had been sweeping. I had the broom and was making sure I remembered every corner and under the bunks. Lindsay crouched down with the dustpan and pointed out any tiny piece that I missed. I thought it was good teamwork because when we were finished, there was absolutely no trace of paper, dirt, or dust bunnies in the cabin. The only things on the floor that didn't belong there were a dark stain under one of the windows and another lighter one in the middle of the aisle, both of which had probably been there forever.

"I've seen cabins lose for all kinds of reasons," Brenda said. "Once my cabin lost on Thursday because the deans found a padlock on one of the windowsills. Apparently, the staff members had put it there in May when they opened the cabins for the season."

"And the deans didn't find it until Thursday?" Kate asked.

"Nope."

"That doesn't seem fair."

"The clean cabin award isn't fair sometimes," Brenda said. "That's why we have to do such a perfect job that they can't find anything wrong with it."

"We should make sure all the curtains are open," I said, trying to think of other reasons my parents had marked cabins down at junior high camp. "And maybe leave them a bribe."

I love when campers leave my parents bribes for clean cabin award. Usually, the bribes involve candy, and I get the candy.

"No padlocks," Autumn announced from the back of the cabin. "I checked all the windowsills."

"A bribe would be fun," Kate said, straightening the shampoo bottles and contact solution on her dresser. "But we haven't had canteen yet, so we don't have any candy."

"What other kind of bribe could we leave?" Teresa asked.

"I know!" Carin shouted. "Fresh picked flowers!"

"Yeah," Jennie said. "There are pretty blue ones all the way down the path to the beach. Let's go get some."

Jennie and Carin bolted for the door.

"Hold it!" Brenda said, and Carin's hand froze on the doorknob. They both turned around. "Some of the flowers around camp are illegal to pick. We don't want to get in trouble because we were trying to bribe the deans."

"I think we should stick to doing the best job cleaning that we can," Kate said, "and forget the bribe."

Lindsay and I went outside with Teresa to straighten the clothesline and look for garbage around the cabin. Both turned out to be easy jobs because the only things on the clothesline were a couple of towels, and there was only one tissue under a bush since we had only been there for about twenty-four hours—less actually.

We went back inside and sat on our bunks, waiting for everybody else to finish cleaning, trying to be as dirt-free as possible so we didn't undo any cleaning we had already done. Kate put a paperback book and a lined notebook into a drawer, and that gave me an idea.

"Hey, you guys. Sometimes at junior high camp, cabins leave the deans notes with poems or drawings or messages in them."

"We should do that," Lindsay said.

"Good idea," Brenda agreed. "And somebody should wash the mirror. It's pretty filthy."

"I'll do that," Teresa volunteered. She left the cabin to get a wet paper towel from the bathroom.

Lindsay took a package of pastel markers out of her suitcase, then slid the suitcase back under her bunk neatly. Kate ripped a piece of paper out of her notebook and then had to brush a few stray scraps into the trashcan. Lindsay folded the paper in half to make a card and drew a picture of a cabin on the front. On the inside she drew flowers all around the outside edge for a border. Then she handed the card to me.

"Here. You do the writing. I have messy handwriting."

"No, you don't," I said because we had written to each other this past year, and her handwriting was fine.

"You have nicer writing though," Lindsay said.

I put the card on Kate's dresser and chose a purple marker. Linds leaned over my shoulder and watched me write. She was the only person who had to stand on the balls of her feet to see over my shoulder. Everybody else was taller than me, but Lindsay was almost an inch shorter. Last year, we were the same height. It was nice to be taller than somebody.

"Dear Dean Ron and Dean Jamie," I wrote. "We hope you are having a nice day. We are having a great week at camp so far! We would have left you candy, but we haven't been to the canteen yet, so maybe tomorrow. Also, if you tell us what flowers we are allowed to pick, we could leave you a beautiful bouquet later in the week. See you at lunchtime. Love, Chipmunk Cabin."

"Perfect," Lindsay said when I was done.

"Is everybody finished?" Brenda asked. "The bell for chapel is going to ring in about two minutes, so we should all grab our Bibles and start down the path so we aren't late."

Teresa wiped the mirror faster, I set the card on Kate's dresser where the deans would be sure to see it, and we all found our Bibles in the pile on Brenda's dresser.

"I think we're going to win," Carin said confidently, with one last look into the cabin before Brenda flipped off the lights and joined us on the porch.

"I hope so," I said as we went down the steps to the path.

"We cleaned the mirror and left a note," Teresa said. "How could we not win?"

"What do you guys have after chapel?" Lindsay asked.

I thought about the schedule we had made up last night, but we had talked about so many things that I couldn't remember what we were supposed to do when. I asked Kate.

"Craft time," she said, looking at her piece of paper with the schedule on it.

"Rats," Lindsay said. "We have skit planning. You know how two groups usually have swimming, crafts, and free time together?" I nodded. "I was hoping your group would be with my group."

"That would've been cool," I said.

"We'll have to do as much together as we can in the cabin," Carin said. "Don't forget about rest time and secret note passing. Too bad Rachel isn't in our cabin. She was the best at flinging gimp mail across the cabin."

The best part of rest hour is writing notes to each other, folding them up, tying gimp (lanyard that we use to make bracelets) around them, and chucking them across the cabin to each other. I would really miss Rachel's gimp mail. Hers were the best.

We walked across the slight hill to chapel, and Car and I had to sit in a pew with Kate, Steve, Teresa, and the boys, while Lindsay went to the other side of the chapel with her group. I wished Lindsay could have sat with us.

CHAPTER EIGHT

Pierre vs. the Bullies

We made these really cool grassheads today in the craft cabin. Grass-heads are balls of dirt that have grass hair that really grows out the top of them. We got to decorate them however we wanted, and it looked like something that you couldn't mess up even if you were awful at arts and crafts like I am. Carin had already picked one out, so I sorted through the box of grasshead lumps until I found one that was fairly round. I didn't want a grasshead with a funny-shaped head.

After I found a fairly round grasshead, I got to look through Cammie the craft lady's box of decorations. She had everything from wiggly eyes to felt to buttons that we could use to dress our grassheads up.

I took my time picking out the perfect accessories, and by the time I brought all my things to the table, Carin had already glued eyes on her grasshead and drawn a mouth. Teresa had decided to make a foam football that we could play with at the beach, and she had two pieces sewn together with yarn.

It turned out that grassheads were not as foolproof a craft project as I thought. The glue to my wiggly eyes oozed out from underneath them, and I had to wipe it off with a paper towel. I guess I wiped one eye too hard because it slid to the middle of the grasshead's forehead, and I had to push it back over. It left a glue streak, but I was planning on giving him eyebrows anyway.

I thought things were going pretty well until I heard a loud, somewhat screechy voice say, "C'mon, girls. Let's go over here."

I looked up from my grasshead's crooked mouth and saw that crabby-looking counselor with the black hair and lots of make-up from the reg-istration line yesterday walking towards a table past us. Rachel and two other girls were with her. That meant that the other group who would have crafts, swimming, and free time with us was Dane's and Rachel's group, which was the next best thing to it being Lindsay's group.

Wade, a boy from our group, ran towards the steps and cut sharply in front of the crabby counselor and her campers. The counselor stopped and pulled back the tray of beads she had in her arms before Wade could bump into it and send beads flying.

"Watch it, you little brat," she said.

I would have been utterly embarrassed if a counselor called me a little brat, but Wade didn't seem to care. He took a quick backwards glance at her as he ran up the steps, two at a time. I know that going to the second floor of the craft cabin without a counselor is against the rules because Cammie had told us so when she went over every rule during the first ten minutes of craft time. I thought the counselor would yell at him about it, but she didn't. She just made an irritated face and kept walking.

Her campers passed our table. I was just about to say hi to Rachel when one of the other campers in her group, a girl with long, blond curls and a smug smile, stopped right next to me and looked down at everything on our table.

"What is *that*?"

Carin had been watching them, too. "It's a grasshead," she said, in a tone as if they were dumb not to know. The girl's question had sounded like an insult, and Carin gets really fired up about being insulted.

The already unpleasant look on their counselor's face got even uglier, as she crinkled her nose and curled up her lip. "Aren't those things kind of dirty?"

I wanted to tell her that camp, in general, is kind of dirty and that the white pants she was wearing didn't stand a chance of staying white until lunch, but I didn't open my mouth, of course. Most people have trouble coming up with a good comeback when somebody says something rude to them. I don't have a problem with that. It's actually being bold enough to say whatever comes to my mind that I can't do.

"Well," Car said, pursing her lips and shaking her head like one of those people on the talk shows my sister watches and laughs at, "they have dirt in them."

That was not such a good comeback, but at least she had said something to defend the grassheads. If Car and I could be telepathic, I would send her my ideas and she could say them, and we would be the greatest comeback team ever for any insult.

"That's stupid," said the other camper, a brunette with really long eyelashes.

I felt bad for Rachel being stuck with these jerky girls. Their insults made me feel like crying. Great. Girls like that are bullies and love when other people cry. I tried to hold it in because I didn't want them to see, but it was hard. They looked at us and smirked like they thought we were babies. I hate, hate, hate when people think I'm a baby.

I looked at Kate so I wouldn't have to look at the campers' snobby smiles. Kate had her mouth open and stared at their counselor like she couldn't believe a church camp counselor would let her campers make fun of other campers. I wondered if she had heard the counselor's comment about Wade being a brat. I thought counselors were supposed to be nice.

It was Rachel who ended it. She poked the blond girl in the back and said she wanted to start her craft project. The girl went to her table but not before saying, "You guys are lame." The counselor laughed. Rachel looked back at us as she followed them and rolled her eyes to show us what she thought of the other girls in her group.

I looked at my grasshead, feeling like I couldn't hold back crying any more. It did look stupid now that I thought about it. A ball of dirt that grew grass hair? No wonder they thought we were babies. So much for being tough and outgoing this year. It had lasted a whole nineteen hours, and now my old, sensitive self was back to cry about something again.

Kate got up from where she was sitting across the table and moved to the spot next to me. She put her arm around me, and I hoped those other girls were too interested in their beads to notice me getting comforted by my counselor. She told me that she thought grassheads were cooler than beaded bracelets, but I know she was just saying that to make me feel better. She's a year younger than my sister, and there's no way Angela would think a silly grasshead was better than beaded jewelry.

Carin said she thought they were jealous because we thought of making grassheads first. I didn't think that was true, but I also didn't think Car was saying that to make me feel better. I think she actually thought that.

Teresa told me to ignore them. That's what everyone says when somebody makes fun of you, but I've always had trouble doing that. How can you ignore somebody who hurts your feelings or laughs at you? It's nice to say but hard to do.

That was when the counselor I had seen Kate talk to that morning walked by with her tray of beads. She stopped at our table and asked what was going on.

"Noelle's campers said we were lame for making grassheads," Car reported. Once she said the counselor's name, I remembered hearing it in the registration line. I noticed, for the first time, the two pink spots on Carin's cheeks and the wrinkle in her nose, the two things that happen when she gets mad.

"What did they do?" the counselor asked, frowning. "They're my campers, too, and I'll talk to them if they were rude."

Kate filled her friend in on the rest of what had happened, and the two counselors decided to make a grasshead together. Kate's friend made a big show of putting her beads back and saying that grassheads were much better. I think they were pretending at first because what teenager would really think a ball of dirt with wiggly eyes was cool? But then they got into the project and had fun for real, at least it seemed like it. They laughed a lot at the things they put on their grasshead.

We talked all craft hour, about grassheads, foreign countries (they decided their grasshead was from France), and cabin clean-up time. The other counselor introduced herself to us. Her name was Julie, she was a C.I.T. (counselor in training) in Noelle's group, and she didn't think her cabin was going to win the clean cabin award because they spent most of the time deciding which earrings to wear instead of cleaning. Kate talked about what a good job we did.

"I hope you guys win then," Julie said. "You deserve it more."

Julie and Kate made the best grasshead. His mouth was not crooked and his eyes did not have glue clumps under them, and he had a polka dotted tie. His name was Pierre. Car named her grasshead Zack after her dog, and I named mine Simon because it was a funny name that popped into my head when I was trying to name him.

By the time craft hour was over, Kate and Julie had me convinced that Pierre, Zack, and Simon were a lot better than those other girls' lousy beads.

***

The only really terrible thing about camp besides the pathetically small and shallow area we get to swim in is skit night. It's terrifying having to perform a short skit in front of the entire rest of camp, and I wouldn't wish it on my worst enemy (as Carin's mom would say).

We had our first skit practice after crafts, and it took us a while to come up with a skit idea, partly because the boys decided that no matter what skit we did, we had to have a part about the deans' underwear in it. That idea was a little hard to work with, but we ended up deciding to do a game show skit and have the dean's underwear be one of the prizes.

We didn't have enough time during skit practice to hash out our whole plan, so we whispered ideas about our game show skit as we ate our chicken soup and grilled cheese sandwiches during lunch. There's something about the new dining hall that makes it hard to hear when a lot of people are making noise, so we had to repeat our whispers several times. We didn't want anybody else to hear any of the ideas and copy us.

"I don't want this," Mason said, as he chewed a piece of grilled cheese sandwich.

"Did you get a burned one?" Steve asked.

"No. I don't like processed cheese, and this is processed."

"It's just cheese," Chad said. "Eat it."

"Think I could get some pickles again?" Mason asked. He had gone up to the counter and asked the kitchen staff for pickles at breakfast this morning. His eggs with pieces of pickles in them had looked grosser than Aunt May's bread pudding from last year, but not as gross as the bug he had eaten yesterday.

"Why don't you just eat your grilled cheese plain?" Steve suggested.

I thought the grilled cheese was good, and so was the chicken soup. I don't know why every television show and book about camp says the food is gross. The food at our camp is yummy, especially DTC, a weird casserole with tater tots on top of it that's named after the initials of a counselor who used to eat the whole serving bowl of it by himself. (That's the legend anyway. I don't know the person and have never seen him do that before.) DTC looks odd, so Mason would probably like it.

When everything was cleaned up, Dean Jamie passed out the mail. Last year, he just sorted it and gave each cabin's mail to the counselors, but this year he announced the mail. He called Carin's name and held up a brown box. She got the best care package last year filled with soda and candy and magazines. I hoped this care package was like the last one. When she brought it back to our table, I could tell she loved that everyone was watching her and wondering what was in that big box. The only people who would get to find out were the people in Chipmunk Cabin.

Dane, at the table next to ours, leaned his chair back so it balanced on two legs. He ended up between Carin and me this way.

"I get something out of that box, right?" he asked.

"Sure," Car said. "I'll bring you something after rest hour."

"Sweet."

We sang songs (which were much less irritating this year now that I was used to the elementary camp songs), and then Dean Jamie said, "I have one more announcement. The winner of the clean cabin award."

I had forgotten about cabin clean-up and how hard we had worked. It was only a few hours ago, but with all the activities we had done that morning, it seemed like a week had gone by since we had been in the cabins. Dean Jamie held up a piece of yellow paper. He read everything that was wrong with the boys' cabins first. None of them sounded very clean, especially the one that had toothpaste on the walls. I bet T-Camp had done that. He and his toothless grin looked suspicious when Dean Jamie mentioned the toothpaste.

"The two best cabins were Chipmunk Cabin and Blue Jay Cabin."

Our cabin and Rachel's cabin. I wanted to win, not only because we had worked hard, but also because I didn't want those mean girls to win. I wanted Rachel to win but not the other two girls in her group.

"I hope it's us," Carin said. I nodded but never broke my gaze on Dean Jamie.

"It was a very hard decision," he said, "but in the end we felt that Chipmunk Cabin put forth a little extra effort—"

I didn't hear what he said next because Carin screamed in my ear. We could tell by half his sentence that we had won. Teresa held up her hands from her seat across the table to give us both high-fives at the same time. We cheered, and so did Brenda's girls from across the room. I smiled at Lindsay, and she smiled back. That was one exciting thing we could share with Linds.

Kate went up to Dean Jamie to get the clean cabin award, this cool yellow and green stick. The boys were complaining to Steve about getting beaten by us girls when I heard one of the girls from Blue Jay Cabin whining to her friend at the table next to us.

"They just won because they're goody-goodies, and the deans like perfect little campers."

"No way," Rachel said. "They probably won because you wouldn't sweep under the bunks."

"I wasn't going to crawl around on the floor," the girl said.

I turned around. I've learned that when you look at a person's lips, you can understand what they're saying better, and it was hard to hear with everybody else in the dining hall talking. The girls were watching Kate bring the award back to our table.

"Maybe they won because their counselor is pretty," the brown-haired girl said.

"People don't win clean cabin awards because they're pretty," Rachel said. "You guys are being dumb."

"Besides," the blonde girl said. "I heard Noelle tell her friend Felicity that their counselor isn't pretty at all. Noelle said the only thing that saves her from being totally ugly is that she has blond hair, and blond hair can make anybody look ten times better than they actually do." The girl wound her pointer finger around a strand of her own blond hair.

"Well, I heard my brother tell Steve Koski that she's hot," Rachel said. "So who are you going to believe?"

"All I was saying," said the brown-haired girl, "is that they must have cheated to win."

I almost stood up and yelled at her that we weren't cheaters, but then Dean Jamie said everybody could go, so we all stood up at the same time. They were such sore losers. It's kind of scary to think I could have ended up in a cabin with them. I know there's a line on the camp registration forms where you can request somebody to be in your cabin, but is there a place on the form where you can request to *not* have somebody? If there was, I was going to find out what those girls' names were and reverse request them for next year.

CHAPTER NINE

Canteen Time

The rule about not running around camp unless you're playing a game on the ball field is especially hard to follow one time of the day: canteen time. I always have to force myself to just walk fast instead of run down the dirt and stone path to the little brown cabin and its screened-in front porch. On the other side of the windows are candy, soda, potato chips, gum, fruit drinks, and some other less important items like postcards, stamps, batteries, and T-shirts with the camp logo on them.

Kate and Brenda were good counselors. They had our canteen cards sitting on their dressers before the bell rang. Carin's, Teresa's, and mine had been in such a neat stack that you couldn't tell if there was one card or twenty in the pile. Lindsay's, Jennie's, and Autumn's canteen cards had been tossed onto Brenda's dresser so that you could see there were three of them.

I spent the first ten minutes of rest hour craning my neck up and down, trying to see two canteen cards poking out from underneath the top one on Kate's dresser, but I finally decided I had to trust that she had one for each of us, and I read a book instead.

Sure enough, as soon as the bell rang, she got up and took the pile off her dresser and handed each one of us our own card. Brenda told her campers to grab their cards off of her dresser on their way out the door.

I like counselors who are prepared; we got into the canteen line when it was pretty short that way. Last year, Eva was always looking for the canteen cards in her dresser after the bell rang.

I read the choices off of one of the big signs on the back of the open wooden window. Ahead of me, I could hear different campers ordering candy and soda, Elissa repeating their orders, and Ben joking with everyone as he and Elissa served them.

"Hey, Abby Dabby," Ben said when I got to the front of the line. His curly brown hair looked shorter than usual. I bet he does not stand in front of the mirror trying to blot out his freckles like Car does. "What would you like this afternoon?"

I ordered my favorite kind of Jenga's Soda (a brand of soda I've only ever seen at camp) and a chocolate bar. Ben turned around to get my raspberry soda out of the refrigerator and tossed it to Elissa. Elissa wrote down how much the soda and candy cost on my canteen card and then slid everything across the counter to me.

I took my food outside and sat down at our favorite picnic table, the one with a great view of the tetherball. It also, unfortunately, is right next to the bug zapper, which isn't the best sound in the world, but most of the other picnic tables are in the direct path of any wild throws on the nuke 'em court.

The screen door slammed, and Carin came out of the canteen with an ice pop. She sat down with me, and Lindsay and Teresa walked out just a few minutes later.

"What do you guys have this afternoon?" Lindsay asked, unscrewing the top of her fruit drink. It was the kind with the lids that make clicking noises.

"Nature hike and swimming," I said.

"Bummer," Lindsay said. "I have crafts and skit practice."

"We did that this morning," Carin said. "Wait until you see our skit. It is going to be the best skit in the history of Camp Spirit skit night."

Our skit was funny, but there's no way I would say it was going to be the best ever. Then again, Car has never seen Blane Adams from junior high camp do his skits. The guy should really be a stand-up comic instead of a teacher.

"You should make grassheads in craft hour," Teresa said. "But don't show Dane."

The three of us giggled. When we had introduced Dane to Pierre, Simon, and Zack the grassheads, he had freaked out. He called them a gang and said Pierre was creepy and walked away from us. I bet he's the kind of person who gets freaked out by clowns at the circus. Just thinking about the look on his face as he walked away, stealing suspicious glances at the three harmless craft projects sitting on a shelf, made me want to laugh again.

"What?" Lindsay asked. "What's so funny?"

"Dane," I said. "When he saw our grassheads."

Carin and Teresa started laughing again.

"It's a grasshead gang!" Carin said, lowering her voice to do an impression of Dane.

Teresa stood up and pretended to run away. "I'm out of here!"

Car and I laughed harder, and I hiccupped raspberry soda breath.

"That doesn't seem so funny to me," Lindsay said grumpily.

"I think you had to be there," Car said.

Lindsay clicked her juice lid a couple of times and stared at a fly that sat in a puddle where Carin's ice pop had dripped.

"I wish you were in our group, Linds," I said.

I knew she felt left out. I wished we could trade Teresa for Lindsay. Not that I don't like Teresa. She's nice and all. But Linds is my best camp friend, and I wanted to spend all day with her, not just rest hour, canteen, and cabin clean-up.

"Did anything else interesting happen this morning?" Lindsay asked, but I couldn't tell if she really wanted to know the answer.

"Not really," I said. Is lying bad when you do it to make somebody feel better?

"Mason ate a wiggly eye that was supposed to go on a grasshead," Carin said. She apparently hadn't caught on to the fact that Lindsay felt left out and that we shouldn't go on and on about all the funny things that had happened.

"Who's Mason?"

I scanned the nuke 'em court for him, but I didn't see him.

"Over there," Teresa said, pointing.

Mason stood next to where Steve and Kate sat on the rocks overlooking the nuke 'em court. Steve looked like he was yelling about something and had his hand held out. Mason bent over and spit something into Steve's hand. Kate leaned back away from whatever Mason had just spit, and Steve made a grossed-out face. Mason ran to the nuke 'em court, and when he turned around, I saw him grinning.

"Hey!" Rachel sat down on the bench next to me.

"Hi, Rach," Carin said.

"You guys, wasn't that funny in craft time when Julie and Kate named their grasshead Pierre and said he was from France?" Rachel asked, cracking open her soda can.

Lindsay let out a noise that sounded like a cross between a grunt and a sigh.

"I feel bad for you," I said. "You know, being in a group with those snobby girls."

Rachel shrugged and popped a round piece of candy into her mouth. "They're not that bad."

It was a good thing Rachel was the one stuck with them because if it were me and those two mean girls, I would've asked to go home last night.

"Alana is an only child, so she's bossy," Rachel said, "and Imogen has two older sisters who are mean to her, so she's kind of a bully. But I told them that you guys are my friends and if they said anything else rude to you, I'd punch them both in the face."

I laughed like it was a joke, but I think that Rachel really would do that. I was very glad that she was my friend and not my enemy. Now I knew those girls' names, so I could request to never be in their cabin. Alana and Imogen.

"Now, the boys in my group," Rach went on, "they're cool. Well, Hunter's not all that cool. He's afraid of everything. But T-Camp is hilarious, and Sam's nice."

The bell rang, and I chugged the rest of my soda, ending up with a fizzy throat.

"Time for hiking," Carin said.

We all got up, threw our garbage away, and headed off in different directions. Kate met us at the path going up to the cabin. We had to change into our swimsuits, then put our regular clothes over them for the hike and douse ourselves in bug dope.

As we walked up the path, I heard Dane yell, "T-Camp, don't pop the volleyball!"

Kate turned around at his shout and waved at him. "See you at swim time!"

I turned around, too, in time to see Dane pull a somewhat flat-looking volleyball out of troublemaker T-Camp's hands.

"Hopefully our entire group will be alive by swim time," he said.

Kate laughed at his remark, but I don't think he was joking. With a camper like T-Camp in their group, there was always a chance that somebody would be hit with a flaming marshmallow or pushed off the big rocks on Mount Spirit.

CHAPTER TEN

Mission Night

It started raining as we were standing outside the dining hall, waiting for the deans to ring the bell for dinner.

"Everybody inside," one of the counselors ordered.

"But the bell didn't ring yet," said a camper who I couldn't see through the crowd.

The rule is that nobody is allowed in the dining hall before meals except for the hoppers and some counselors.

"It's okay," Vanessa said, pushing the door open. She held it, and motioned for us to go inside. "You can go in to get out of the rain."

The rain was kind and waited until everybody was inside at their tables and Dean Ron had said grace before it decided to stream down harder.

After our chicken nuggets, French fries, vegetables that nobody ate, and cherry cheesecake that everybody except Mason ate, we sang some songs, led by not-so-nice Noelle the grasshead-hater, then headed down to the chapel. It was still raining—not pouring but still raining pretty steadily.

The rain had changed our plans for our evening program. We were supposed to have water Olympics, but the deans switched it to mission night because mission night is always held inside the chapel, so it didn't matter if the rain let up or poured harder. I didn't see why we couldn't have water Olympics in the rain. We were going to get wet anyway. Although, as we walked to the chapel and the cold raindrops hit my face, I agreed with the switch. We had already frozen during the swim tests. We didn't need to freeze again.

I sat in a pew between Carin and Kate. Teresa sat on the other side of Carin in the aisle seat, and the boys sat on the other end of the pew, using Steve as a shield between them and us girls.

I heard a big screech come from somewhere behind me. My whole pew turned around in time to see Dane lifting T-Camp off of two of the other kids in his group.

"You can't sit on the other campers, T," Dane said.

"But I want to! These benches are hard!"

Julie patted a spot on the wooden pew next to her. "I think you need to sit right next to me."

"No way," T-Camp protested. "I don't wanna sit by any girls or any counselors."

Dane looked like he was going to blow up (Who knows what else T-Camp had done all day to drive him nuts?), but before he could, Julie shrugged and said, "It's either sit by me or sit by the deans. Your choice."

T-Camp looked into the aisle. I think he was checking out his escape route, like he was going to bolt and run out of the chapel into the rain and down to the beach to have his own private water Olympics.

"Don't even think about it," Dane said, stepping between the pews to block T's exit.

T-Camp glared at Dane, a scary glare that looked like a creepy kid in a horror movie, but he moved down the pew past two of the girls and sat next to Julie.

"Do we have to do this?" one of the girls asked. She was the girl with the long blond hair, the lucky one who now had a seat right next to T-Camp, the terror. I didn't know if she was Alana or Imogen. "Because I don't want to. It's boring."

"How do you know if it's boring or not?" Dane asked. "It hasn't even started."

"I can just tell," she said.

"Good evening, campers," a loud voice said from the front of the chapel.

I turned around, as did the rest of the people who had been watching T-Camp's interesting group.

"Thanks for being such good campers, girls," Kate whispered as we focused on Dean Ron.

"Tonight," Dean Ron announced when it had quieted down to just whispers instead of loud talking, "we're going to talk about mission trips."

I used to think mission night was boring when I was a little kid and had to listen to it during junior high camp. Now that I'm older, I don't have trouble paying attention anymore. I don't have to resort to things like counting the number of people wearing blue shirts to pass the time. I just listen to the speakers.

"I've asked my friend Roger to talk with you tonight." Another man stood up in the front pew and walked the few steps to where Dean Ron stood. He was kind of old, probably a grandpa, and had gray hair and a few wrinkles. "Roger and I led a mission team to Haiti last fall, and we'd like to tell you a little about missionaries."

"Boring," I heard that girl behind me say, which was followed by a few giggles from her friend and a loud, annoyed-sounding, "Shh!" from Dane. I bet he wished he had us for campers again. Car and Chad and I would never say that in the middle of chapel, even if we thought it.

I looked down my row to see what everybody else was doing. Kate and Steve were watching Dean Ron and his friend, of course. So were Chad, Mason, and Wade. Wade squirmed around a little in his seat, but he wasn't noisy about it, and he watched the speakers all the time.

"We were in Haiti for two weeks," Roger said. "In some ways, it felt as if we had to leave the day after we got there, but in others, it felt as if we had been there for years."

Camp is sort of like that, too. It goes by fast but slow at the same time, kind of like summer vacation does in general.

"We spent most of our time at an orphanage," Dean Ron continued. "There were some wonderful nuns who ran this orphanage, but there were too many kids for the number of workers, so sometimes the kids wouldn't get very much attention."

"The teenagers who went with us had a great time playing with the children, even though they didn't speak the same language," Roger continued. "I brought some pictures that we can pass around."

He handed a pack of pictures to the counselor sitting in the first pew on the other side of the chapel, then gave another pack to the camper sitting in the first pew on our side.

"These kids don't have nice things like you and I do," Dean Ron said. "They only have one small toy box for all of them and old, dirty clothes. The nuns are very good to them and try to give them all they can, but it's a very poor country, and they can only give them what they can afford."

I hadn't heard much out of T-Camp, so I turned around to look at him. The girls had bored looks on their faces, but T sat up straight and leaned forward, staring at Dean Ron and Roger like they were his favorite television show instead of two old guys talking about missionaries. I guess Julie's plan to make him sit next to her had worked. That, or he liked stories about orphanages.

Dean Ron and his friend told several stories about their time in Haiti and the children they visited in the orphanage. Some of it was sad, like how whenever they would pick up one of the little kids, the kid would cling to them because they didn't get picked up or hugged often. Some of it was funny like a story Roger told about some of the mission workers getting lost when they were taking a walk and having to get directions from people who didn't speak English.

The mission workers smiled in all the pictures and looked like they were having fun. I don't know how fun it would have been though. The little kids from the orphanage looked skinny and sick. I think it would have been depressing to see that in person—as depressing as going to your friend's funeral even.

"I hope that you will all want to help these kids," Dean Ron said when they finished telling their stories. "You have the opportunity to donate any leftover canteen money you have to continue this mission, so that other groups may travel to Haiti."

"Unfortunately, you are all too young to be missionaries," Roger said, "but please make a generous donation for those who can go to Haiti. Every part of this mission is important: those who sacrifice time and energy to make the trips over there and those who give money to help fund the mission."

We said a prayer and sang some praise songs, and it was then that I noticed Carin. She looked down at the floor, didn't sing, and looked very sad.

***

Dean Ron did our devotions in the chapel instead of around the campfire because it was too wet outside. He talked about Zacchaeus and how Jesus loved everybody no matter how many sins you had.

Dean Jamie left the chapel when we sang one final song, and then Dean Ron said that we could go to the campfire area to have the snack that Jamie was getting ready. I wanted some of the chocolate chip cookies, but when everybody else got up to leave, Car sat there still looking sad.

I couldn't leave her behind, no matter how good I knew those chocolate chip cookies were.

"Carin?" Kate asked. "Are you all right?"

Carin didn't say anything, but I knew she was upset. Best friends know these things.

"There's something wrong," I said to Kate.

"Do you want to talk about it?" she asked, reaching her arm around me to touch Car's shoulder.

Most of the other campers and counselors had left already. Chocolate chip cookies are good motivation to go outside even into the sprinkling rain.

Carin shrugged. I had no idea what was wrong. It might have been that she felt bad for the kids in the orphanage, but Car doesn't usually get all worked up about things like that.

"One of those pictures made me sad," she finally admitted in a very small voice.

"Why?" Kate asked. I don't know how she could hear her. I could barely hear Car, and I was sitting next to her.

"There was a little black dog in it that looked like my dog."

I started remembering things about Zack. He had been a great, old doggie. He used to let us dress him up with bandannas, and we had dog shows with him as the star before he got too sick.

"Are you homesick for your dog?" Kate asked, not knowing that just a few days ago Mrs. Morgan had discovered that Zack had died in his sleep.

Carin shook her head, and tears started falling out of her eyes. I put my arm around her. She must've been really upset because Car doesn't cry very often. She's the tough one, and I'm the wimp who cries at things.

"Her dog died last week," I said, so Kate and Teresa would know.

"Oh, hon, that's too bad," Kate said.

"I feel like a baby," Carin choked out, wiping off tears. Welcome to my world, Car. "It was just a dog."

"No, it wasn't just a dog," Kate said firmly. "It was *your* dog, and pets can feel like part of the family as much as people."

"I want to get a cookie," Car said. She stood up and pushed past Teresa, heading to the back of the chapel.

We followed her. We almost had to run to keep up with her quick pace, but at the door she stopped and sat down on the steps and started crying again. Kate sat down next to her, and I sat on the other side.

"It's okay," Kate said. "You don't have to feel embarrassed. I would cry, too, if my dog died."

Carin put her head on Kate's shoulder, and our counselor hugged her. I didn't know what to do, so I sat next to Car and thought about Zack some more. I thought about all the tricks he could do and how we charged fifty cents to the neighbor kids for those pet shows. I thought about how whenever I slept over at Carin's house, Zack would sleep on the floor with us right between our sleeping bags.

Pretty soon, I thought I was going to cry, too. I tried to hold it in to keep the promise I had made to myself about not crying at camp, but my eyes wanted to cry.

Finally, the bell to go to our cabins rang. Car had been calming down from sobs to the occasional sniff, so Kate hugged her and stood up. We all stood up with her, and Carin and Teresa both took one of Kate's hands. I put my hand on Car's shoulder, and we started walking back to the cabin. I could tell that we were going to have a very close cabin by the end of the week.

As we passed the nurse's cabin, Car said, "You guys didn't get chocolate chip cookies."

"That's all right," Kate said. "I wasn't hungry anyway."

"Me neither," Teresa said.

"Me neither," I said, but I really had wanted a chocolate chip cookie. Ben makes them, and they're really good.

I wouldn't tell Carin that though. I wouldn't want her to feel bad about it.

CHAPTER ELEVEN

The Second Annual Taco Eating Contest

Another line for the showers greeted us when we got to the bathroom the next morning, this one even longer than yesterday's. It made me think about going to the boys' side, but only for about half a second. I don't know how people can take a shower in that thing where everyone else can see them. If I'm ever a millionaire and have a lot of money to donate to charity, I will buy shower curtains and walls for the boys' side of the bathroom at camp.

Carin, Lindsay, and I stood in line until seven thirty-five when Carin said, "Forget this," and went back to the cabin to get dressed.

By that time we were almost to the front of the line, so I stayed. So did Lindsay. I figured I'd waited in line that long, so why quit now? Plus, I always get dressed by throwing on the first pair of jeans and T-shirt I find in my suitcase. It's not like I needed a lot of time like Car.

Waiting almost paid off because at seven forty-three, I was at the front of the line, and Teresa came out of the shower with a towel wrapped around herself.

"I was in the one with the good water pressure," she told me.

"Excellent."

"It's not even cold yet. Just a little, like lukewarm. But not cold."

That was pleasantly surprising news, since long lines in the bathroom usually mean a freezing shower. If Car had been just a little more patient, she would have gotten Teresa's shower with the good water pressure and lukewarm temperature.

I reached back to grab my towel and bathroom bag off the shelf, and somebody brushed by me.

"Hey," Teresa said, and Noelle turned around from her spot in front of me.

"Counselors can cut," she said in a snippy voice.

Noelle did not have her make-up on yet and actually looked better without black caked around her eyelids. I wished I was brave enough to tell her that, not only because I was mad that she had cut in front of me but also because it was good advice about how she could look better in life.

"But Abby was next," Teresa said. "And they've been waiting a long time."

"Too bad," Noelle said. "I'm a counselor, and you're just a dumb camper. All the counselors cut. Deal with it, losers." She snapped the shower curtain shut behind her.

I could not believe that a counselor had just called Lindsay, Teresa, and me losers. Who ever heard of a mean counselor before? And it was a lie that all the counselors cut in line for the showers. Just yesterday Kate and Julie had moved to the yucky boys' side of the bathroom to take their showers instead of going in front of the campers in line.

"I don't think we have time to wait anymore," Lindsay said.

"No," I agreed. "We don't. Not if we don't want to be late for breakfast."

Linds got her things off the shelf, and we headed back to the cabin with Teresa to get dressed. There was nothing I could do about Noelle this week. I was "just a dumb camper" at elementary camp, like she had pointed out herself. She could be a big jerk all she wanted. But at junior high camp, I'm not just a camper. I'm the dean's daughter. I was going to tell my parents to never, never, never as long as they lived let Noelle be a counselor at junior high camp.

There are very few things at camp that really irritate me. Some of the dumb songs they make us sing after meals is one thing. Another is not getting a shower when I want one. Counselors who cut in the bathroom should be banned from camp. There should be something on the counselor evaluation form about it.

***

Bad luck in the bathroom is usually a sign that the day is off to a bad start. It didn't get much better as the morning went on. Breakfast was oatmeal, which I happen to think is disgusting and should never be served to kids. None of us campers even touched the oatmeal. Steve ate it, but even Kate wrinkled her nose at his heaping bowl and ate cold cereal instead. I ate Fruit-os cereal out of the dispenser and drank watery hot chocolate.

The hot chocolate machine must not have gotten filled with chocolate that morning.

Cabin clean-up was okay, but I knew we wouldn't win today because we had won yesterday. The deans said that just because your cabin won didn't mean it couldn't win again, but I know they just say that so the people who already won don't slack off or trash their cabins. They always try to let all the cabins win, if possible. It takes away some of the motivation to clean when you know you won't win again so soon unless all the other cabins look like disaster zones.

I had to resort to counting the number of people who were wearing blue shirts in chapel in order to stay awake because it was so boring. Dean Ron didn't tell a Bible story. He talked about the Ten Commandments for twenty-five minutes. That is a long time to have to listen to a speech about the Ten Commandments. I was bored by the time he got to commandment number three.

Then we had to play volleyball when some people got sick of our nuke 'em game. I'm okay at most sports. Not a star, but not the kid who gets picked last, either. Volleyball is hard for me though because I'm so short. My growth spurt could happen any day now—that would be okay with me. I'm sick of being shorter than everybody else.

I somehow survived not getting a bloody nose like this kid once did in gym class. Nobody was very good at volleyball except for Steve (major height advantage), Dane (natural athlete), Noelle (played volleyball in high school), and Teresa (loves sports). Even Kate and Julie weren't so good at it, and they were counselors.

The only really good part about the morning was craft time. The girls got to sit at one table and make sand art while the boys went to the totally opposite part of the craft cabin and made bugs with wheels on them. I don't know why the bugs had wheels. They just did. It seemed like a dumb craft project to me, but all the boys acted hyper about it, like it was the best thing ever. Kate and Julie sat with us and created Pierre's wife, a grasshead named Laurette, who had cool earrings made out of blue milk carton rings.

I was glad that the boys sat at their own table because we really needed a break from having to watch Mason eat gross things and making sure T-Camp didn't get close enough to put "kick me" signs on our backs like he tried to do during the Ten Commandments speech in chapel. The grossest thing about craft time was that Mason ate a piece of felt and washed it down with glue.

***

Lunchtime brought the first really fantastic part of the day: tacos.

"Welcome to the second annual taco eating contest," Carin said when we had all found spots around our lunch table—a table filled with bowls of lettuce, tomatoes, sauce, cheese, and more.

She held a spoon in front of her mouth like a microphone. I think she was trying to get into the mindset of a game show host for her role in our skit. Once she had to play a cat in our first grade Old MacDonald play, and she walked around her house on all fours and only said, "meow," and, "hiss," for a week.

"Second annual?" Steve asked, with a chuckle. "I hate to break it to you, Car, but we had very full and interesting lives here at camp before you started coming, which actually included taco eating contests."

Steve had won last year's taco eating contest, and Dane blamed it on eating a bunch of pancakes for breakfast.

"How many taco eating contests have you had?" Mason asked.

A taco eating contest would be right up Mason's alley, only the kind of tacos he'd probably want to eat would have something disgusting on them like bugs or at least spicy guacamole. I wonder if Mason has ever eaten a marble like T-Camp.

"I'm not sure how many taco eating contests there have been. I guess one every week that we've been at camp together."

Steve stood up a little and leaned forward towards Carin and me and the other table. Car and I had good spots, on the side of the table that was back-to-back with Dane and Julie and Rachel's table so we could swivel around to watch the action from both sides.

"Dude, how many taco eating contests have we had?" Steve asked.

"I don't know," Dane said, turning around.

Dean Jamie walked to the middle of the clusters of tables and raised his hand. Everybody stood to sing the Johnny Appleseed song for grace.

Dane turned around again as everybody sat down. "Seven."

"Seven what?" Kate asked.

"There have been seven taco eating contests at camp, and one at Border Grill that involved not only us but Scott and Billy, and you have to switch spots with Steve."

Kate, next to me, gave him a funny look.

"It's for the contest," he explained.

Steve and Dane went up to the counter to get the bowl of taco meat. I grabbed a soft shell taco and put it on my plate before Steve could eat all of them. Kate stole Steve's seat when he was getting the taco meat so he was left with hers, which put him back to back with his competitor. He turned around in his chair and asked Dane if he had a witness, and Dane motioned at his table that was full except for one spot—Noelle's. That was okay. She'd probably make fun of a taco eating contest anyway. That or she'd eat all the tacos herself and not let anybody else have any.

"We should have a taco eating contest," Chad said. "I mean us campers."

I think he said that because he knew he could win. Boys can usually eat more than girls. Not always, but a lot of times. Plus Mason was probably too full from eating a spider or something, so that left him with Wade as his main competition. I wished I could eat fifteen tacos and prove Chad wrong. I can't stand boys who think they're tougher than girls. And to think, I had saved Chad's life last year by checking that the medication The Scary Nurse brought to our table every night actually had his name on it and wasn't poison.

Steve dribbled salsa onto his taco. "Your counselors are about to consume more taco ingredients than anybody ever should." He took a big bite of the taco and said with his mouth full, "Do not attempt this at home." It was sort of hard to understand him with the taco in his mouth.

For the record, Steve still looks cute even when he talks with his mouth full. Wait until I tell Car about this whole having-a-crush thing. She'll go bonkers. I can't tell her until camp is over though because she will be way too loud about it and he'll end up finding out.

Chad smiled, then picked up his hard shell taco and shoved it into his mouth.

"Don't attempt it here, either," Kate said. She pulled Chad's plate away from him and made him swallow what was in his mouth before he took another bite. "I don't want anybody to throw up."

I finished making my taco, which required looking away from Steve and Chad and down at the table. I could probably only eat two. Kate was watching all of us like we were going to start eating bugs like Mason. I think she was mentally totaling the number of tacos each of us ate to make sure we didn't overeat and get stomachaches.

Sure enough, after two tacos, I was pretty full, so I watched Steve eat instead.

"And the reigning champ goes for taco number three," Carin announced into her spoon.

I don't know why we had silverware for taco day. I guess the hoppers didn't put much thought into what we would need for the meal.

"He shows no sign of being full," Car went on. In all the excitement, she hadn't finished her first taco. She was too busy commentating, and half of the taco sat on her plate. "I am going into enemy territory to see how Steve's rival is doing." Car leaned back near the other table. "What number taco are you guys on?"

Dane swallowed and stuck his tongue out to prove he had finished his taco.

T-Camp stood up, pointed at Dane, and shouted, "That's three!" He looked over at our table and said, "Eat that for breakfast!" That cracked up Kate and Julie, and they both sat there giggling really hard. It wasn't breakfast though. It was lunch. T-Camp really is a strange boy.

"It's a fierce battle locked at three tacos each," Carin said so seriously that you would have thought she was a news reporter talking about a deadly tornado or a war.

The contest went on for quite a while. Chad made it to a couple bites of round four, but then he had to stop. The hoppers had started clearing the dishes at most of the other tables by the time the contest got to six tacos. I knew that it was only half over. Last year, Steve had to eat eleven tacos to win. There probably wouldn't be much time left after the meal to sing songs. Wahoo! Maybe we could go right to rest hour and throw gimp notes and not have to watch Noelle-the-shower-stealer sing songs.

"Yum, yum, yum," I heard T-Camp say in a weird voice that sounded like a cartoon alien.

I turned around to look at him. He was covered in taco stuff. His face and hands had sauce all over them. He had dropped pieces of shredded cheese on the table and in his lap. But the funniest thing about T-Camp's mess was that he had a rather large chunk of lettuce stuck to his cheek.

I took a napkin out of the metal dispenser and wiped my face. I was pretty sure I didn't look like T-Camp, but you never know on taco day. I wiped my fingers off, but I needed another napkin. The napkins they have at camp are pretty wimpy. If you need one napkin at home, you'll probably need two or three of the camp kind to do the same job.

"Are you a freak?"

I turned around again. All the good stuff seemed to happen at the other table. We had a pretty normal group except for Mason's bug eating habits and Carin's serious play-by-play commentary about eating tacos. Dane's and Julie's group, on the other hand, was never quiet and didn't usually do what they were supposed to.

Noelle had come back to their table. I don't know where she had been, but she was back now, hands on her hips, glaring at T-Camp.

"Go to the bathroom and wipe all that crud off of yourself, you disgusting little monster!"

Seriously, how had Noelle managed to find a pastor and "two unrelated adults" to sign the form that she had to turn in to the deans who thought she would be "an asset to the camping program"? (I've seen those forms at home, so I *know* the counselors have to fill them out.)

T-Camp didn't seem to mind Noelle's insult. He giggled and said, "No thanks," about wiping up.

Noelle sat down and made a funny noise that sounded like a drawn-out sigh and a grunt. I don't know what the big deal was. Taco day is always messy. Not as messy as T-Camp had made it, but messy. Once at junior high camp I filled my taco with too much sauce, and it ran all the way down my arm to my elbow. This was in the old dining hall that didn't have bathrooms, so my mom had to take me into the kitchen, and I held my arm in the dish window by the dishwasher so Ben could spray me with the dish sprayer.

I was thinking about that time and the old kitchen and how I still wasn't used to this new dining hall with its bright white walls and no screened-in porch when I heard Dane exclaim, "Aw, Noelle!"

Carin, Steve, and I turned around, and the people on the other side of the table leaned forward. Dane held half of a taco in his hand, but he didn't eat it.

"Is that eight or nine?" Steve asked.

"Eight," Dane said, sounding disgusted.

"You going to finish that or what?"

Dane pointed at Noelle. "Interference! I call interference. She said something gross."

T-Camp laughed as he shoved food into his mouth. "Fingers, yum, yum."

What did that mean?

"If you don't eat that, I win," Steve said.

"I know." Dane put the half taco up to his face, and it looked like he was going to eat it, but then he groaned and dropped it onto his plate.

"The champion!" Carin shouted, grabbing Steve's arm and holding it in the air.

"The *undefeated* elementary camp champion, two years in a row," he corrected her.

The hoppers for our two tables could finally start cleaning up. All the other tables were done and waiting for the song leading. As Mason and Chad stacked plates and cups, Carin interviewed Steve about his victory.

"What was your motivation?" She stuck her "microphone" up to his face.

"I wanted to beat Dane."

"Do you train away from camp?"

"Why, yes. I frequent Border Grill quite a bit and do most of my serious training there."

"Tell us all, how did you manage to eat eight tacos this afternoon?"

"I thought I was finished on taco number six," he said seriously, "but I then burped, and suddenly there was room for two more tacos."

"That's disgusting, Steve," Kate said.

I think the purpose of day groups is that girl counselors and boy counselors are good at different things. Girl counselors are good at making sure you remember your towels and sunscreen for swim hour, but boy counselors are the ones who make things like eating lunch fun and interesting.

"I want a rematch," Dane said. "Noelle and her meat packing plant story interfered with my taco eating abilities."

"That's why you stopped eating?" Carin asked. "Because Noelle told a gross story?"

I knew it had to be something about Noelle. She ruined a lot of things. The grassheads. The taco eating contest. Taking a shower. Somebody needed to push her in the lake or something. I'd volunteer, but I don't think I'm big enough or brave enough.

CHAPTER TWELVE

Noelle Makes a Splash

"I wish this lake was more like the pool at the community center," Carin said, as we treaded water in the middle of the roped-off swimming area.

"I know," I said. My foot had touched the bottom several times already. "There aren't any good games you can play when the water is so shallow."

I watched Teresa as she dripped on the sand near the buddy board. She had just decided to get out because she thought it was too cold, and now she had to take her buddy tag off and switch Carin's and mine to doubles.

"Here comes Kate," Carin said. "Maybe she will have an idea of what we can do. And there are the boys." Car turned her back to me and pointed at a bunch of boys shoving each other.

Kate walked by us through the water, but she wasn't out for a relaxing swim or trying to play Marco Polo. She seemed in a hurry to get somewhere, but she looked down at the water as she walked instead of ahead to where she was going.

"What's wrong?" I asked as she passed us.

Kate looked up with a smile I could tell was fake and said, glumly, "Nothing, hon. Not really, anyway."

One thing I can't stand is when grown-ups lie to kids because they don't want them to have to worry about something or they think that kids can't handle hearing about a little problem. I knew she was upset about something. People don't randomly have teary eyes for no reason.

What could have made my counselor look like she was going to cry in the middle of swim time? There's nothing sad about swim hour. Mission night can be sad if the mission is about starving orphans or something, and nighttime can make you feel homesick. Not swim hour though. I guess I'd cry during swim time if the lifeguard was mean, like this one guy who lifeguards at the community center and yells at you if you even accidentally splash somebody with your foot while you're swimming by. Cord and Tony weren't like that though, so I didn't see anything to be upset about.

Poor Kate. Maybe her pet died last week and somebody said something that reminded her of it, just like Carin was upset about Zack last night. I didn't want her to be sad. She was a really nice counselor. I hoped it wasn't anything worse than missing a pet that was bothering her, like missing a person, the way Steve was.

The only thing that made me stop wondering what was wrong with Kate was Carin's shout of, "Whoa!" and the sound of a big splash. I turned around just in time to see somebody's hand go under water in the middle of a huge wave of splash.

Car grabbed my arm. "Did you see that? That was awesome!"

"All right!" I heard Chad yell from somewhere behind me.

I hadn't seen it, but I could guess what had happened when Noelle stood up next to the dock completely soaked. She turned around sharply and looked up at Dane, pointing and yelling something I couldn't hear.

"Good job!" Car screamed. She had a little pink spot on the cheek I could see, and her nose had wrinkled up as it always does when she gets mad. "She laughed at Pierre!"

Since I hadn't actually seen Dane push Noelle into the lake, I tried to picture what it would look like in my head. That made me giggle. That's what happens to people who cut in line in the bathroom. I hadn't seen what her hair looked like before her dunk in the lake, but now it was messy and wet, probably like my own ponytail that had started out in the center of my head but had worked its way to one side like on those music videos of people from a long time ago that Angela watches on *Totally 80's Weekend*. Noelle kept pulling at her swimsuit, and even though I couldn't see her face I could tell by the way she moved her head that she was still yelling at Dane, like her yelling at him would bother him.

Dane actually had a smile on his face. He pulled off his shirt, dropped it onto the dock next to Steve, and jumped into the lake. His jump splashed Noelle again. They said something to each other that I couldn't hear, and then he swam by us, too, and ended up on the raft with Kate and the lifeguards.

The whole rest of swim time, all any of the campers could talk about was Noelle's unintentional dive into the lake. T-Camp, Chad, and their friend Sam even reenacted it twice. T-Camp played Noelle by prancing around the dock on his tiptoes, pursing his lips, and batting his eyes. Then Chad said in a deep voice, "Take that, jerk face," and shoved T-Camp in the shoulder. T-Camp let out a high-pitched shriek and made a big show of falling into the lake with a great belly flop. Sam's only part in this, as Steve, was to turn around, look at Chad, and give him the thumbs-up sign.

The only bummer about the whole thing was that I hadn't gotten to see it live. I had been too busy trying to find out what was wrong with Kate. The gift of compassion strikes again. Carin hadn't noticed or cared that Kate was upset about something, and she had witnessed Noelle's plunge into Lake Spirit.

It wasn't fair. Thinking about other people sure makes you miss out on some good stuff.

Plus, I had the idea way before Dane did. I had thought that someone should push Noelle into the lake during the taco eating contest.

**

We had our group camp picture in front of the chapel after dinner. It was supposed to have been yesterday, but the photographer canceled because of all the rain. The ground had completely dried out by now, leaving the grass a brighter shade of green, not that anybody would be able to tell in a black and white photo. Some of the counselors went to the craft cabin to get benches and others started to organize the group into rows.

"Okay, guys," Kate said, as more groups joined us on the hill. "Stay together."

One thing I will never get used to at elementary camp is how the campers have to stay with their groups all the time. I think I'm too used to junior high camp and all the free time those campers get. On the other hand, staying with my group wasn't all that bad because I got to see Steve and his awesome eyes and great thick, dark hair almost every second of the day. Oh boy. I have to stop thinking like Carin and go back to thinking like myself. Although, if I did think more like Car, I'd probably be a more exciting and fun person.

Steve and Dane came back with benches. Steve had my favorite bench, the tan one that people had graffitied over the years. Angela and I had written our names with a wood burner in one corner. I was about to point out the star my sister had burned when Dane dropped his bench, a brown one with a big blue paint stain on the seat, and it rolled down the hill a couple of feet.

"I still can't believe I lost the taco eating contest because Noelle was disgusting," he said, shaking his head. "There's going to be an interference rule next year. There need to be more clear-cut rules."

"Well, you can train all you want for next summer's taco eating contest," Steve said. "But I'm going to beat you again, and then these campers will go to junior high camp knowing that I am the master of all things taco."

"Let's get ready!" the photographer shouted from down the hill. He had his camera and tripod set up and held out a little black box.

The counselors shooed campers into rows. Car, Teresa, and I stood in front of Steve, Kate, Dane, and Julie, who stood on the back bench. The boys sat on the bench in front of us.

Lindsay and Rachel ditched their groups to stand by us. We would have to be smarter next year about requesting each other so the four of us could get in the same group. Car and I had requested to be with each other on our registration forms, but I hadn't thought about making sure my mom requested Lindsay and Rachel when she filled out the form.

The deans, hoppers, and camp staff came down the path from cleaning up the dining hall just in time to jump into the picture. Ben climbed onto the bench between Kate and Steve. By then the photographer was ready, and he held up that little black box thing again.

"You guys all know what to say, right?" he asked. "Toby."

A big, black dog with pointed ears stood up in the back of the photographer's truck when he heard his name.

"Hey!" Teresa exclaimed. "A dog!"

Toby always comes with the photographer. If the campers get their picture taken without fooling around too much, the photographer has Toby show off his tricks.

"On the count of three," he announced, positioning his finger over the button on the camera. "One, two, three."

"Toby!" we all chanted, giving our best smiles.

This year of camp had started off much better than last. I remember thinking that Toby the dog was the best part of camp when we had our picture taken last summer. Toby is pretty cool and all, but there's no way he was the best part of camp this year.

We said, "Toby!" three more times so the photographer would have four pictures to choose from in case some wise guy boys decided to give each other rabbit ears or stick their tongues out.

"Okay, everybody," Dean Jamie announced, his hands cupped around his mouth. "Go get your suits on for the water Olympics, and we'll meet you at the beach!"

The counselors jumped down from the benches, and we all headed in different directions. Car, Teresa, Lindsay, and I followed Kate back to the cabin after Toby had done his tricks.

"Did you have water Olympics last year?" Kate asked as we crunched the pebbles on the path.

"Yep," I said. "And it was fun."

"Our team won," Carin said. "Me and Abby and Lindsay and Chad. We're the champions." She put one arm around me and one around Lindsay.

"Maybe we'll win again," Kate said.

"We can't all win," Lindsay said softly.

Yep, next year we were definitely going to have to make better use of that line on the registration forms where you can request a buddy.

CHAPTER THIRTEEN

Defending the Water Olympics Title

After a milk crate game (that I helped my team win by squishing myself into a big, red milk crate while Chad and Wade pulled me through the water) and a greased watermelon game (that was slimy and gross), we had a beach nuke 'em tournament. Two teams at a time played each other, and then all the winners would play until they had an overall winner. Vanessa and another counselor read off the pairings. There were two games before our team had to play, so we got some time to hang out or swim if we wanted to. Our group stood together by the buddy board.

"Are you guys going in the water?" Kate asked.

"Yeah," I said. "C'mon, let's go."

Mason and Chad ran for the lake while Car, Teresa, Wade, and I searched the other side of the buddy board for our tags. Before we could get one toe in the water, Steve said, "Uh oh, here comes trouble."

Dane walked barefoot in the grass over to us, trailed by Sam and Hunter, two of his campers. I didn't know where T-Camp was. Hopefully, Dane did because knowing that kid, he could be hitchhiking to Marquette or blowing up the canteen.

"Hey," Dane said, holding out part of a watermelon. "Want an early snack?"

"Sure," Car said, and we all held our hands out as he hacked at it with a pocketknife.

"Are you about done with my knife?" Steve asked. "I'd like it back before the deans see that it says, 'James Koski,' on it, link that to me, and write, 'aids and abets criminals,' on my counselor evaluation sheet."

"What's aiding and betting on criminals mean?" I asked Steve.

We watched Dane stab the leftover watermelon with his knife and watermelon juice squirt all over the sand.

"It's when a well-behaved, law-abiding citizen gets conned into hiding their criminal friend or driving the getaway car or giving them a gun or something," Steve said.

Dane ignored him and handed the first piece to Carin, who had the most outstretched and jumpy hand. "All I'm doing is cutting pieces for hungry campers to eat," he said innocently.

"Ew!" Car said, making a face and letting go of the watermelon piece with one hand and shifting it in the other so that it dangled between her index finger and thumb. "It's all slimy." She flapped her right hand back and forth, splattering something on everybody.

"Stop it, Car," I said as a couple of drops landed on my leg.

"Yeah, there's grease on the rinds from that game," Dane said. He gave Teresa, Wade, and me pieces and wiped his hand on the side of his swim trunks.

"You're going to ruin your swimsuit," Kate said, pointing to the grease spot on the waistband of his swim trunks.

"Then I'd better find another place to wipe my hands," he said, brushing the palm of his hand all the way down her arm.

"Gross," she said, shoving him away but laughing at the same time. "Our campers are learning some interesting things this week. I don't think their parents will let them come back."

"What are you talking about?" Dane asked, taking a big bite of watermelon. "They're learning a lot of important things."

"Yeah," Steve joked. "Like how to hit people with watermelon rinds."

"That was funny," Sam said. From what I had seen of Sam this week, he was a pretty decent boy. He hadn't pulled anybody's hair or made fun of any girls, at least as far as I had noticed, and he could be a bully if he wanted to with his size—tall and solid but not chunky.

"Who are you hitting with watermelon rinds?" I asked.

"Noelle," Dane said, his mouth full of watermelon. "Six times. Six direct hits and one that went off target and accidentally hit Bruce in the side of the head." He held up the rind. "This'll make some good ammunition."

"I think you should stop throwing things at Noelle," Kate said.

"Why? She was totally mean to you during swim time today. All that rude stuff she said ticked me off."

"I know, but I don't want you to get in trouble. Plus, it's not nice."

Dane looked across the beach at Noelle. I could tell he really wanted to throw the rind at her, but he twisted around and tossed it into the garbage can behind him instead.

"We learned lots of good things this week so far," Car said. "Like how to make a grasshead."

Dane stuck his tongue out and said, "Bleck."

"That's gross, Dane," Kate said. I think she said that because he had pieces of chewed-up watermelon on his tongue.

"We also learned how to eat a lot of tacos," Sam said.

"And about the meat packing plant," Hunter said. He and Sam both laughed, but I had no idea what made a meat packing plant so funny. It must be a weird boy thing, like how to a normal person farting is only mildly funny but to a boy it's hilarious.

"If you value your canteen card, you'll stop talking," Dane said. "Hey, check this out. See that rock over there?" He nodded at a rock about ten feet away. Then he launched a watermelon seed out of his mouth. It bounced off the rock and landed in the sand.

"Awesome," Wade said.

"How old are you?" Steve asked.

"Eighteen." He shot another seed that also hit the rock. "And ten months. How old are you?" he teased back.

"Too old to spit watermelon seeds at inanimate objects."

Dane's response was to spit a seed at Steve. It hit him in the forehead and fell on the ground. I watched him, waiting for his reaction. He just looked at Dane, stunned for a moment.

"You're not an inanimate object," Dane defended himself.

Steve reached over, grabbed a piece of watermelon, and took a big bite out of it without saying a word. He slowly chewed and swallowed.

"Oh, it's on," Steve finally said, still looking serious.

Three seeds popped out of his mouth at Dane right after each other.

"Hey, awesome!" Wade yelled. "It's like a machine gun with watermelon seeds."

"Show us how to do that," Sam said, reaching for another piece of watermelon.

"Yeah," Teresa said. "Take all these boys somewhere else for a seed-spitting class." I think Teresa had the same opinion I used to have about boys, that they were immature and not good for much besides entertainment.

"But give my knife back first," Steve said.

Dane dropped the leftover watermelon in the sand and handed Steve his knife. He held his gooey hands out at Kate and wiggled his fingers.

"Don't touch me," Kate said. She twisted her arm to look at the spot he had already coated. "This stuff is drying on my skin."

He dropped his grin and looked serious. "Sorry. That was not very nice of me. I should help you wash it off."

"Yes, you should. You should go to the bathroom and get a paper towel and bring it back—"

He ducked down and scooped her into his arms. "One shower coming up."

"No," Kate protested. "Don't you dare."

"By the end of the night, my plan is for everybody to be soaked except for me. It's nothing personal. You're just a casualty of the plan."

"Do it!" Car shouted, pumping her fist into the air. "Throw her in the water!"

"Thanks, Carin," Kate said. "I'm glad I have such loyal campers."

"Don't do it," I said. I actually thought it would be funny, but somebody had to take Kate's side.

Car and I followed Dane to the lake, shouting at him until he reached water that came up to the bottom of his baggy swimsuit and dropped Kate in.

"Just you wait," she teased him when she stood up, a dripping mess. She looked a lot better drenched than Noelle had though. "By the end of these water Olympics, you won't be dry either."

"This is it," he said, smacking the skin above his knees where the water ended. "This is as wet as I'm getting."

Kate smiled at him and headed for shore.

"I think you're in trouble," I said.

"I'm not worried."

Vanessa announced into the megaphone that it was our group's turn for a beach nuke 'em game, so we had to dry off and join our team on the court.

***

We had a plan. A secret plan. The only people who knew about it were Kate, Carin, Teresa, and me. Car almost ruined it out of loyalty to the only crush she's kept almost as long as that singer Ridge Stone, but when she found out Kate's plan revolved around Car and me touching Dane, she was all for it.

We lost our first nuke 'em game of the tournament to Vanessa's and Donnie's campers, but none of us cared except for Teresa, who was really big into sports and super competitive. I liked hanging out and getting to have fun in the lake more than playing the games. Lindsay and Rachel got to join us when their groups weren't playing.

"Go, now, girls," Kate said as soon as Dane strolled out to the end of the dock. He didn't have any more watermelon or watermelon seeds.

Teresa hopped onto the dock, and Carin and I jumped around in the water.

Dane hadn't gotten wet all night, just like he planned. Everything was dry from his hair and his Camp Spirit T-shirt down to his swim trunks and bare feet. The very bottom of his feet were probably wet from standing on the dock, but that was it. Carin made enough noise so that he stopped his conversation with another counselor to look over at us and flash us one of his dimpled half-smiles.

"Watch me do a handstand!" Carin yelled.

She dunked herself under the water, and the next thing we saw of her were her feet and knees wiggling above the surface. I half-swam-half-walked over to the end of the dock and looked up at Dane. I slowly shifted my eyes to Teresa who stood a few feet away from him. She lifted up her fingers in the "Okay" sign. I looked back at Dane so he wouldn't notice Teresa lurking behind him and get suspicious.

Carin's feet splashed me, and her head reappeared. "What did you think?"

"That was pretty good," I said.

Dane clapped a couple times. "Nice."

"I want to stand on the dock, too," I said. "Are campers allowed?"

"Sure?"

"Help then."

I reached up and grabbed his hand.

"Me, too," Carin said. She lunged through the water and clamped onto his other hand.

Dane braced himself with his feet and said, "Okay, you guys ready to jump?"

I had to hold my mouth shut tightly to hide a grin. As soon as he started pulling us up, Car and I hung back instead of jumping, and Teresa came running down the dock to give him a good shove in the back. All four of us fell into the water.

The three of us campers stood up laughing, and Dane surfaced looking shocked at first, but then he glared like he was trying to be annoyed, but cracked a smile after about half a second and ended up looking more impressed than annoyed.

"Very sneaky," he said, standing up and holding his arms away from his soaked shirt. "I like it."

I looked up and saw Kate smiling on the end of the dock. "Looks like somebody got outsmarted by a bunch of campers."

"Yeah," he admitted with a smile. "You girls got me." He reached out towards Kate. "Now help me onto the dock."

"No way." Kate backed away from his outstretched arm. "You'll pull me in like they did to you."

"I wouldn't do that." With a grunt, he pulled himself and his wet clothes onto the dock, then hopped to his feet. "But you look entirely too dry to be at the water Olympics."

He put his arms around her and hugged her close to him. Kate shrieked and tried to push him away, but he held on, getting her soaked again.

"I'm entirely too dry for the water Olympics!" Carin shouted, even though there wasn't a single part of her that didn't look like a drowned rat.

Car scrambled onto the dock, trying to get his attention and the dripping wet hug that Kate was attempting to escape.

"Let go," Kate said, but she was laughing and not trying all that hard to get out of his hug grip. "You're wet and cold, and I just dried off."

"Not until you admit that you made your campers do your dirty work for you."

"I did the dirty work!" Carin shouted, grabbing his arm.

I've gotten squeezed on the arm before by Car, and she pinches hard, so I don't know how he didn't notice her, but it didn't seem as if he did. He was too busy holding onto Kate and teasing her. I had the awful thought that this was going to end up the same way the Stacey thing did last year; Dane getting a camp girlfriend, and Carin upset and crying to me about it.

What was life going to be like when we were actually old enough to have boyfriends? If Car was this crazy over eighteen-year-old boys who didn't know she existed, what in the world was I going to go through with her when we were teenagers and the boys she liked had the potential to like her back?

***

We had to get off the dock and go to our teams for the last event, a swimming relay.

"Okay," Steve said to our tight huddle. He was the only dry one. "You guys heard Vanessa. We need one boy and one girl."

"Abby and Chad," Car said right away. "It has to be them. They won the swimming relay last year."

"I'll do it," Chad said. "If nobody else wants to."

"Yeah, you do it," Wade said.

Mason nodded. "You're the best swimmer."

"Chad and Abby then?" Kate asked.

Teresa looked like she wanted to protest, but everybody else seemed excited about having Chad and me, last year's winners, represent our team. Teresa's more athletic than I am, but she doesn't know what a good swimmer I am. That made me want to win extra hard, to prove to her that I deserved the spot in the relay.

"Swimmers, line up!" Vanessa announced into the megaphone. "Girls first, then boys."

It was the opposite order this year. Last summer, the boys had gone first. At least this meant I wouldn't be the one having to cross the finish line when it counted the most. I stood next to Rachel, my toe just touching the line Vanessa had drawn in the sand, and waited for the signal to go.

"Good luck," Rach said to me.

"You, too."

I didn't like having to compete against my friend, especially not a friend who had long legs and a killer competitive edge. Rach would probably punch anybody who beat her, or at least loook at them with that scary glare of hers. Luckily, we were going first, so we wouldn't know who won until the boys finished and I could get away from her.

Chad stood behind me, and everybody quieted down, waiting for Vanessa to start the race.

"Come on, Abby," Chad whispered. He punched me in the shoulder blade, which I think is how boys pump each other up for sports, but it still stung. "We have to win again."

I planted my feet in the sand and leaned forward. This was a lot more stressful than I remembered last year. Then again, last year Chad and I were two new campers who nobody expected to win the swimming relay.

"Go!" Vanessa yelled, and I ran.

I ran as hard as I could, splashing water behind me until I got to the first set of buoys. I dove over the rope and swam underwater, kicking my legs furiously and keeping them as straight as I could. I surfaced, took a breath, and started pulling through the water with my arms. I didn't see anybody in front of me, so I knew I was in the lead as I got to the second set of buoys where we had to turn around. I stretched my arm out and hit the rope with my hand, then tried to turn around as fast as I could.

Right before I turned, I saw another hand hit the rope. I wanted to know who was right behind me so bad I almost looked, but I knew stalling would break the rhythm of my swimming strokes, so I pushed on. I didn't feel tired at all, just excited to be at the front of the pack.

I swam until my knee scraped pebbles, then jumped up and sprinted to tag Chad. As soon as I slapped his hand, the energy escaped out of me and into him. I fell onto the grass at the end of the sand, and Chad took off running faster than anybody is supposed to at camp.

"Yea, Abby!" Kate yelled. "First place for your leg of the race."

Carin and Teresa ran over to me and hugged me, and we all ended up in a pile on the grass. I sat up and watched Chad dive over the rope and begin his swim. The boys couldn't be bothered congratulating me because they were too busy watching Chad and cheering for him to win.

Steve leaned down and took my hand to help me up. He had big, strong hands like I remembered Scott having. I wondered if he could do the small, round gimp braid. Scott had told me that his large fingers were too clumsy for that braid. Maybe I could make Steve a gimp bracelet like Car did last year for Dane. My gimp bracelet would look a lot better than hers had. How do you make a gimp bracelet for a cute counselor without it being obvious that you have a crush on him?

"Good job, Abbers," Steve said, giving me a pat on the shoulder that was a lot nicer than Chad's punch had been. That broke me out of my gimp thoughts.

"Oh no!" Wade yelled. I looked over and saw Mason cover his face with his arms. "He got passed!" Wade said. "Go, Chad! Go!"

I felt a poke in the back and turned around to see Rachel breathing hard. "Good race. You beat me by this much." She held out her fingers about an inch apart.

"Good job to you, too," I said.

"Rachel, get over here!" I looked at the blond girl who was yelling. She wasn't wet at all. Her blond hair was completely dry. "Stop talking to the enemy."

"Hang on, Alana!" Rach yelled back. So Alana had the blond hair and Imogen had the brown hair. At least now I could tell them apart. If Alana were a teenager instead of a ten-year-old, I have a feeling she'd be a candidate for an entirely-too-dry-for-water-Olympics attack from Dane, the Noelle version, not the flirty kind Kate got. "See ya later," Rach said, running back to her group.

I shook my floppy, tired arms and followed Carin and Teresa to where the boys stood watching the race. Sam, Rachel's teammate, now had a gigantic lead over Chad. We cheered as hard as we could, but nothing could help Chad catch Sam, and our team ended up second.

Chad walked right past us when he finished the race and collapsed in a pile by the volleyball net. Mason tried to put his hand on his shoulder as he passed, but Chad shrugged it off and glared. Sam and Rachel got mobbed by their victory-chanting team, and Chad rolled over in the grass onto his back, panting.

I walked over to him and sat down, listening to his sharp breathing.

"You did a good job," I said.

"I lost."

"So what? Nobody could have beaten Sam. Look at him. He's ten like us, but he looks like he's in junior high."

"You were awesome," he said between gasps, as he struggled to sit up. "You left me in first place. Sorry I didn't finish it."

"No problem," I said, punching him in the shoulder the way he had me. "We're still the Totally Awesome Coolest Campers Ever To Set Foot On Camp."

We sat on the grass together for a minute. I looked back and forth between Rachel's and Sam's cheering group and our bummed-out group.

"Thanks," Chad said. He stood up and walked over to the other campers as Vanessa announced into her megaphone that we had some free time.

I stayed on the grass for a little while longer. I hate losing. I really do. I don't do many competitive things, but when I do, I'm in it to win. Stuff like volleyball games or soccer games, those don't bother me. You can't control a bunch of players on a team. But swimming races that were up to me to win, it bugs me to lose that.

It wasn't all Chad's fault, even though he must have felt like he let us all down. We were a team. If I had given him a bigger lead, we would have won. I tried to think about every stroke I had made. Could I have somehow gone faster? Losing is hard, even if it is just a swimming relay at summer camp.

CHAPTER FOURTEEN

Foul Moods

I watched the groups break up for free time. Dane and his campers and the boys from our group got another watermelon and went to the end of the dock to spit seeds. I stood up and walked over to where Kate, Carin, and Teresa were talking about the nuke 'em tournament. I might as well enjoy free time as best as I could even after a relay race defeat.

That's when I noticed Steve. He should have been spitting watermelon seeds into the lake with Dane and their campers or standing in a circle and laughing like a bunch of other counselors were doing. Instead, he stood away from everybody else, leaning against one of the poles of the volleyball net and looking absolutely miserable.

"And then Rachel from Blue Jay Cabin grabbed the ball just before it went out of bounds," I heard Carin continue her recap of the game.

I looked back at Steve's miserable expression, and suddenly, I felt like maybe it wasn't such a big deal to have won that milk crate game or lost the swimming relay. I wanted to go over to him and tell him something that would make him feel better. But what could I say? My dad has to visit sick people in the hospital and family members of people who die. I wonder what he says to them.

I turned around to listen to Carin's and Teresa's play-by-play of the action. Who was I kidding? I was just a kid, one of the campers. It wasn't my job to help people this week. That's what the counselors and deans did. I couldn't go over there and start talking to him. I felt too shy, especially around Steve.

"That milk crate race was fun," I said, trying to get back into the excitement of the game.

"You did a great job in that event," Kate said.

"And Teresa had that idea for Chad and Wade to go in front of each other," Carin said. "That was so smart."

Carin must've been incredibly impressed with Teresa's plan. She doesn't usually give other people credit.

"I couldn't believe how fast Chad and Wade could run through the water that way," Teresa said. "It was much faster than the campers who ran side by side."

I snuck another peek at Steve. I hoped he would be having fun, but he was still just standing there glumly like we were at that Ten Commandments sermon instead of the fun water Olympics.

I couldn't stand it anymore. I had to say something to him. Nobody should be sad on water Olympics night. That's like being sad on Christmas or a school snow day. I took a couple of steps towards the volleyball court. But what if he could tell that I had a crush on him? That would be totally embarrassing. I stopped.

I couldn't do it. My throat felt dry, and my hands were sweating. He would think I was a big dork if I walked over there and started talking to him. Any minute now somebody else would notice that Steve was upset and go over and fix it. That's what counselors do.

I looked around the beach for counselor help. Julie was talking to Tony the lifeguard. Dane slapped Sam's hand, and the other boys cheered with their arms in the air. I think Sam had just spit a watermelon seed really far into the middle of the lake. Carin and Teresa dodged around Kate moving their arms as if they were swimming, probably telling her about the swimming relay.

I wished really hard for somebody to talk to him. Nobody did. Everybody just did their own thing and didn't even notice, not even the deans, who I always thought were supposed to be like the counselors' counselors.

The old Abby would have given in to the shyness and run back to Kate. But hadn't I promised myself I would be braver now?

I went back to the bench, wiped my hands on my towel, and walked over to Steve as quickly as I could so I couldn't think about it and chicken out. At first he didn't notice me. He leaned against the pole, one arm wrapped in the net, and gazed at Chad's summer cottage on the other side of the volleyball court. His other arm hung down at his side.

I reached up and put my fingers in his big Scott-like hand. He looked down at me and smiled.

"Hey, Abbers."

I didn't know what to say, so I blurted out the first thing that popped into my head.

"Why don't you have fun at camp?"

What a stupid thing to say. This was a mistake. I knew exactly why he wasn't having fun at camp. Why couldn't I come up with good conversations like Carin can?

"I do have fun at camp," Steve said. He squeezed my hand a little. "I'm just sad right now."

I didn't want him to be crying. That would make it worse. I looked at his eyes. They were dry. He must not have been *too* upset. I had a sudden flashback to last summer, looking up into Scott's eyes in the craft cabin. They had the same blue eyes with a couple little brown flecks in them. Angela and I don't have the same eyes. Hers are blue, and mine are brown.

Now I felt like I was the one who was going to cry. I couldn't let go of his hand and run away though. I tried to swallow the dryness out of my throat. Why were my eyes getting wet but my throat dry?

"I want to tell you that I think Scott was a really good person. He was my very favorite counselor last year."

Steve looked away from me and squinted at the lake. I couldn't stop saying stupid things. That probably upset him even more. But I didn't know what else to say. I just wanted to say something that would make him feel better.

"Thank you," Steve finally said, looking back at me.

Dad always says that when you don't know what to do about something that you should pray. Praying always helps no matter what your problem is. That's what I could do.

"My dad says that when somebody dies, we need to pray for their family members. He's a minister."

He smiled at me. There was something different about that smile than the one he had given me when I first walked up to him.

"Yeah, I know your dad."

So that's what was so funny. Of course Steve knew my dad. He was his dean at junior high camp and did Scott's funeral and everything. Jeepers, why do I say such dumb things?

"I'm going to pray for you to start having fun at camp," I said. I would, too. I couldn't think of anything else that would help. "I'll pray for you every single day."

I thought about Scott again and how sad it was that he had died and how much I missed him. I had to get away before I started crying. I smiled at Steve one last time and ran to the beach area to Kate, Carin, and Teresa.

"Abby, hey," Kate said. "We just came up with another great plan. You have to help us."

"Okay," I said, even though I didn't feel like helping with any great plans. My whole stomach and chest felt funny—like something inside me was pushing everything down and squishing my happiness into a tiny box instead of letting it spread all over me like it had been during the rest of the water Olympics. I wished there was a switch I could flip to lift the weight off my fun time at camp.

It hurts to feel bad for someone. I never knew how much until now. I don't know which is worse, missing somebody or watching someone else miss the same somebody even more.

***

Carin's mom has a saying that she uses whenever somebody acts crabby: "My, aren't we in a foul mood today?" She says "we" even if she's not the one who is mad and also if there's only one crabby person. I'd heard that expression all my life, even at times when Car and I were just talking about something unfair that happened at school, not actually grumpy about anything.

Ever since rest hour, Dane had been in one of those "foul moods" Car's mom talks about. I thought maybe it had to do with Noelle ruining the eating contest for him, or Noelle being mean to Kate at the beach, but after he got her back with the watermelon rinds for being so rude all day, he still looked crabby. The only thing that broke him out of those scowls was water Olympics. Once they were over, he was back to looking blah.

It was the way, back at the fire bowl, during free time between water Olympics and campfire devotions, that he sat on the grass away from everybody. Kind of like Steve had been at the Olympics. Then when T-Camp was hanging on the volleyball net, Dane bellowed, "T! Off the net! You know better!" without giving him any second chances or anything.

When it was time for us to gather around the campfire, I told Kate where I was going and sat next to Dane on the top bench.

"Hey, Squirt."

"Hi."

The rest of the campers filled in around the fire. Most of them were still fooling around or laughing about things that happened during the water Olympics.

"Are you in a foul mood today?"

For some reason, this made him laugh. Nobody has ever laughed at Mrs. Morgan when she says it, at least not when I was around.

"I guess you could say that," he said.

"Is it because of Noelle?"

"Noelle could put anybody in a foul mood. But no…it's not her."

I sat on the bench and waited to see if he would tell me anything more. My feet barely touched the first row of benches below me, but Dane's feet reached easily, and his knees came up high enough so that he could rest his arms on them.

"We had a potato chip war in our cabin at rest hour today," he said.

Dean Ron had his hand in the air, trying to get everybody to calm down for the devotions. It didn't seem like that was going to happen anytime soon since everyone was still fired up about the water Olympics, so Dane and I had a few minutes left before we actually had to be quiet.

"And you had to clean up all the potato chips?" I guessed.

"No, they were actually really good about sweeping everything up."

"But you don't like potato chip wars?"

I was starting to realize how much work being a counselor must be. I had spent a whole evening talking to upset people. It was hard. I always thought counselors just had to tell you when it was time to go to the dining hall for food and remind you to be quiet during chapel, but there was other stuff like talking to someone whose dog had just died.

"Potato chip wars are awesome."

"Then why were you kind of crabby this afternoon?"

"I learned about potato chip wars from Scott. He was the best at launching those tiny crumbs at the bottom of the bag." He smiled, just a little bit. "I learned a lot of stuff from Scott. And then after the potato chip war, Kate and I were talking at the beach about the funeral and everything. It just got me thinking about all that again."

I leaned over and put my head on his arm. "It's really sad, isn't it?"

Dean Ron, Dean Jamie, and the counselors had almost gotten all the campers under control by then, so he had to whisper.

"Yeah, Squirt, it's really sad."

CHAPTER FIFTEEN

The Longest Prayer

"Tonight I am going to tell you about an event that is recorded in the Book of John," Dean Ron said.

The last few campers who were goofing around finally stopped poking each other and paid attention. I'm not sure if they knocked it off because the dean had started his story or because Steve, who was sitting near them, had given them a "quiet down" look that all the counselors are so good at.

"There was a man who was good friends with Jesus who was sick," Dean Ron began. "His name was Lazarus, and he lived in a town called Bethany. He had two sisters who you might have heard about in other stories. Their names were Mary and Martha. Have any of you ever heard of them before?"

I knew who Mary and Martha were. They were these sisters who invited Jesus to their house, and one of them did all this work like cleaning and cooking to get ready, but the other one just sat there and hung out with Jesus, and the one doing all the work got mad. I can't remember which one was the worker and which one hung out with Jesus, but that doesn't matter. The point of the story is that you should spend time with Jesus and love Him and not be too busy for God.

I knew about that story because whenever we have company, Dad says, "Remember, we need to show the love of God to our guests." Unfortunately, the Martha and Mary story doesn't get me out of vacuuming the living room before guests come over, even though I've tried.

Even though I knew the story, I didn't want to raise my hand and have to tell it in front of everybody.

A girl on the other side of the campfire wasn't as shy. Her hand flew into the air. "Mary, Jesus' mother?" she asked.

"That's a Mary from the Bible," Dean Ron said. "But this is a different Mary."

Nobody else seemed to know about Martha and Mary, so Vanessa finally spoke up and told the story after Dean Ron asked the counselors for help. I don't know why he didn't just tell us. Maybe he thought we would get sick of him talking, like we had during the Ten Commandments sermon.

"This Lazarus is the brother of the women from the story Vanessa just told," Dean Ron went on. "Martha and Mary sent word to Jesus saying that their brother was sick. Now, I don't know about you, but when I hear that somebody I love is seriously ill, I get very worried. Not Jesus, though. He wasn't worried. He said, 'This sickness will not end in death. No, it is for God's glory so that God's son may be glorified through it.' Jesus was so confident that God would heal Lazarus that He didn't rush to his house to help him. He took his time and finished what He was doing."

I wondered what it would be like to be friends with Jesus. I mean really friends, like in person, not just through prayer and reading about Him in the Bible. What would it be like if Jesus was your teacher at school or your camp counselor? I think it would be weird, but nice.

"By the time Jesus got to Martha and Mary's house, Lazarus had been dead for four days."

"This story stinks!" T-Camp shouted, not even bothering to raise his hand. "I thought it was going to be one of those stories where Jesus healed someone, like that blind guy."

"That's why you need to be quiet and listen to the entire story," Dean Ron said. He took a breath and refocused after T-Camp's outburst. "But you do bring up the very point Martha did. When Jesus finally got there, she said, 'Lord, if You had been here, my brother would not have died.' It seems as if the story had an unhappy ending, but Martha knew the power of Jesus, and she went on to say, 'But I know that even now God will give You whatever You ask.'"

I wondered if anybody else at camp had a mom or dad who was a minister. I'm not saying I know everything about the Bible because of Dad, but I have learned a lot from him over the years and from all the church services we have had to go to. I remembered the ending to the story, but it didn't look as if most of the rest of the campers knew what was going to happen.

"Jesus asked if Martha believed that those who believed in Him would never die, and she said that she did. She got her sister Mary, and they went to the tomb of Lazarus. Jesus cried when He saw the tomb, but He told them to take away the stone that blocked the entrance. Martha protested this, since a person who has been dead for four days doesn't smell or look particularly good."

I thought that some of the boys would snicker at that, but nobody did. The mood was pretty serious as we all listened to Dean Ron and watched the flickering campfire do its blazing dance.

"So Jesus said to her, 'Did I not tell you that if you believed, you would see the glory of God?' Then, as they rolled away the stone, Jesus prayed that the people would believe that God sent Him to save them. He called out very loudly, 'Lazarus, come out!' And, what do you know, out came Lazarus, just fine. Jesus had raised him from the dead. That is just one of the miracles of Jesus."

Some of the counselors started leading songs. I knew all the songs by heart from last year and all those years at junior high camp with my family, so I could sing them and think about the story at the same time.

It would be great if Jesus was on Earth now instead of a long time ago. If He were, I would have found Him when I heard that Scott had died and told Him what happened. Then He would have gone to Scott's house and made him come back to life just like Lazarus. I know He would have because of the part where He said, "If you believe, you will see the glory of God."

I believe that Jesus could have saved Scott. I wished He had. Those people from the Bible were so lucky.

Jesus wouldn't have wanted everybody to be sad. Dane was sad. I was sad. Steve was very, very, very sad, the saddest. I knew there had to be other sad people, like my dad and Ben and all the people who had been at the funeral.

I remembered that big poster with all those pictures of Scott on it. He had looked happy and real in all the pictures. It was still hard to believe that he wouldn't walk out of the craft cabin doors and join us, late for campfire because he had been finishing up a project. I turned around to look at the craft cabin, just to make sure. All the lights were off, and it was dark. I could barely see the outline of the rainbow in the windows because of the automatic streetlight next to the canteen.

There was no more Scott, and he wouldn't be like Lazarus.

***

When we were getting ready for bed that night, I opened my Bible and found the card from the funeral with Scott's name on it. I read the part with his name and the dates and my dad's name and then flipped it over. "God grant me the serenity to accept the things I cannot change." That's how the saying started. I still didn't understand that part. I think it meant we were supposed to not be sad that Scott died because there was nothing we could do about it, but how could I not be sad?

I needed to find out what serenity meant because the last part of the saying was about having wisdom to know the difference. How could I have wisdom to know the difference when I didn't know what serenity meant in the first place?

Funerals should have easier to understand cards. It's hard enough to understand why somebody you love dies. You shouldn't have to use a dictionary to look up any big words on the cards.

I bet Steve would know. I didn't want to ask him though. I couldn't go up to him and be like, "I was looking at your brother's funeral card thing, and I was wondering what serenity meant."

"Abby, hurry up," Carin said. "I'm waiting for you to go to the bathroom. Teresa went with the other group, and I need a buddy."

I put the card back in my Bible. I had tried to be careful with it, but already one of the corners had bent and there was a smudge on the bottom from when I looked at it after I had eaten chocolate cake.

I grabbed my bathroom kit off the shelf and went with Carin, understanding why Dane had been in his foul mood after thinking about Scott. I was in a pretty foul mood myself.

***

I prayed for Steve for the first time that night, after we had all gotten ready for bed and finished cabin devotions. I lay in my bunk and tried to ignore Carin rolling around and thumping the bed from her top bunk. I shut my eyes.

Dear God, I would like to pray for Steve tonight. He's my counselor at camp. Camp Spirit. I think You know that, but I wanted to make sure. His brother died. I think You know that, too. Please help him feel better. He's pretty sad right now, and so am I. Why do people have to die? I think that's very scary. I don't mean to be rude. I know it shouldn't be scary because of heaven and all. But it is. I don't want to die ever, and I'm sad that Scott did. It's not that I don't want to meet You, but I like my life. Anyway, that's not the point. What

I want to pray about tonight is for Steve to feel better. Please, God, help him to have fun at camp, and help him to not feel so sad. Amen.

I opened my eyes again and stared at the bottom of Carin's bunk. I couldn't see much in the dark. I lay there in silence and the complete stillness, since my bed (and Car) had stopped wiggling.

That was the longest prayer I had ever said. I never had much to say before.

CHAPTER SIXTEEN

Underwear Saves the Day

My group was sitting in the canteen porch trying to decide which items we could have people guess the price of for our game show skit when all of a sudden, something funny popped into my head. I don't know how I thought of it, but it made me giggle. Then the giggle turned into a laugh, a pretty loud laugh, and Carin looked at me.

I had thought of something that would be hilarious to put into our skit. The boys had been talking about underwear again, which must have been what got me thinking about this. I couldn't imagine how funny this would be if it really happened. Just the thought of it made me crack up.

"Hey, you guys," I said, but I started hiccupping. I didn't mind nearly as much this summer when everyone in the group looked at me, so hopefully that meant I was becoming less shy. Maybe this meant I was on my way to being outgoing and fun like Car.

"What is it?" Kate asked. She smiled at the sight of me and my crazy giggles.

"I just thought of something hilarious."

"We noticed," Steve said. That morning he was wearing a bright blue shirt that said "Marquette Boosters 3-on-3 Basketball Tournament." When he had walked into the canteen and turned around to shut the door, I had seen that the back said, "Team Koski/McAllery," which must have meant him and Scott and Ben. I bet he is a very good basketball player, being so tall and all. Plus, he could probably do that thing that the Bucks basketball players do where they hold the top of the ball with just one hand. "Wanna share it with us?"

I did. I really did. But I couldn't stop laughing. What I had thought about was Dean Ron's underwear. Dean Ron, who seems shy and quiet, who is a minister, kind of old, and not very funny like Dean Jamie. For some reason, I had gotten a picture in my mind of Carin holding up Dean Ron's underwear during our game show skit and saying, "This is the next item you need to guess the price of."

Everyone looked at me, waiting to hear what was so funny. Whoops. Maybe it wasn't that funny. Maybe it was one of those things that is only funny to the person who thinks of it, and when you say it out loud, it loses its funniness and people think you're strange.

We had to write these "self poems" for an English project last year where we printed our full name down the left side of a piece of paper and then put adjectives that described us on the lines. I didn't put the word, "funny." That's partly because there's no F in my name, but also because I don't think I'm funny. I could have put, "amusing" or "hilarious" but I didn't.

But when I told everyone what I had thought of, they all started laughing, too.

"I wonder what kind of underwear he really wears," Chad said.

"Maybe the kind with the days of the week on them," Car suggested. Car used to have those, and she'd get really mad if the pair for whatever day it was ended up in the wash.

"I bet he has Spider-Man underwear." You would think that would have been Wade or Mason, but Steve was the one who came up with the Spider-Man crack. He was laughing so hard that he leaned forward with his arms over his stomach. "Oh, that's funny, Abby."

Kate said she didn't think we should put that in our skit. Chad thought Dean Ron wouldn't have much of a sense of humor about underwear the way Dean Jamie would. Kate looked at her list. I think she was trying to get back to the skit planning, but Steve wasn't helping because he kept encouraging the underwear conversation. Carin had come up with an idea for the skit, and Steve started laughing again.

He had the best smile. It wasn't like Dane's sneaky half-smile with dimples. It was a broad smile that showed a lot of teeth, but not like Eva's annoyingly bright white teeth, just normal straight teeth. I could see more of the brown specs in the overall blue of his eyes when he smiled.

His laugh was not like Scott's. Steve let out low chuckles. Scott had had a weird, snickering laugh. I noticed that last summer because ever since Car told me she thinks my laugh is funny, I listen for other people's weird laughs.

Car's cheeks got pink and she crinkled her nose, putting her hands on her hips and glaring at our counselor. "What's so funny about my idea?" I don't think he had heard her latest idea though because he was still stuck on my underwear one.

Steve looked at her with a straight face for about a second, then started laughing again. "I'm not laughing about that." I saw him swallow and take a large gulp of air. "I just keep thinking about..." He put his face in his hands, and his shoulders shook as he tried not to laugh. He looked up, gave up trying to stop laughing, and burst out, "Dean Ron's underwear."

The rest of us laughed again, even Car.

"That would be funny," she admitted. "Boxers or briefs." That finally sent Kate over the edge from a tolerant smile at the topic to a real laugh.

Steve stood up and did an imitation of what Dean Ron would do if we really put his underwear in our skit. He should be a comedian because he really sounded and moved like Dean Ron during the impression. Kate kept telling him that we had to get back to work on the skit, but that didn't happen for several minutes.

We talked about underwear for a while longer and made a few more guesses as to what kind of underwear Dean Ron wore. Mason's idea, Scooby Doo, was the funniest, but also the least likely to be the truth. I can't picture a dean wearing Scooby Doo underwear. Even Rick, my dad's junior high camp co-dean, wouldn't do that, and he has done some pretty goofy things over the years. Kate's idea was the most boring, but the most likely to be true. She thought he probably wore plain, old white underwear.

Despite the underwear start, we got a lot done for the skit. We finished the script and got to practice it twice. It was going to be a very funny skit, especially when Wade, who played the devil, said he thought a roll of gimp was worth a thousand dollars. It was brown gimp, too, not the sparkly kind or anything.

It was the best skit practice I'd ever been a part of, and not only because I had managed to work it so I didn't have any lines in the skit. I had made Steve laugh. Big, uncontrollable, joyous laughs, too, not just a little snicker. The kind of laugh he and Dane used to share last summer.

He got into this skit practice, yelling out ideas and laughing when the boys goofed around. He was acting much differently than he had yesterday when he let Kate run the whole practice and just sat there with a neutral expression on his face, staring at a floorboard.

Steve looked happy, and it was my idea that had made him laugh so much. Granted, it was stupid and about underwear, but it had still made him laugh.

When the bell rang and everybody else headed for the craft cabin, I stood there, watching him. He still had a smirk on his face, I think about Dean Ron's underwear. The only other funny thing that had happened during skit practice was when Wade yelled, "Devil time!" and started doing an odd dance. I don't think that was as funny as the underwear.

"You're a pretty funny kid, Abby," he said, which was weird because nobody had ever said that to me before.

I think most people would probably call me shy or nice instead. I liked being called funny. Funny people are interesting. They make people happy. I'd rather be funny than a compassionate crybaby. Maybe if I could keep coming up with these funny ideas, my dad would say, "Oh, Abby Leah, you have the gift of making people laugh," instead of that boring gift of compassion.

"I told you I would pray for you," I said.

"I think it's helping. I haven't found underwear that funny in a long time."

I laughed again, thinking that I hadn't found underwear that funny in a long time either, not since second grade or so.

We talked for a couple more minutes before pushing open the squeaky canteen porch door and going to the craft cabin, but I don't remember what we talked about. I was too busy staring at his smile. The dark, brooding look was handsome, but he was even cuter when he smiled.

I like that God can use anything and anyone to make people happy. He used a kid and something as dumb as underwear to make Steve laugh that day.

CHAPTER SEVENTEEN

Broken Picture Frame

We made popsicle stick picture frames in craft hour. I had made one once a long time ago, but Angela had helped me with it. This was the first time I had to gather my own four sticks and make a picture frame out of them all by myself.

I painted two of the popsicle sticks green and wrote "Camp Spirit" across one in fancy red letters. On the other one, I wrote, "Sisters." I found a glue bottle that worked (it took checking three bottles to find one that didn't have a glued-shut hole) and wrote the date in glue going up and down the other two popsicle sticks. I used some of Carin's glitter and sprinkled it all over the popsicle sticks. When I shook the sticks over the glitter container, the extra glitter fell off and I was left with two popsicle sticks with glittery dates on them.

This craft project was going surprisingly well for me, the arts and crafts dud, and I hadn't even needed to ask anybody for help.

"Oh, that one is awesome!" I heard Julie shout.

I stood up so I could see over everybody else. Julie stood next to Kate at another table. They both had grassheads and every type of decoration imaginable on the table in front of them. I could only see the tops of the grassheads because of the sea of colored paper, netting, cotton balls, cups full of markers, and fabric the grassheads sat in.

Rachel sat at the other end of their table stringing beads. The other girls from her group were at a different table laughing and pointing at some boys. I still felt bad for Rachel getting stuck with those snobby girls even though she said she didn't mind. She and Lindsay should have both been with us.

"I love the gimp eyelashes," Julie was saying about Kate's grasshead. "And the shape of her lips. That's cute."

"Yours is cool, too," Kate said. "But what's that supposed to be on its forehead?"

"That?" She pointed at something I couldn't see.

"Yeah."

I got up from my bench and went over to where the counselors stood. I wanted to see these grassheads if they were that great.

"That's a tattoo of the letter M. I named it Marquette. It was the only French name I knew besides Pierre and Laurette."

Kate laughed as I got to their table and took a look at Marquette. "Oh, awesome. I like it."

Marquette had one brown eye and one blue eye, a rather large nose, and a mouth that curled up into a sneer. The tattoo also made him look like he was scowling. Marquette must've been the crabby teenager of the grasshead family.

"What do you think, Abby?" Kate asked.

I looked at Kate's grasshead, which had the gimp eyelashes and a pouty, full, red mouth that actually looked a lot like Julie's. Both of the grassheads were pretty funny.

"I think they're even better than the other ones," I said.

"What did you name yours?" Julie asked, pinching one of the girl grasshead's gimp eyelashes with her thumb and index finger.

"I couldn't think of a name," Kate said. "I don't know many French names. Marquette was a good one though. There's that *Star Trek* character named Jean-Luc. I thought that would make a good grasshead name, but I can't come up with any female names."

"Hmm," Julie said, sitting back down on the bench. "Know any French names, Abby?"

I shook my head. "Not besides the ones we've already used."

"Coritza."

All three of us looked at Rachel, who had just made the suggestion. She dropped two beads onto her piece of fishing line.

"Where did you hear that name?" Kate asked. "That sounds familiar."

"My brother Billy lives in France, and he married a lady named Coritza."

Julie's eyes got big and she scooted down the bench so she ended up right next to Rach. "Was it romantic and beautiful, a French wedding?"

"Did you get to be a bridesmaid?" Kate asked. "I was a bridesmaid in my brother's wedding two years ago."

"Oh," Rachel said, looking into her jar of beads again. "I didn't go. He didn't tell us about it until after they were already married. He sent us a picture of them standing in front of the Eiffel Tower and said they were on their honeymoon."

"Why didn't your brother tell you he was getting married?" Julie asked.

"Because he sucks," Rachel muttered into her beads.

"Is Billy as gorgeous as Dane?" Julie asked.

Rachel made a face. "He's much cuter. Taller and bigger and less annoying."

"I think I'd like to meet him," Julie said with a pout bigger than Coritza the Grasshead's. I think Julie is an older, even boy-crazier version of Carin.

"He's also married to this Coritza person," Kate said.

Julie waved her hand. "Details. Now, I have an idea about how to make a grasshead with a Mohawk."

"Great," Kate said. "He can be Jean-Luc." She turned her head and looked at the clock on the wall. "But we only have twenty minutes left."

I went back to my table. I needed to get to work if I was going to finish my picture frame. Lot of times I think an art project I'm working on is going all right, but when I take another look at it, I realize it's horrendous. That didn't happen this time when I looked at my popsicle sticks. They had turned out pretty good. The glitter was an especially nice touch. All I had to do was glue it together.

"Where'd you go?" Carin asked when I sat down next to her.

"To look at the new grassheads."

"New grassheads? Where?"

I pointed at Kate and Julie, and Car took off. I looked over at her pile of arts and crafts materials. She had finished her popsicle stick picture frame and had tilted it against one of the supporting beams the table leaned against so it could dry. It said "Dane and Carin's Wedding" across the top and had little hearts and a ton of purple glitter all over the rest of it.

I hope Car never finds out about Billy or she will get on an airplane to France, and Coritza better watch out.

I opened the glue bottle and put little dabs of white on both ends of my top popsicle stick (the one that said "Sisters"). Then I placed the popsicle stick over one of the side ones and squeezed it together hard. When it seemed like it had stuck, I tried to glue the other side onto it, but the glue must have dried enough so that it wasn't gooey anymore because when I squeezed, instead of smashing together like the other side had, the popsicle sticks slid from between my fingers and onto the table.

I put more glue on the top popsicle stick and tried to stick the second side onto it again. This time they stuck together fine. I waved the picture frame around in the air to help it dry faster, and the first side I had glued fell onto the table.

Stifling a "grr" I picked up the popsicle stick and tried to stick it back to the top one before the glue dried. It didn't work, so I put more glue onto it and pinched it together even harder than I had before. I held my almost-finished picture frame with both thumbs and index fingers pinching a side to the top and watched the second hand on the clock go around three full times.

That should be enough drying time. I picked up the bottom popsicle stick, quickly put two dabs of glue on it, and stuck it on the side popsicle sticks. I held the bottom just as I had held the top and looked at my completed project. Awesome! That was the only word for it. Angela would love it.

I set it down on the table, and one of the sides popped off. Why was I so lousy at arts and crafts? Carin had had no trouble at all getting her popsicle sticks glued together. I bet when Lindsay had arts and crafts that afternoon, she would make an amazing picture frame with twenty popsicle sticks or something.

I wished Scott were there. He could have helped me with my picture frame just like he had helped me with my Noah's Ark last year.

I put more dabs of glue on the popsicle stick that had fallen off and stuck it back on. I must've put too much glue on because a big glob of it oozed through and covered the last "s" of "Sisters." I got a piece of paper towel from Cammie's counter and wiped the glue glob off. Some of the glitter came off the letters.

The top popsicle stick inched upward on the right as I wiped, and the whole thing ended up crooked. I tried to push the popsicle stick down on one side to straighten it out. The left side came unglued as I pressed the right side down. I put more glue on the top popsicle stick and stuck it where it belonged.

I looked around the craft cabin, as if Scott would magically appear out of thin air to help me.

My hands were all gluey now, and I had glitter all over them and smudges on the picture frame.

I had that feeling in my nose and behind my eyes that I get whenever I'm about to cry. I was probably the only camper who couldn't glue four popsicle sticks together.

Maybe one of the counselors could help. I looked at Kate and Julie. Kate held the bottom of a grasshead while Julie fussed with pulling seeds out of its head with a pair of tweezers, I guess to form the Mohawk instead of leaving seeds to grow grass all over its head.

I tried wiping my fingers off with the paper towel, but that just spread the glue all over my hands. I looked over campers' heads and found Dane writing something on the wall at the other end of the craft cabin. He snickered, looked around, and started writing again.

I tried yet again to glue the top popsicle stick to the sides. I squeezed one side together. Not wanting to bump the bottom off, I held the side popsicle stick in the middle instead of the bottom. I twisted it in my hands just a little to see if the glue had finally done its job, and the side popsicle stick snapped apart in the middle, making my beautiful glittered numbers jagged.

I looked around one more time for somebody to ask for help and saw Steve sitting a couple tables over, staring up at a plaque on the wall that had his brother's name on it. He was not laughing about underwear anymore or even smiling. He looked like he had that crying feeling in his nose, too.

Why do people die? Especially, why do people who are needed so much die?

The crying wasn't just in my nose and behind my eyes anymore. A bunch of tears dripped onto my popsicle stick mess and sticky hands.

Why did I always have to act like such a baby and cry about things? It was just a dumb camp arts and crafts project. All I had to do was glue it back together.

I wiped my eyes with my arm because my hands were still gluey. That sounds like something I'd do. Get glue in my eye. Lindsay wouldn't because she's perfect at crafts. Rachel wouldn't because she seems older than the rest of us somehow and above childish glue messes. Carin wouldn't because clumsy stuff never seems to happen to her. Only dummies who cry about silly things would be dumb enough to get glue in their eye.

I grabbed the uncooperative glue bottle, turned it upside down, and squeezed hard, hard, hard right over the middle of my broken popsicle stick. A big blob of glue squirted out, but it landed on the table instead of the popsicle stick, so I slammed the bottle on the table. It flew between the two by fours separating work stations, bounced off the table in front of me, and soared across the room, jumping on the floor a couple of times before rolling to Kate's and Julie's feet.

Kate handed the grasshead to Julie, bent down, and picked the glue bottle up. She brought it back to me, her face filled with concern.

"Are you okay, Abby?"

"Yes," I said, even though I felt like I was going to cry again.

"Do you need help with anything?"

"No, thank you," I said quietly.

"Are you sure?"

"Yes."

I started wiping up the glue with my battered paper towel and tried to act like everything was fine so she would go away. She couldn't help me anyway. Kate could probably fix my picture frame, but she couldn't bring people back from the dead, and that's what I wanted.

I managed to clean the glue off of the table and dump the pile of paper towels and my popsicle sticks into the garbage right before the bell for lunch rang. We got to go to the beach for a picnic, and I think that was the only thing that could make me forget about Scott and my awful project for an hour.

CHAPTER EIGHTEEN

Parent Talk

When the bell rang after rest hour, Car dragged me down the path. I wasn't feeling quite awake yet, so she had to pull me behind her to get there at her top speed. I think Car couldn't stand spending a whole hour in a cabin with just girls and needed to get to the canteen quickly because there would be boys there. The boys always make it to canteen first because their cabins are closer.

Dane was already sitting on a bench in the canteen when we got there. He was almost finished with his bag of potato chips, but he had a second bag on the bench next to him. Kate got to get her soda and candy from Ben in the back of the canteen without waiting in line because she was a counselor.

I got into the line behind Lindsay and looked at the rows of candy. It's hard to choose just two things from so much awesome junk food. Did I want potato chips or candy that afternoon? Soda or a fruit drink? Taffies or gum?

Kate came back around the side of the canteen to the porch and sat with Dane while we inched along in the line. I can't wait until I'm a counselor and can go in the back of the canteen to get my candy and not have to wait in line.

"Here. Eat one of these. They're the best."

I turned around and watched Kate shake her head at Dane's open bag of potato chips. She made a puckered face.

"Salt and vinegar? Those are so gross."

He tilted the bag on its side and shook it, then put it up to his face and tipped his head back to get all the crumbs. He made a big show of licking his lips and opening the other bag.

"Yum. Sure you don't want one?"

"Your breath is going to smell disgusting," Kate said.

He leaned closer to her and gave her a charming smile complete with both dimples.

She stood up and pointed at something across the grass. "There's Steve. We have a canteen date to share our candy." She looked at Dane and nodded her head towards the screen door. "You can come, too, as long as you keep your salt and vinegar breath away from us."

He followed her out of the canteen.

We were at the front of the line, and Lindsay ordered a soda and candy bar. I got a soda and salt and vinegar chips to see whose opinion I agreed with. I wasn't sure how much I was going to be able eat though because my stomach hadn't felt the best since the beach cookout where I had watched T-Camp and Mason have a very disgusting eating contest that involved worms, ketchup, and T-Camp hurling all over the sand. The only other interesting things that happened at lunch were that Dane ate ninety-two potato chips, beating last year's record of eighty-six, and Noelle cut in front of everybody in the food line.

Lindsay, Car, and I met Rachel at our favorite picnic table. Teresa came with us, but she chowed down on her candy bar and ran to the nuke 'em court before we got to any topics of conversation more interesting than chapel.

"Hey, you know how that one Paul counselor talked about being in a gang today?" I asked. It had been a shock when right in the middle of his story about how he became a Christian, he told us he used to be part of a gang in Chicago. I didn't think people who were in gangs ever quit, moved to the U.P., and became camp counselors. It made me wonder about all the other counselors, like what they did before they came to camp.

"Yeah?" Carin asked.

Lindsay put down her soda and leaned forward towards Carin and me. "I couldn't believe that. He's so nice. I think of gang members as scary people with guns and stuff."

"We got mugged once," Rachel said.

"With *a gun?*" Car asked, opening her eyes so wide that bugs would have flown into them if we hadn't been sitting at the picnic table next to the bug zapper.

"I don't know," Rach said. She pulled her legs up so her feet rested on the bench. I opened my chip bag while she told the story. "He had his hand in his pocket and pointed it at us like it was a gun, but I never actually saw a gun. It could have been a candy bar or a pen or his hand."

I ate my first salt and vinegar chip. At first I thought I liked it, but it had a weird aftertaste, sour or something. I almost made a face like Kate had.

We sat there eating our snacks for about a minute before Lindsay said, "What does that have to do with what we're talking about?"

Rachel shrugged. "I don't know. Abby was talking about Paul being in a gang, and it reminded me of the mugger."

"Oh, yeah," I said. "When he said that, all I could think of was when we showed Pierre, Zack, and Simon to Dane, and he said there was a gang of grassheads. I almost started laughing in the middle of chapel."

"At somebody's story about being in a gang?" Lindsay asked. I have a feeling that Lindsay would never have a giggle fit at an inappropriate time.

"Yeah," I said. "I had to hold it in because I didn't want him to think I was laughing at him."

"Don't you hate that?" Car asked. "When something makes you laugh somewhere that you aren't supposed to? Like this one kid in front of me farted during a math test once, and I kept snickering, and the teacher looked at me a lot. I wanted to say, 'I'm not cheating. Tyler just farted.'"

We all giggled at the thought of somebody saying that to the whole class during a math test.

"My mom calls it giggle fits," I said. "And I better not get them in the middle of church, or she gets mad."

"I get giggle fits in the middle of church," Rachel said. "Especially when we go to Annoying Jim's church. There's this lady there who is a really bad singer, and she has blue hair, only it's not blue on purpose, I don't think, and Dane and I always get in trouble for laughing when she sings during the offering. But she's one of those people who adds, 'Amen!' and, 'Hallelujah!' to the song even if it's not supposed to be there."

"Abby's dad is our minister," Car said. "So nothing weird like that happens at our church."

"Except when Manny is the lay leader," I said. Manny is this really nice guy, but he's also unorganized, and he usually ends up reading the wrong Bible verses and having to say, "Oops. Back it up there, folks."

"Oh, yeah," Car said, giggling some more.

"Your dad is a minister?" Rachel asked. I nodded. "I didn't know that."

"Do you have to go to church a lot?" Lindsay asked.

"Sort of."

"More than most people, but not all the time," Carin said. She knows my life as well as I do. I guess that happens when you've been best friends since first grade.

"Yuck," Rachel said. "Doesn't that suck?"

"It's not that bad," I said. "I'm not used to going to church less, so it's not a big deal to me."

"You must be perfect," Rach said.

"Not really." Lots of people think that. I would say Angela and I get in trouble less often than most kids, but that has more to do with our personalities than what our dad does for a living. "We get in trouble sometimes."

"My dad could never be minister," Rachel said. "He'd get kicked out right away because of Dane and me getting in trouble."

"You can't get kicked out of being a minister because your kids get in trouble," Carin said, as if she were the expert. Then she added, "Right, Abby?"

"Yeah," I said. "They care more about if you give interesting sermons and visit sick people when they need you than if your kids have good be-havior."

"What does your dad do, Rachel?" Lindsay asked.

"My real dad owns a computer company, and my step-dad annoys me."

Car, Linds, and I got another giggle fit.

"That's his job?" I joked. "What he does for a living?"

"Yep."

"So if someone came by with a door-to-door survey, he would have to write in the blank under job, 'annoy Rachel'?"

"Yep. If he got paid a dollar for every time he annoyed me, he would be richer than my real dad by now."

"My dad's a dentist," Carin said. "And my mom is a mom and works in the dentist office sometimes if his secretary goes on vacation."

"You must not have any junk food at your house," Lindsay said.

"We do so." Car sounded offended. "It's just sugar-free junk food."

"That must suck," Rachel said.

"No, it's good. It tastes just like regular junk food, right Abby?"

"Well…" The Morgans have lots of good sugar-free cookies, but once we had this sugar-free chocolate ice cream that made me want to gag and I had to choke it down so I wouldn't look rude. "Some of it's good, and some of it's not so good," I said honestly.

"What's your dad?" Rachel asked Lindsay before Car could argue with me.

"A truck driver. And my mom works at Shop-Mart."

"Does he swear and burp and fart a lot?" Carin asked.

"No!" Lindsay shouted just as I exclaimed, "Car!"

"Most truck drivers aren't gross," Rachel said. "Just like not all dentists get rid of their junk food."

"And not all pastors have perfect kids," I added.

"My dad is really polite and nice," Lindsay said.

"But is he annoying?" Rachel asked. "That's what really matters."

"Not usually."

"It's never the real dads that are annoying. It's the step-dads."

"Is your step-*mom* annoying?" I asked. We never heard anything about her. Just Annoying Jim the step-dad.

Rachel thought for a minute, scrunching her lips together and glancing to the right with both eyes. "No. She lets me eat dessert before dinner and has lots of pretty clothes she lets me try on. Plus she's not old like most parents."

"How old is she?" I asked.

"Twenty-six."

"Wow," I said. "My mom's forty-one."

"So is mine," Rachel said. "But Kylie my step-mom is twenty-six."

"How old is your *dad*?" Carin asked.

"Forty-three. I think. Or maybe forty-four. I don't remember. Annoying Jim is forty-six. That's pretty old, huh?"

I was too busy trying to figure out what forty-three minus twenty-six was to answer her question about Jim being old. I'm not so good at math in my head.

"I don't think you're right," Car said. "Whose dad would marry someone who was seventeen years younger than them? Think about it." Apparently Car's mental math was better than mine.

"I know how old my own step-mom is, Carin," Rachel said. "Ask Dane."

"It all seems old to me," Lindsay said. "I don't think adults care about things like how old people are."

"But to be married?" Carin asked. She made a face that looked more grossed out than Kate's face had been about the salt and vinegar chips. "And to kiss and hold hands with? When I'm twenty-six, there's no way I'm going to date anyone who's forty-three. That's gross. That's grosser than gross. I mean, not that your dad is gross, Rach."

"Car," I said, "you like eighteen-year-old boys, and you're ten. That's almost like being twenty-six and having a husband who's forty-three."

"No, it's not. And I would never marry someone who was in his forties." Then she took a bite of her candy bar and thought. Car makes a funny face when she thinks, sort of like a squinting baby who has gas. "Unless he was rich...and cute."

"My dad *is* rich," Rachel said. "You should see my house. We have a swimming pool. And he used to be cute like in pictures from his prom and stuff."

"Does he have a limo?" Carin asked.

"No, Car," Rach said, sounding annoyed. "That's movie stars. Real people don't have limos. He has a Viper and an old Corvette. And Kylie has a purple SUV." Her mouth twisted and her eyes narrowed into a glare, although she wasn't glaring at any of us. "But I only get those cool cars every other weekend. The rest of the time, at my mom's house, I'm stuck riding around in Annoying Jim's ugly truck with rust spots on it. And horse poop."

"Ew," Car said.

I was about to ask Rach why her step-dad's truck would have horse poop on it when Dane and Steve walked over to us. Steve had a volleyball in his hand and popped it up with a hit from his other fist, then caught it over his head.

"You guys want to play nuke 'em?" he asked. "We're trying to start a tournament, but we only have ten minutes until activity time."

Rachel ignored his question and came back with one of her own. "Dane, how old's Kylie?"

"Don't even talk to me about that," Dane said, his face going from camp-happy to crabby. He grabbed the volleyball away from Steve and chucked it over to the dirt under the volleyball net. "Let's forget about the game. There's not much time left anyway."

I stood up on the bench and ended up eye level with Dane. Steve was still taller than me, even when I stood up as tall as I could. Maybe I would be taller than him if I stood on the table part, but it looked tippy and I didn't want to fall off and have to go to The Scary Nurse. Once in a lifetime was enough for that experience.

"Do you want these?" I held up my bag of salt and vinegar chips, which had only lost about eight chips.

Dane's face got less crabby. "Awesome!" He snatched them and put a couple in his mouth, acting like he hadn't seen a bag of them in ten years, not like he had just eaten two bags twenty minutes ago. "You rock, Squirt." The smile and his good mood were back.

Boys are pretty easy to make happy. Something Rachel said made Dane really mad, but one little bag of potato chips brought my happy, carefree counselor back.

Kate walked by and threw her soda can in the green recycling bucket near the picnic table.

"Are you guys ready for the sleep-out tonight?" she asked. She had taken her hair out of her ponytail, and now she shook it and ran her fingers through the messy sides.

"Sleep-outs are awesome," Carin said.

"Yeah," Lindsay said. "But we need a scary story."

"Don't worry," Dane said in a confident voice. "I've got a story this year that will make last year's story look like it was for mini-campers."

Kate looked at him and made a face. "*More* of those potato chips? You really are going to have the most disgusting breath out of everybody in this entire camp." She smiled at him and shook her hair so that the long blond locks brushed over her shoulders and landed on her back. "You girls better throw your stuff away. It's almost time for skit practice for my group."

We got up from the picnic table and threw all our wrappers in the trash and cans in the recyclables. Rachel headed one way, Lindsay took off for the rocks where Brenda and her co-counselor were, and Car followed Kate to the spot behind the craft cabin where we were supposed to meet for skit practice. My soda can didn't make it into the bucket, thanks to my bad aim and a gust of wind, so I lagged behind, having to crouch down and reach behind the garbage can where my soda had rolled. I found three other soda cans back there.

"Dude, that was definite interest," Steve said quietly, but not so quietly that I couldn't hear him.

"What was?" Dane asked.

"That hair shake and the comment about your breath. She's interested, and pretty and nicer than most of your other girlfriends, so don't screw this up."

"Seriously? Or are you messing with me?"

"I'm as serious as Dean Ron on counselor evaluation night," Steve said. "I'm with her all day long, and she doesn't smile like that for me. Me, she watches the kids for when I have to go to the bathroom and gives the candy she doesn't like to. You, she flips her hair for and teases about garlic breath."

"Salt and vinegar breath," Dane corrected, holding up the empty bag.

"Whatever."

I had found my soda can around the time Steve had said something about Dean Ron and counselor evaluations, but I pretended to still be looking for it. I know it's wrong to listen to other people's conversations, but in my defense, it was a *really* interesting conversation. Plus, Steve was smiling that great smile throughout it.

"I don't know," Dane said. I snuck a peek at him from my position, slowly picking up the four soda cans and dropping them one by one into the gigantic green bucket. He shook his head and frowned as he crumpled my potato chip bag up. "Every girl I date ends up hating me."

"Because you get bored and dump them."

"I know. So it would be a bad idea."

"Yeah," Steve said with a laugh, like he didn't believe him. "That would stop you."

"No, I mean it. Usually, I don't care if some girl ends up hating me, but Kate and I have done the whole camp friends thing—instant bond after a couple of hours at camp. How can I date her and not mess it up somehow?"

"With your track record, you can't."

"That's my point."

Steve grabbed Dane's crumpled up salt and vinegar chip bag and walked towards the garbage can. I had to "find" my soda can and put it in the recycle bucket quickly in order to not look suspiciously like an eavesdropper. Steve didn't seem to notice I was listening though. He just turned around when he was done.

"All I'm saying is that you could probably go all camp romance at some point this week. And by the way, you still owe me the whole Stacey Radkey post-camp story."

"Yeah, I know. Tonight. I gotta go get ready."

Dane headed back to his cabin, and I went with Steve to the grassy spot behind the craft cabin where everyone else in our group had already met for skit practice. You can learn a lot of interesting things by pretending to lose your soda can. I would have to do that more often.

※

On our way back to the cabin later to change for swimming, we ran into Rachel. I don't know how she ended up by herself because usually the counselors are pretty strict about the buddy rule. She stomped her feet as she walked, causing little poofs of dirt to fly up behind her tennis shoes.

We caught up with her near our cabin. She must have been planning to take the back path up the hill to her cabin. Kate and Teresa went right in to Chipmunk Cabin, but Carin and I stayed outside.

"Is something wrong, Rach?" I asked.

"I can't *stand* him," she said, punching a blue towel on the clothesline so hard that all the other towels wiggled around.

"Who?" I asked, although I could probably guess: T-Camp, the wildest camper I'd ever met.

"My stupid, lame brother. He thinks he's the boss of me, but he's not."

"He kind of is your boss this week because he's your counselor," Carin said, which was the wrong thing to say because it caused Rachel to glare at Car. Rachel has really good glares, the kind that make you realize what exactly a "glare of death" is.

"I can't wait for him to go to New Hampshire. I should have a countdown. It's something like a week and a half away now."

"Why is Dane going to New Hampshire?" I asked.

"For college. I suggested Africa, but I guess New Hampshire will be far enough."

"New Hampshire," Car said. "That sounds very far away. Is it by Florida?"

"No, Car," I said. "It's by Maine and Vermont." That made me wonder how she did on Mrs. Simon's third grade U.S. geography pages two years ago.

"What's by Florida?"

"Um, Alabama?" Rachel suggested.

"This is so sad," Carin said, looking even more devastated than some of the people at Scott's funeral. "How will we ever see him?"

"At camp," Rachel said.

"It's not like we see him any other places besides camp," I said.

"New Hampshire just seems so far away."

"It is," Rachel said. "That's why I can't wait for him to go there."

"Is New Hampshire by California?" Carin asked, grinning. "Maybe he'll meet some movie stars and tell them about the best actress he knows, a camper from church camp."

"It's not by California," I told her.

"Maybe he'll go away and never come back," Rachel said. "Not even for summer vacation."

"That would be awful!" Car wailed.

"I don't think people do that," I said, thinking of Angela. There's no way she won't come home during school breaks when she goes to college a year from now.

"Yes, they do," Rachel said. "That's what my other brother did."

The door to our cabin opened, and Kate stuck her head out. "Hurry up, girls. It's time for swimming. You don't want to miss out."

"We have to go," Car said.

Rachel started up the path to her cabin, stomping like she was still mad at whatever Dane had done to annoy her.

"See you at the beach!" I called after her, but it sounded really lame.

CHAPTER NINETEEN

All-camp Sleep-out

Last year at the sleep-out, I froze. The only time I felt warm was when we went to Eva's husband's cabin and watched an episode of *Campfire Tales*. The rest of the time, I tried to snuggle in my sleeping bag until I somehow fell asleep, even though I felt like I was sleeping in the big walk-in refrigerator in the camp kitchen.

That wasn't going to happen to me this year. This year I would be prepared.

After dinner we had some free time. We played—what else?—nuke 'em. When the sky had just started to go gray, one of the counselors stood up and asked, "Who wants to go to the sleep-out?"

This stopped the game and broke up the clusters of campers scattered around the area who were talking or gimping. Lindsay and I had been watching the game and working on our gimp bracelets. I was trying to spend as much time with her as I could, but that wasn't easy, being in different day groups. I had to find her whenever the whole camp did things together.

We started walking back to our cabins to get ready to sleep out. Carin caught up with Lindsay and me on the way up the path.

"Remember last year's sleep-out?" Car asked.

"*Campfire Tales* and flashlight tag," I said.

I couldn't wait to get down to the beach. The sleep-out had been one of the best parts of camp last year, except for the cold and having to worry about getting eaten by wild animals. This year would be even better because I wasn't such a little kid, so I wouldn't be afraid of wild animals. Besides, wild animals prowled the woods, not the beach, where the entire camp was going to sleep. And even if they did, a wild animal could not possibly eat everyone in the whole camp, so I would wake up and could run to my cabin long before it got to me. Plus I had a plan to stay warm.

"Remember the ghost of the pit toilets?" Lindsay asked, giggling about the ghost story Dane had told last year.

"I hope Dane will tell another story," Car said. "He's very cute when he tells ghost stories."

"He will," I said. I think that Dane's favorite part of camp is scaring the campers. That and doing inappropriate things with the watermelons at the water Olympics.

We got to the cabin, and Kate held the door open as we filed in.

"Is Dane telling a ghost story tonight?" Car asked, as we passed Kate.

She put her finger up to her lips like she couldn't let us in on the secret, but then she nodded and smiled.

"Told you," I said, poking Carin in the back. I know my counselors better than anybody.

I opened my suitcase and dug through it, knowing exactly what I wanted to wear. My jeans were fine. The rest of my outfit needed work. I took off my shoes and socks and accidentally got sand from the nuke 'em game I had played earlier all over the floor. I put on a clean pair of socks and then a big, gray pair over my normal white ones. I took off my T-shirt and traded it for a long-sleeved, fuzzy, red shirt and a gray sweatshirt over the red one.

Just rolling up my sleeping bag with all those clothes on made me sweat, but that was in our cabin with the heater going. As soon as the sun went down and we were outside, it would be freezing, just like last year.

"Does anybody need help with their sleeping bags?" Brenda asked.

"Me!" Autumn yelled.

I looked at her sleeping bag sitting on her bed in a rumpled mess. I quickly rolled mine up and helped Car. Kate helped Teresa, but it didn't look like they made much progress. I've always been good at rolling sleeping bags. Is being good at camp stuff genetic? My parents were campers and counselors and deans here for years. That must be how I got so good at rolling up sleeping bags.

"Don't forget to bring extra warm clothes," I reminded Lindsay and Car.

Lindsay pulled up the bottom of her sweatshirt to show that she had another shirt underneath. Carin grabbed her sweater off the end of her bunk before we left the cabin. On the way down the porch steps, I saw that Kate was wearing pajama pants and a long sleeved T-shirt. I hoped she wouldn't be cold. Maybe she had one of those extra thermal sleeping bags for fifty-degree below zero weather.

"I hope we can sleep wherever we want," Lindsay said on our way down the hill to the beach.

"Me, too."

Ben and Mr. Newman had the camp truck parked on the hill near the girls' cabins, and we got to throw all our stuff in the back of it. Then they drove down the long way around to the beach, and we got to take the shortcut down the hill the other way.

The first thing I saw when we got down to the beach was the campfire Steve was working on. It only had a few, little flames, but he fussed with the logs and sticks, trying to find an arrangement that would make the fire bigger. A couple of counselors helped, positioning sticks and calling out advice whenever the flames shrunk.

Carin, Lindsay, and I got our sleeping bags and pillows out of the camp truck that had just pulled around the corner and stopped near the tarps.

"Girls on that side," Vanessa said, pointing to the area where we had already put our things near some other pink and flowered sleeping bags. "Boys over there." She pointed to another tarp set up a little ways away.

"Hey, Abby, Carin, you guys!" I turned around and saw Rachel waving wildly at us. "Over here."

We picked our things up again and lugged them over to Rachel's.

"It's just like a night in our cabin last year," Lindsay said.

"Only we're outside," I said.

Sam and Chad walked over to us, their arms full of sticks.

"You guys can't be over here," Rachel said. "This is the girls' tarp."

"It's okay, Rach," Car said, smiling at the boys. "We don't mind visitors."

Chad held up his arms full of sticks. "Don't worry. We don't want to bother you. We're looking for some firewood."

"Seen any good driftwood around?" Sam asked.

"Not really," Car said.

"Okay," Chad said. "We'd better move on then."

"See ya," Sam said, as he followed Chad.

We sat down on our sleeping bags to talk while we waited for the ghost stories to start. Rachel brushed a pile of dirt off of her sleeping bag.

"They got my new sleeping bag all dirty," she muttered. "Boys suck."

Teresa was standing by her still-rolled-up sleeping bag and pillow a few feet away from us, looking around nervously.

"Teresa!" I called. "You can sleep by us."

"Don't invite her," Carin whispered, elbowing me in the ribs. "We want it to be just us."

Teresa picked up her sleeping bag and pillow and started walking towards us.

"She's okay," Rachel said. "The more friends we have, the more fun it will be."

"I remember last summer when I didn't know anybody at first," Lindsay said. "It was awful."

Teresa put her things down by ours, but she didn't unroll her sleeping bag, as if she expected us to tell her to go way after all.

"We were all in a cabin together last year," Car told Teresa, playing with a strand of her red hair. "That's how we know each other. Rachel is Dane's sister."

"You don't have to tell everyone," Rachel said. "It's okay if the new kids don't know that I'm related to that dweeb."

"He's not a dweeb!" Carin cried.

"I've seen him do some pretty dweeby things," Rachel said.

"Like what?" I asked.

We all leaned forward and made our little circle even smaller. There's nothing better than telling stories with your camp friends outside at dusk.

"Well," Rachel said, "one time he asked a girl to a dance, and he barfed on her new shoes when she came over to our house."

Carin sat back and gave Rachel a shove in the shoulder. "He did not. You made that up."

Rachel laughed. "Yep. He did. And I have the home video to prove it. My other brother took it."

Lindsay turned around, and I looked at what she was looking at: Dane holding his hands out to Kate. Without Carin giggling in my ear, I could hear them talking if I listened closely.

"Your hands are freezing," Kate said, taking one of his hands in hers.

"Told you."

"But it's not cold out."

He shrugged. "It just happens a lot. It's an old snowball-related injury."

"A what?"

"I had a snowball fight with a barn, and I got frostbite."

"You did not," Kate said, but she put her hands over his and pulled him over to the fire that Steve had managed to build up with the help of Sam's and Chad's kindling.

"Ask Steve. He knows the whole long tale," Dane said. "Actually, you don't want to know that story. It's a bad one."

"You're such a joker," she said, letting go of his hands and hitting him on the arm.

"It doesn't look like he has any problem being around girls," Lindsay said.

Rachel rolled her eyes. "Not now. Now he has all kinds of girlfriends. I'm talking about a long time ago. In junior high. That was so funny." She laughed again, as if she were remembering what it looked like when her brother had puked on some poor thirteen-year-old girl's shoes.

"I still don't believe you," Carin said.

"It happened. It smelled like dog food."

"Ew!" Lindsay and I both cried.

Teresa made a grossed-out face. So far she hadn't said much, but she looked like she was having a good time. I asked her what she thought about camp, and she started talking about the water Olympics. We gave Rachel and Lindsay the same play-by-play of our milk crate win that we had given Kate the night we won. The conversation centered around the water Olympics for the next few minutes.

"Why is he doing that?" Carin asked with scrunched-together, mad lips.

"What?" I asked, confused. We had been talking about the swimming relay that Rachel and Sam won.

"Look," Carin said, pointing at the fire where Dane, Steve, and Kate still stood, with Vanessa and a couple other counselors.

Dane, Steve, and a guy I didn't know talked as Steve fussed with the fire. The bits that I caught were about hockey and something called a salary cap, whatever that is. Dane had his hands around Kate's heap of long blond hair and had started combing it with his fingers, all the while talking to Steve and the other counselor about hockey. I was pretty sure that was why Car had narrowed her blue eyes.

"He's flirting because she's pretty," Rachel explained.

"She's not *that* pretty," Car muttered.

One thing about being boy-crazy is that you get jealous a lot. Carin sure does. This boy she liked gave two Valentine's Day cards to another girl in our class last year, and Carin glared at her throughout our entire spelling test, even the challenge words.

"Is she prettier than the girl who got her shoes thrown up on?" Lindsay asked.

We all giggled at that, even Carin. Then she shook her head, brushed her own red hair with her hands, and stood up.

"I'm going to go request the ghost story," she said, marching over to the campfire. She pushed herself right between our counselor and her crush. "Will you tell us a ghost story like you did last year?"

Chad must have heard her because he stood up from the boys' tarp and yelled, "Yeah, but this time make it even scarier!"

Dane smiled his half grin and ruffled Car's hair. "I think I could do that." It wasn't exactly the way he had played with Kate's hair, but Car turned around and gave us a victorious smirk. Rachel rolled her eyes, the biggest eye roll I had ever seen, complete with half a head roll and an irritated sigh.

I stood up right away and moved closer to the fire to get a good spot. Lindsay and Rach came with me. I turned around and offered Teresa a hand. She took it, and I pulled her up.

"You're going to want a good seat for this," I said. I must say, I really liked being an elementary camp expert this summer. Knowing all about camp was way better than being a new camper.

We squeezed in next to Lindsay and Rachel. Kate and Julie sat down with us, and most of the other campers and counselors got ready for a scary story.

CHAPTER TWENTY

The Ghost of Lake Spirit

Dane stirred the fire around with a long stick while he waited for everyone to find spots on the tarp. Carin squeezed between him and Steve on the bench and sat kicking her legs back and forth. Some of her kicks came within an inch of melting the sole of her tennis shoe in the fire.

"Once there were two campers named Frank LaBoyer and Elizabeth McAllery," Dane began in this very ominous tone. Just that one sentence creeped me out because Frank LaBoyer is the camp manager, so this meant the story might be true and not something funny Dane just made up. "They had gone to camp together for years. On their last night of high school camp they decided to sneak out and go for a midnight swim."

"Maybe we can go to high school camp together," Lindsay whispered to me.

"That'd be great. We should try to go to all ten years of camp together. And be in the same cabin together every year."

"Shh," Car said from the other side of the fire, looking right at us, like she was the hall monitor of the ghost story just because she had pushed her way onto the bench so she could sit by her big crush.

I looked at Dane in time to see him frown and say quietly, "But they didn't make it into the water."

Teresa gasped. I didn't because I was expecting the story to be freaky. A bunch of kids on the next tarp over looked up at Dane. A couple of girls sat down and put their fingers to their lips, glaring at the boys in their group who were still roughhousing near the volleyball net. Everyone was gathering for the story.

"Frank and Elizabeth met at the top of the hill by Elizabeth's cabin." Elizabeth must have been in Bunny Cabin since it's the one with the good meeting spot on the way to the lake. "They walked down to the lake in silence, not wanting to wake any of the counselors. They stepped onto the end of the dock. All of a sudden, Elizabeth heard a noise."

He paused, and I waited for the ghost's creepy noise.

"Reeet, reeet, reeet. 'Frank, did you hear that?' Frank froze and tipped his head towards the water. He heard it. Reeet, reeet, reeet!"

I leaned towards Kate, who was sitting between Teresa and me. It's always good to be next to your counselor in scary situations.

Dane stood up and walked sideways a few paces with his hands in his pockets. He pulled one hand out and pointed at the dock. It looked more rickety in the dusk than it did during the day. I had never noticed how crooked it was before or how there was a little chunk missing from one of the corners that made it look like some monster had taken a bite out of our dock.

"Frank was scared," Dane continued, "but he didn't want to look like a wimp in front of his friend. 'I think it's just the board squeaking,' he said. They walked further onto the dock." He turned around to face the dock, his back to us, and just looked at it for a minute. "Then. . ."

I watched the dock for signs of spookiness and just about jumped over the fire when Dane whipped around and let out that funny noise again of, "Reeeet, reeet, reeet!"

It reminded me of the sound effects my friend R.J. made at junior high camp last year when he told us a story about a murderer who killed people with a hand saw.

"I don't think that was the boards," Dane said in his slightly high-pitched "Elizabeth" voice. "Just then a man appeared on the end of the dock. He was completely gray: his hair, his body, and his swimsuit. 'I am the Ghost of Lake Spirit,' he moaned. 'I was a kid who snuck out of his bunk to go swimming, and I drowned.'"

"That's not true," T-Camp said. "How could you drown in this lake? It's too low."

He had a good point. Once I asked my mom if anyone could actually drown in the lake at camp, and she said people can drown in two inches of water. I don't see how that's possible, but my mom isn't one of those parents who make things up to get you to stop bugging them the way I think Carin's mom does sometimes.

"It was higher back then," Dane said, not getting stumped by T-Camp. "Much higher." He held his hand over his head to give us an idea of how high the water was. "Elizabeth and Frank were so scared that they took off up the hill and woke up Elizabeth's counselor. They told her what had happened. 'I know,' the counselor said. 'The Ghost of Lake Spirit comes out at night and tries to get campers who sneak out of their bunks to go swimming. You must have barely escaped.'"

Sam coughed. Dane stopped the story to look at him.

"Uh, no offense," he said, pushing his glasses up on his nose. They must've slipped down when he coughed. "But that seems too corny to be true."

Dane nodded. "That's what Vanessa LaBoyer said when her dad told her the story. She didn't believe it, either. But one night, she couldn't fall asleep and thought it would be fun to go for a swim."

"Oh, no!" Teresa yelled, putting her hands up to her face. "Don't tell any more!"

Chad made a noise that sounded like, "Pfft!" and shook his head, his mouth twisted into an unbelieving smirk. "It's all just make-believe." His confidence made me feel silly for leaning so close to Kate, so I sat up straighter again.

Dane chose to ignore Chad's comment. "It was family camp, so Vanessa went to the cabin that the Koski/McAllery family was sharing. She woke up her friend Ben and told him to get on his swimsuit. You see, even though Vanessa didn't believe her father's story, she was too afraid to go to the beach by herself. So Ben changed, and the two of them headed towards the lake."

I looked around for Vanessa to see her reaction to being in the story, but I couldn't find her in the crowd of campers and counselors.

"How did Ben get on his swimsuit without waking up the other people in his cabin?" Alana asked. She *would* try to ruin the story. Who cared how Ben got his swimsuit on? Did that make any difference to the story? I highly doubted it.

"He changed in the bathroom, smarty pants," Dane said, and I smiled at his good comeback to Alana. "Anyway, Vanessa and Ben went down to the lake. They were younger than Frank and Elizabeth had been when they first encountered the Ghost of Lake Spirit, about twelve or thirteen. They got to the dock and were going to step onto it when...reeeet...reeeeeeet... reeeeeeeeet!"

The reeeeeeets were somewhat ruining the story because every time he did that I thought about R.J. sticking his flashlight in his mouth when he got to the part in his scary story when the murderer attacked again. R.J.'s lit-up face was hilarious.

"Then there he was. The gray, shriveled Ghost of Lake Spirit. 'Who are you?' Ben asked. 'I am the Ghost of Lake Spirit. Come join me for a swim.' Vanessa and Ben were scared out of their wits. They ran back to the cabin. They slammed the door, not caring who they woke up. Ben's father turned on the lights and asked what was going on. They told the whole story, but Ben's family was not amused. His older brother and sister laughed at them. His mother put an arm around Ben and one around Vanessa and told them they had imagined the whole thing. 'Doesn't anyone believe us?' Vanessa asked."

Vanessa had the same voice as Elizabeth in the story. I wondered if they really sounded similar and Dane was trying to be realistic or if he had one generic voice for every girl in any ghost story.

"They were all silent for a moment, and then Ben's aunt spoke: 'I believe you.'"

Dane sat down on the bench again, the flames in front of him making his face a lot scarier than R.J.'s had been when he had his flashlight crammed into his mouth at junior high camp. Carin grabbed Dane's arm, either because she was scared or she wanted to hang on him. It was hard to tell which.

Dane went on with the story.

"'Do you really believe us, Aunt Elizabeth?' Ben asked. 'Don't encourage this nonsense,' Ben's dad told his sister. She looked him straight in the eye—" at this Dane looked down at Car and locked eyes with her "—and said, 'I was there.'" He looked up at us again. "Ben's Aunt Elizabeth was the same Elizabeth who had first seen the ghost with Frank, Vanessa's dad."

I don't know what most of these people sounded like in real life, but the Ben voice didn't sound much like Ben. Dane was much better at telling the story than doing the voices.

"It took a long time, but finally Vanessa calmed down enough to go back to her cabin. Ben's dad said he would walk with her. He got a flashlight, and the two stepped out onto the porch. Immediately, Ben's dad felt his slippers become soaked. He looked down and saw that the porch was covered with water. 'How did you two manage to bring back so much water from the lake?' he asked. Vanessa trembled and turned white, reached out and grabbed his hand. 'But Mr. McAllery,' she whispered, 'we didn't go in the water.'"

Yikes! I grabbed on to Kate's arm. A ghost who followed campers back to their cabins? That was creepy. When I dared to move, I saw that Lindsay was leaning forward so far that her chin almost touched the tarp. Sam and T-Camp even looked freaked out, with their mouths hanging open, Sam looking uneasily at the lake. Next to Sam, mouth slightly open, Chad didn't look like he thought it was all pretend anymore.

"The end," Dane finished with a sneaky, twisted smile.

I dropped my hold on Kate and let my hands fall on the plastic of the tarp.

"What kind of ghost would pour water on somebody's porch?" Kate asked. She was looking at Teresa, who had Kate's other arm in a grip that looked tighter than mine had been. " Seriously, hon," she whispered, giving Teresa a little shake of a hug, " it's just for fun."

Teresa laughed, and so did I. Dane was now calmly roasting a marshmallow, and T-Camp and Wade shouted at each other, both trying to claim the first one.

"That was a good story," Lindsay said.

"Much better than the Ghost of the Pit Toilets," I agreed.

Carin snagged the marshmallow off the stick while T-Camp and Wade fought over it, not even noticing what she had done. Next to her, Steve frowned, his arms folded across his broad chest. He gave Dane a funny sideways look, and Dane shook his head, putting one index finger on his lips in a quick gesture that I don't think anybody else caught.

"No, it's not," Steve said quietly. "That's not the end of the story."

Car looked over at him and paused, the marshmallow half in her mouth and half on her fingers. T-Camp and Wade stopped bickering right in the middle of an insult.

"Huh?" T asked.

"Shh," Dane said, holding the stick out at Steve. "That's the end."

"Right." Steve took the stick from him and stood up. But the look they gave each other made me know they were lying to keep us from hearing the real end of the story.

We didn't let them get away with that. Everybody started talking at once, wanting to know what the rest of the story was. Dane tried to distract us by asking who wanted the first s'more, evidently forgetting that Carin already claimed it. The story must've been terrifying to make him lose count of something food-related, and after we bugged them long enough, they caved in.

"You should be the one to tell it," Dane said to Steve, handing over the storyteller job, "since it happened to you, too."

His voice sounded so serious and spooked that Carin screeched and wrapped both of her arms around one of his. Steve took a while, watching the fire, before he began the end of the story.

"I was in that cabin the night the Ghost of Lake Spirit almost got Vanessa and Ben."

Lindsay gasped. "Can you imagine meeting a ghost?" she whispered.

I shook my head hard.

"Ben is my cousin," Steve explained, "and his Aunt Elizabeth is my mom. So you see, it was destined that I would someday meet the Ghost of Lake Spirit."

"You saw it?" T-Camp asked. "Like really *saw* it?"

Steve nodded solemnly once and went on with the story. "I was only seven when Vanessa and my cousin had their run-in with the ghost. I always wondered if it was real or not, but I was too afraid to go to the lake at night. Then, my last year of junior high camp, Dane and I were in the same cabin." He looked at Dane. "As we were getting ready for bed one night, I took him aside where our counselor couldn't hear us and told him the whole story. He said he would check things out with me as soon as our counselor fell asleep."

"We didn't change into our swimsuits," Dane said, evidently unable to let Steve take over telling the story. "We didn't want to go swimming."

I watched him turn his head to glance back at the lake as Steve went on.

"We only wanted to find out for ourselves if the Ghost of Lake Spirit was real or a figment of Vanessa's imagination."

"We went to the dock," Dane said.

Now I looked at the dock for about the bazillionth time. If that ghost was going to show up, I wanted to know about it before it tried to haunt me or slime me or make me go for a swim.

"We stood there as still as we could, listening, for probably five minutes," Steve continued. "I started to think that Ben and Vanessa had poured a bucket of water on the porch and made the whole thing up to scare us. But right when we turned to leave..."

"Reeet, reeet, reeet!" This time, I didn't think of R.J. and his flashlight. I thought of a misshapen, old gray ghost floating around a couple of junior high campers.

"There he was!" Steve shouted. I jumped, thinking he meant the ghost was here now. Then I realized he was still telling the story. "The Ghost of Lake Spirit."

"We started to run, and we heard him behind us. He was saying, 'Why doesn't anybody ever want to join me for a swim?'" Dane's ghost voice that had sounded sort of corny before now creeped me out. It sounded old and feeble but powerful, in a weird, ghosty way.

Steve creaked the bench standing up. "We ran as fast as we could, but he was still behind us."

"Join me for a swim. Join me for a swim." Dane even added creepy hand gestures to his quoting the ghost that looked like bony ghost fingers trying to grab us. I don't think even Car would try to hold those hands. She let go of him and scooted away on the bench.

"We made it back to the cabin," Steve said, his voice getting quieter, the panic gone. "Our counselor was a heavy sleeper, so he didn't even know we were gone. We started to get into our bunks, and I looked down." My eyes dropped down to his tennis shoes as his did. "My shoe was gone. I figured it had fallen off when we were running up the hill and that I just hadn't noticed because we were so scared."

"But then," Dane said, "when we went swimming the next morning, we found Steve's shoe drenched and sitting on the end of the dock."

"The Ghost of Lake Spirit stole your shoe?" Chad asked.

"Was it a nice shoe?" Alana asked, like it only mattered if it was an expensive shoe. I was more worried about how we could tell the ghost was about to come back than the quality of the shoes he had stolen in the past.

"I've never been at the lake after dark since then," Steve said, shaking himself as if a shiver had just run through him. He glanced towards the lake with just his eyes, as if he was worried about the ghost but didn't want us to know. Then he shifted his eyes back to us. "Until now."

I didn't care how much of a baby I looked like, I screamed. Loud. And grabbed Kate again, almost hitting Teresa in the face because she was hugging our counselor, too. Everybody else was screaming, so I screamed louder. Lindsay hugged me, screaming in my ear. "That's not really a true story, is it?" I heard somebody ask, the voice muffled from underneath a sleeping bag.

"Should we be sleeping down here?" Rachel asked.

My ear started to ring thanks to Lindsay's scream.

"I'm sure the Ghost of Lake Spirit won't come tonight," Dane said. Then he half-grinned. "Unless he wants someone to swim with."

This time I thought my sleeping bag might be better protection, so I ran back to it, lifted up the flap, scrambled underneath it, and let everybody else bother with screaming. A ghost can't get you if your head is covered with a sleeping bag, can he? It's like home base in tag, right? I thought I heard somebody snickering, but I didn't dare look because it could have been the Ghost of Lake Spirit. The air was hot and smothering inside the sleeping bag, but I wasn't coming out.

"Abby," I heard someone say, and then my sleeping bag shook.

It was the ghost trying to shake me out of my sleeping bag so he could get me! On the bright side, this meant that the sleeping bag *was* home base and that if I could stay inside it, I would be okay. I squeezed my fists, and the sleeping bag together, tighter.

"Abby, come out of there."

Or maybe it was just Kate. I backed out of my sleeping bag and pulled my head out last. The inside of my sleeping bag had made my hair crazy-looking, and I tried to press it down, but it kept popping up in frizzy waves.

"It's just a story, girls," Kate said to Teresa, Lindsay, and me, as all of us hovered close to her. "Now let's eat some s'mores."

She made us get up and go closer to the fire, even though that put some distance between us and the safety of our sleeping bags.

"Should they be standing over there?" Car asked. She pointed at some of the counselors who were talking near the lake.

Kate smushed the marshmallow Steve had roasted between two graham cracker pieces and slid it off the stick. "It's just a story, Carin," she said, giving the smoking s'more to Teresa.

Teresa took it with a trembling hand. "I'm not going to be able to sleep at all tonight. Maybe the Ghost of Lake Spirit is hiding out in the woods waiting for swim time." She was looking at Chad's summerhouse that was surrounded by trees. She had it all wrong. It was the Ghost of the Pit Toilet who haunted the woods. I decided not to tell her that. She looked scared enough as it was without knowing about any other ghosts.

Kate tried to convince us there were no such thing as ghosts, but we didn't believe her until Steve admitted that he and Dane had made it up before the sleep-out and planned the whole second ending to scare us more. It kind of ruins a ghost story to be told your counselors made it up, but it also made me feel more like eating my s'more and sitting back on the tarp with Carin, Teresa, Rachel, and Lindsay.

"That was scary," Linds said.

"Scarier than last year," Car said.

"Much," I agreed.

"Let's talk about something else," Teresa suggested.

"Okay," Rachel said. "How about skit night. What are you guys going to do?"

"Oh, it's going to be really funny," Car said, and I started thinking about our underwear skit instead of ghosts.

But before we could tell Rachel and Lindsay anything about our game show skit, someone said loudly, "Hey!" We all looked in the direction of the shout and saw Noelle kneeling on one of the tarps. "Has anybody seen my shoe?"

"Yikes!" Car exclaimed. "The *ghost* stole shoes. Remember?"

"I took my shoes off to go boating, and now I can only find one," Noelle said. "It's a red sandal with straps, and if I don't get it back in the next minute, I'm going to be very angry."

I wasn't taking any chances. I dove for my sleeping bag. I don't know who was scarier, the Ghost of Lake Spirit or Noelle. Hopefully my sleeping bag would protect me from both of them.

CHAPTER TWENTY-ONE

Sick at the Sleep-out

After some of the counselors had led us in a group prayer, I burrowed into my sleeping bag and pulled it over my head. I wasn't going to be cold this year. Last summer made me feel bad for homeless people. If I was that cold on a one-night sleep-out in the middle of summer, it must be really awful for them in the winter, especially in Wisconsin or the U.P.

I didn't feel cold yet. I actually felt hot, and it was pretty stuffy underneath that heavy sleeping bag. I poked my head out and felt the cool air on my face. I took a couple of deep, clear breaths, then ducked back under my sleeping bag. I had to stay warm.

I could hear the muffled sound of Carin and Rachel whispering and giggling about something. I wanted to know what it was, but I didn't want to risk getting cold.

I stayed under my sleeping bag in the pitch-blackness until I started to sweat. I sort of felt like I was going to throw up. I wiggled to the top of the sleeping bag and pushed the material down.

It wasn't very dark out. There were a lot of stars and an almost-full moon. It was cooler outside the sleeping bag, but sweat still made the back of my neck itch, and my stomach felt like I was doing a bunch of back handsprings down a gymnastics mat instead of lying on a tarp.

Throwing up in front of everybody at the sleep-out would be way too embarrassing, so I got up and stepped over people until I got to Kate. She rolled over and sat up as soon as I knelt down next to her.

I should have known better than to tell a counselor I was sick because her first suggestion was to go to the nurse. I tried to talk her out of it. I told her I didn't want to go because the nurse would make me sleep in her cabin, and I didn't want to miss the sleep-out. I could not tell her the real reason—that I was afraid to go to the nurse's cabin because my friend R.J. and I used to think she was a witch who put campers into her laundry detergent cauldron. Looking back on it during the day, I feel silly that we used to think that, but at night, it doesn't seem that crazy. It also seems like the kind of thing that, if you admit, the counselors would give you a stern look about and tell you not to be ridiculous.

I thought about pretending I felt better, but as soon as I tried to stand up, something weird happened in my throat, something that felt like throwing up was on its way.

"I think I'm going to throw up," I said.

Which would be worse: barfing on somebody's sleeping bag at the all-camp sleep-out or having to face The Scary Nurse?

Steve came over to us and suggested going to the bathroom and getting a drink. I got to hold his hand and Kate's as we went up the steps to the bathroom. I held Steve's hand because he offered it, and I wanted to hold it. I held Kate's so it wouldn't be weird that I had Steve's. I am much more subtle than Carin and her arm clinging. I didn't run up the stairs like we usually do. Bouncing up steps can't be good when you're trying not to throw up.

The little round clock by the mirror in the bathroom said two-ten. They couldn't make me go to the nurse's cabin now. She gets mad if you go in there five minutes after bedtime. What would she do if I knocked on her door at two-ten in the middle of the night? She'd probably give me three shots or something.

Steve walked right into the bathroom with us. If I didn't feel so awful, I would have thought that was funny, a boy counselor in the girls' bathroom.

"Your face is all red, Ab," Kate said. "I think we should go to the nurse."

I shook my head so hard it made me dizzy. "No."

"Let her use the bathroom first," Steve said.

I went to the farthest stall, the one closest to the showers. I did not want anybody else to have to hear or smell my puke if it came to that. I sat down to go to the bathroom. I could still hear Steve and Kate talking, so my plan of picking the farthest stall probably wouldn't work as far as being less embarrassing.

I started to feel better after I flushed, but then I heard Steve and Kate say something about s'mores, and the thought of gooey marshmallows and chocolate made all that trying not to throw up pointless. Why is it that something that usually tastes so good can make you want to puke when you don't feel well? It's not like I thought of something gross like bananas or a worm milkshake like they have to eat on that one television game show.

"Kate?" I asked, not caring anymore if my counselors heard or even saw me puke. My stomach felt rotten, and throwing up is the worst, especially when you feel like you're going to choke. "Kate, I think I'm going to throw up."

I knelt down on the hard floor. If I was going to puke, I did not want any splatter. Gross. I really hate puking. I can't think of anything more disgusting.

Kate told me I needed to unlock the door, and I somehow got it open right before looking into that toilet and losing my two s'mores. I don't know many counselors who will stand behind you in a toilet stall and hold your hair so you don't get barf in it, but Kate did. I don't think Noelle would do that for anybody.

When we came out of the stall, Steve handed me a paper towel with cold water on it and told me it to wipe my face off and sit down on the cement outside.

As I was rinsing my mouth out at the drinking fountain, I decided that Kate was an even better counselor then Eva. She hadn't yelled at me on the first night when I went to the canteen, and now she had put herself in the same stall as me while I hurled just to help me. I somehow think Eva would have given me a lecture on why you aren't supposed to puke at the all-camp sleep-out. And she would not have let Steve come in to help because boys going in the girls' bathroom is against the rules, and Eva was all about the rules.

I sat next to the water fountain and put my hands on the ground and felt the cold.

Steve figured out what had made me sick. It wasn't having too many s'mores like Kate first thought. It was because I had so many clothes on and had tried to fall asleep with my heavy sleeping bag over my head. He felt my forehead and said I looked a lot better than I had at first, even though my stomach got all jumpy again when he touched the back of his hand to my head. Then he told me I had to take off my extra sweatshirt and one pair of socks so that I was just wearing a sweater, pants, one pair of socks, and my shoes.

When we got back to the sleep-out, Kate made sure I took off the sweatshirt. That made me feel almost normal, and I stopped sweating.

Steve went to his sleeping bag on the boys' side of the tarp, and Kate walked with me to my spot.

I settled back into my sleeping bag, and Lindsay asked right away, "Where did you go? Are you okay?"

"I felt sick. Steve said I got overheated."

"It's not freezing like it was last year," Lindsay mumbled, sounding tired now that she knew I was okay.

"Did you puke?" Carin asked.

Leave it to Car to wonder about puking. Lindsay wanted to know if I was all right, but Car was interested in details on barfing.

"Yes," I said honestly, even though I really didn't want everybody to know.

Rachel started giggling, which I thought was pretty rude and insensitive until she asked, "Did it smell like dog food?" and I realized she was thinking about that girl her brother threw up on.

"I don't know," I said. "I was trying not to think about it."

"Did you have to go to the nurse?" Car asked. That stopped Rachel's giggles.

"No. They almost made me, but then Steve figured out about the overheating thing, so they said all I had to do was not wear so many clothes."

"It's time to go to sleep, girls," Kate said from another part of the tarp.

I looked up at the stars. I felt all better. As gross as it is, sometimes puking makes you feel better. I'd never been sick at camp before. It was not an experience I wanted to have again anytime soon...or anytime ever.

I felt so much better that when I heard Steve and Dane talking about having a kitchen raid, I tried to get them to bring me along. They wouldn't let me go though. Steve said they would get in big trouble with the deans if they brought a camper, but Dane said he would bring me a cookie.

It was a chocolate chip cookie, the kind we had missed out on Monday because Carin had been upset. It's probably not a good idea to eat a chocolate chip cookie half an hour after you throw up, but it didn't make me feel sick to my stomach. The only thing that was a bummer was that I only got one little chocolate chip cookie, but Dane and Steve and Julie got DTC.

I closed my eyes and forced myself to go to sleep. I had to get a good night's sleep because we were going to Mount Spirit tomorrow for lunch, and going on that long hike is hard enough when you've gotten enough sleep. I couldn't imagine a Mount Spirit hike with no sleep.

CHAPTER TWENTY-TWO

PS—We Went to Mount Spirit Today

Not only did Kate let me walk on the railroad tracks all the way to Mount Spirit, but she tried it, too. This was a huge improvement in counselor behavior from last year when Eva yelled at me because she thought I would get hurt or lost walking on the railroad tracks.

Our group went with Rachel's group, but Noelle didn't go, which was another good thing about this trip to Mount Spirit. It was pretty much the perfect trip—no Noelle, walking on the railroad tracks, sub sandwiches, and the great view from up high. Ben came with us, too, and that made it even more fun because I hadn't gotten to see him much this week. You don't see the assistant manager as often as you see the lifeguards. I wished he were a lifeguard again because he's one of the most fun people to hang out with at camp.

As soon as we reached the railroad tracks, I got up on the track on the right side and tried to do a split leap like we do in gymnastics. I slipped right off the railroad track and jumped into the pebbles along the trail. That was weird because I haven't fallen off the balance beam on a split leap in months. I'm a good jumper, and usually I nail my leaps. It's those tricky full turns that give me trouble.

I got back up on the track and looked behind me to find Kate and Carin. "Watch this, you guys!" I took a running start on the balls of my feet and jumped into a tuck leap. I landed square on the track with both feet and tried a turn, but my tennis shoe slid off the metal, and I hopped onto one of the boards between the tracks.

Kate clapped, and Carin yelled, "Perfect ten!" I think she thought that was my dismount.

I turned around and walked backwards. "Why can't I do any of my tricks?"

Kate looked down at the track. "The railroad tracks aren't much like the balance beam. They aren't as wide, and the train has worn them down

on the edges. See?" She pointed at the side of the inside track, and I saw
that they were more curved than straight edges.

"What kind of gymnastics can we do on them?"

She stepped onto the track and started walking, her arms at her sides
for balance like Mrs. Newman used to make us do on the beam when we
were little. She stepped onto her left foot and raised her right one behind
her in a great arabesque, then leaned forward, making her legs go into almost a split position. She looked just like Mrs. Newman. I wondered who
was a better gymnast between Kate and Mrs. Newman. Kate ducked her
head and stretched her arms down to touch the track, then kicked her legs
into a cartwheel. It was a perfect cartwheel with straight arms, split legs,
and pointed toes, but she didn't land on the track either. Her foot brushed
the side of the metal, and she ended up on the pebbles.

"Not much, Abbers."

Bummer. If Kate couldn't do an easy trick like a cartwheel, I didn't
have much of a chance of doing anything. The only thing I could really do
was walk, and that was totally boring. Then I got an idea.

"We could have a balance competition. We can see who can walk on
the railroad track the longest."

Kate agreed, so I stood on the right track and Kate stood on the left
one. Car and Teresa wanted to try, too, so Carin went in front of me and
Teresa went in front of Kate. We all started walking. Teresa and Carin
fell off after a couple of steps. Teresa laughed at herself and walked in the
middle on the boards, but Car got back on the tracks three more times
before she gave up. She doesn't like to lose, which makes her really annoying to play board games with but great to have on your team for kickball
against another class. She's better at sports when we play girls against girls
and boys against boys instead of co-ed because when it's co-ed sports, she's
too busy watching the boys play to pay attention to what she's doing.

We walked for a long time, balancing on the tracks until I stepped
my left foot half on the track and half in the air. I tried to put my right
foot entirely on the track on the next step, but my weight was too far to
the left, and that foot ended up half on the track and half over thin air,
too. I stepped onto the boards next to Car, and Kate won. I didn't care or
anything. How can you beat a counselor? I was just glad she let me walk on
the track without giving me an Eva-lecture.

I didn't notice T-Camp watching us, but he must have been because he started running and yelled, "I'm a gymnastics man!" He jumped and twisted at the same time, almost making it around in a full somersault, but crashing down the hill at the end. He had a lot of force going into the flip, but he didn't tuck his legs together very tightly. He hit the ground hard and kind of skidded, still rolling.

If it were me, I probably would have cried. Not T-Camp. He stood up, looked at his elbow, and ran back to us with a grin on his face when Dane yelled, "Get back up here!"

We had almost caught up with the rest of the group, so I heard T-Camp say proudly to Sam and Hunter, "Look! I'm bleeding. Awesome!"

"Then you get to go to the nurse when we get back," Dane said.

"No way, man. She's weird. And old."

"She's not weird," Dane said. "Don't say stuff like that about people. She's just the camp nurse."

"She scares me," Hunter said.

"Why?" The way he asked made it sound like he thought Hunter was silly for being afraid of her, the way you would respond if someone said they were afraid of a kitten, even though last year he had seemed not so sure about having to go to the nurse himself. "I think she's funny."

"Hey, Ab," Kate said. "I think T-Camp just tried to do a full-twisting double back."

I laughed because a full twisting double back is one of the hardest tumbling passes, and what he had done would better be described as half a somersault flop.

Having Kate for my counselor was a lot different than having Eva, and not just because I got in less trouble. I liked Eva, but Kate was my friend, like Scott had been. Sometimes counselors are just counselors, but other times counselors are friends *and* counselors both at the same time.

The other group had gotten way ahead of us by the time we made it into the woods and started climbing Mount Spirit, but we passed Alana and Imogen taking a rest by a big rock with Julie. Carin stopped to rest, too, but I wasn't going to. I wanted to get to the top without stopping, to prove I was better at this camp stuff than snobby Alana and Imogen, so I pressed on behind Kate, trying to concentrate on the sounds of Teresa's hiking boots behind me instead of the burning in the tops of my legs.

I didn't run up the second half of the hike like Dane and Ben did, but I didn't stop either, and Teresa and I got to the top with Kate, Steve, Rachel and most of the boys. Dane was lying on the ground. Ben was still standing but just barely, leaning over with his arms resting on his knees. You really should not run up Mount Spirit. It's harder than any exercise they can give you in gym class.

"That wasn't such a good idea," Ben said, sucking in air hard between each word.

"What are you talking about?" Dane asked. "I feel great."

"Then stand up." Ben straightened his body up and put his hands behind his head, breathing in, one very deep breath.

"Just five more minutes," Dane said in a tired, cracking voice.

"You just doomed yourself in the sub sandwich eating contest, you know," Steve said.

"No way," Dane argued, still from the ground. "I have to win this one after Tuesday's devastating taco loss. I'm still appealing that one on the basis of Noelle being annoying."

Julie, Carin, Alana, Imogen, and Wade made it up the hill then, and we all looked for good spots on the rocks to sit and eat our lunches. I found a fairly flat rock to sit on. It was so flat that when I set down my cup of lemonade, the lemonade only shifted a little towards the left in the cup instead of spilling onto the rock, which is what usually happens at Mount Spirit.

Rachel had walked with Alana and Imogen most of the way until they had stopped for that rest, but she sat with Carin, Teresa, and me for lunch. I didn't like having to share her with Alana and Imogen. Most of the time when I saw her, she was talking to them or laughing. I don't know why she sat by us instead of them. Maybe she thought they were wimps for resting on the trail. Car had rested, too, though. Maybe she just liked us better.

Alana and Imogen sat together, and the boys took over the other side of the rocks, amusing themselves by throwing tree branches and rocks off the cliff and listening to the sounds they made bouncing off juts of ground and trees. The counselors and Ben sat on the grassy area next to the big cross by the woods.

Mount Spirit is the most beautiful place to eat lunch in the whole entire world. I'm not exaggerating. The sky is bluer up here, and the clouds look fluffier, and I've never seen so many trees together in one place.

The last thing we did was put a special rock next to the cross, one we had painted our names on during crafts that day. We had to leave, but our names could stay together at Mount Spirit forever. Or until next year when T-Camp, or some other mischievous boy like him, used our rock as something to throw off the edge of the cliff.

***

We got back to camp just as everybody else left lunch to go to rest hour. Back in the cabin, Lindsay and I sat on my bed together, and I told her about walking on the railroad tracks, how Carin brought Laurette the grasshead in her lunch bag, how the boys threw rocks off of Mount Spirit, Dane's and Ben's race to the top, and even how I found a perfect rock to sit on.

She smiled until I mentioned how Rachel sat with us instead of Alana and Imogen. Then the corners of her smile faded down into a frown.

"Why do you guys always do stuff with Rachel's group?"

"I don't know," I said, feeling lousy for saying anything at all that would make her feel left out again. "Because our counselors are friends with Rachel's counselors?"

"It's not fair. How did you and Carin get put together, but the rest of us got split up?"

I shrugged and pretended not to know. Hopefully she wouldn't be suspicious of that because usually I know the answers to anybody's questions about camp, having come here longer than most of the campers my age.

"It stinks," I said. "Next year we'll have to figure out a way to all be together."

Carin and I had gotten in the same group both years by writing each other's names on the line on the registration form where you can request a buddy. I wasn't going to tell Lindsay that though because then she would want to know why I didn't put her name down. The truth was, my mom had filled out the form, assumed I just wanted to be with Car, and sent the registration in.

Brenda said it was time for everybody to lie down, so Lindsay had to take her hurt expression across the cabin to her own bunk. I thought about how I would feel if Lindsay and Car got put together and I was in a different group. Lindsay is just as shy as I am. I felt a lot less shy this year though because I had Car, Chad, and Steve all in my group—people I knew from before.

Next year would be different. Next year we would be smart about the cabin request forms and request each other in a circle. A four-way circle of me, Car, Lindsay, and Rachel. Teresa could be in it, too, if she wanted because sometimes there are five people in a group. That would be perfect.

***

Dean Jamie handed out the mail at dinner because four different groups had eaten out at lunch. Besides us going to Mount Spirit, one group had eaten a floating lunch in rowboats and another had gone to the nature trail.

Car and I both got letters. I felt bad for Teresa because she didn't get one, but then I remembered she had a letter yesterday.

I ripped my envelope open. Angela's pretty handwriting full of curvy letters ran all the way down a whole piece of notebook paper. My neat sister had pulled off the fringes. It's a good thing we've never had to share a room. We would have driven each other crazy—Angela with her perfectly made bed and me with all of my stuffed animals thrown everywhere. At camp she's different though. She's not so much of a neat freak here. Our cabin at junior high camp always looks like a clothes bomb exploded.

"Mine's from Joey!" Carin exclaimed.

She shoved the yellow paper in my face. It had little kid drawings all over it. I think one was of a sun and one was of a car, but I didn't know what the third drawing was. A rabbit maybe? Or a cat with messed up ears? Or it could have been a tree with eyes, I guess.

"What did you guys get?" Rachel asked from the table behind us.

She moved her chair so she could look over our shoulders.

"Drawings from my little brother," Car said. "He's annoying at home, but when I'm at camp, he's so sweet!"

"A letter from my sister," I said.

"Oh," Rach said, leaning in so she could read the first few sentences.

"Did you get anything?" Car asked.

"Uh, my brother would have sent me something," Rachel said, "but it takes like three months for mail to get here from France. By then, *all* the camps would be over, not just ours. That's why he didn't write me. Otherwise, he would have."

I don't know why it took so long to get mail from France. My cousin went to school in England for a year, and whenever she wrote to us, we got her letters within a week or two.

"But what's that?" Car pointed at the long white envelope that lay on the table next to Rach.

Rachel rolled her eyes. "That's from Annoying Jim. 'Dear Rachel, I hope you are having an excellent time at camp. I miss you.' Blah, blah, blah. He does *not* miss me. Plus, he sent me five dollars. Duh! He's so dumb he doesn't even know that we have canteen cards instead of real money at elementary camp. Who doesn't know that?"

I wondered what was so annoying about Annoying Jim. I would be happy if somebody sent me money in a letter.

"Sweet!" I heard Dane shout from further down Rachel's table. I saw him looking inside a card. "Five bucks! Jim, you rock."

"He would think that's cool," Rach muttered. "It's just stupid five bucks."

Dane shot her a glare. "Hey!" Evidently, she hadn't muttered quietly enough. "This is worth at least two trips to the canteen."

"Jim thinks this is a good bribe?" Rachel snapped back. "Five lousy dollars?"

"It's not a bribe, Rach. Jim just wanted to send you five bucks and a letter."

"Well, that would be great," she said sarcastically. "If I *could use real money here.* Kylie would not send me something so stupid."

"Do you see a letter from Kylie and Dad?" Dane asked.

"They'll write me tomorrow," Rachel said, sounding confident. "But they won't write to you because you're mean to them."

"You're mean to Jim, and he still wrote to you."

"That's different. He's an idiot."

Rachel threw the letter away. I know that because I was a hopper, and I saw it in the garbage when I tossed out the dirt that we had swept. The return address on the envelope was a sticker of two beagle puppies and said, "Dr. James T. Mills, DVM." I had two thoughts about seeing Rachel's letter in the trash. One—I wondered if she had thrown the five dollars away, too. Two—I didn't think anyone who liked beagle puppies could be all that annoying.

CHAPTER TWENTY-THREE

Return of Skit Night

I didn't freak out about skit night until, all of a sudden, I found myself sitting in a pew between Carin and Steve and watching a group of campers pretending to be Bible characters going to camp. This was progress from last year, when I was freaked out about skit night from the time we had our first skit practice until about two minutes after the skit was over. It was hard to be scared during skit practice this year when we talked about underwear and laughed so much.

I knew I didn't have any lines since my part was to be a model and show off all the things the pretend contestants were supposed to guess the prices of, but now that it was almost time to do our skit, I felt myself wiggling around and nudging into Carin like I was hyper T-Camp or something.

"I will send great rain after canteen tomorrow, and all of camp will be destroyed," the counselor up front said in a deep voice. "You must gather together two strands of every color of gimp so that gimping will survive this great flood."

Steve snickered and said, "I love this skit." But there's no way I could have told anybody the plot because I was too busy being nervous about my own skit.

They finished, and the next group did a skit about the "Pharaoh, Pharaoh" song we had sung after meals all week. Bruce, the counselor from the registration line, had a sheet wrapped around himself like a toga and leaned on a big stick that he had probably found in the woods. He sang the verses about Moses. The kids had bed sheet togas, too, but it didn't look as funny on ten-year-olds as it did on a teenager. I felt bad for the boy who had to wear Barney sheets. Everybody else had plain sheets or sheets with good cartoons or something. The kids sang the Pharaoh, Pharaoh part. Everybody looked like they were having fun. Even Bruce laughed and got into it. The other counselor, a bigger girl who had her lip curled up throughout most of the skit, stood at one end of the stage and didn't say anything or sing. She had her arms folded across her chest most of the time. She did not look like a fun counselor.

Thank You, God, that I got Kate and Steve, I prayed quickly.

Dane and Julie's group went after the "Pharaoh, Pharaoh" skit. They had even more props than we did. Alana set up a coat rack with several sweatshirts hanging from it in the middle of the stage, and Rachel and Imogen piled about two feet of shorts, T-shirts, and shoes on the two wooden chairs that always sit up front in the chapel. Julie placed a purple case on the podium and flipped it open. She pulled on the top, and several layers of make-up appeared.

"Awesome," Carin said.

"Oh, Imogen," Alana cried dramatically, beginning their skit. "I'm going to camp in three days, and I don't have a thing to wear!"

How would you not have anything to wear to camp? Didn't her parents buy her jeans and sweatshirts?

"I have a great idea," Imogen said with a wide smile plastered across her face. When she talked, she bobbed her head up and down. "We can go to the mall!"

"Oh, dude," Steve muttered next to me, "you can't let Noelle and Julie plan your skit."

"What a great idea, Imogen!" Alana said. "I heard they're having a sale!"

Rachel ran onto the stage and slid between Alana and Imogen. "Can I go, too? I don't know anything about fashion, so maybe you can help me."

"Let's do a makeover!" Alana exclaimed.

"An extreme makeover," Imogen said with another head bob.

I didn't see anything wrong with Rachel's clothes, a pair of khaki shorts and a red sweatshirt. It was pretty much what I was wearing, only my sweatshirt was green and said "Millers Creek" on it. Maybe we were supposed to pretend Rachel looked bad like we had pretended Bruce was Moses.

"Hello, welcome to Noelle's Boutique," Noelle said.

Shoppers were probably allowed to cut in line at Noelle's Boutique. That would be some store. It would drive Angela nuts. One thing she can't stand is line cutting. Noelle better never counsel at junior high camp because if my sister ever caught her going in front of people in line, she'd regret it.

"Our friend would like a makeover," Alana said, pointing at Rachel.

"Oh, I see," Noelle said, making a face like Rachel was wearing something with taco toppings all over it like T-Camp had the other day.

It bugged me that Alana called Rachel their friend. Rachel was *our* friend, and Alana and Imogen weren't. Was it just a line for the skit, or did Rachel really have a bond with these girls? There's no way she would like people who made fun of other campers and were so snobby, would she? When we requested people to be in our cabins next year, would Rachel write down my name or Alana's?

Their skit went on for a long time as Julie put make-up on Rachel, and Alana and Imogen tried on a bunch of clothes and pretended to look into mirrors. I don't think anybody except for Carin, who ooed and aahed at every outfit they put on, was very interested in their skit.

"This is worse than that centipede thing," Steve said. He didn't even bother to mutter it or say it under his breath.

Just when I thought I couldn't take much more of Rachel bobbing her head like Imogen and smiling at Alana like they were long-lost sisters, T-Camp ran onto the stage and started throwing pieces of clothing all over. He chucked a pair of shorts at Alana and rapid-fired T-shirts into the audience.

"I want a makeover, too!" he screamed. Then he let out an animal roar and pounded on his chest with his fists.

The girls screamed and waved their hands next to their faces, pretending to be scared as T-Camp swept the rest of the clothes off the wooden chairs and flipped one upside-down with a loud bang on the stage. I hoped the deans would send him home if he broke one of the chairs. Those chairs have been there for as long as I can remember, and Blane Adams sits in them every junior high skit night when he's the emcee.

Despite the horrible racket the chairs made, neither one broke, at least as far as I could see. T-Camp continued to go wild, screaming and jumping and knocking over the coat rack. At one point, Dean Ron stood up and took a few steps towards the stage, but T-Camp kicked the coat rack and stomped his feet so that he looked like he was running in place and going even more crazy, and Dean Ron sat down again. Finally, after a lot of screaming, T, looking exhausted and panting, lay down on the floor, his arms and legs sprawled out in all different directions.

Sam and Hunter took the stage for the first time and told some kind of joke, but I couldn't hear the punch line because people in the audience were laughing at T-Camp and asking each other to explain the confusing skit.

I'm not sure, but I think the skit was about Godzilla attacking a shopping mall. I could be wrong though. No matter how weird their skit had been, at least it was creative, which was more than I could say for the next two skits, the predictable centipede and Good Samaritan numbers I've seen every year at junior high camp.

Finally the dreaded moment came, the moment when Dean Jamie stood on the stage, looked at a piece of yellow, lined paper, and announced, "The Really Cool Campers are up next."

"Who signed us up?" Carin asked. "That's not our name. It's the Totally Awesome Coolest Campers Ever To Set Foot On Camp."

I thought we had more important things to worry about than what our name was, like not tripping when we went up to the stage. I had to be one of the first people on stage. I stood next to Kate and stared at the back of the chapel so I wouldn't have to look at anybody. I could see out of the bottom of my eyes that there were people in the audience, but I couldn't actually see any one person.

"Hello, and welcome to *Price That Camp Item*," Steve said, clapping his hands together and doing a much better acting job than he had during practice. "I'm your announcer, Steven Koski, and this is your lovely host, Miss Carin Alexandra Morgan." He held his hand out toward Car, who gave a fake-looking wave by pressing her fingers together and wiggling her arm at the elbow. "And these are my models," he went on, stepping between Kate and me and putting an arm around each of us. "Otherwise known as Koski's Cuties."

Everybody laughed at that, even Kate because Steve had added that to the skit right then. I'm glad that hadn't been in the script all along because it was pretty embarrassing to be called a Koski's Cutie in front of the entire camp even though it was a joke, and if I had known he was going to say that, I would have been way, way, way more nervous for skit night the whole week.

"Now all we need are a few contestants."

T-Camp stood up and waved his arms in the air. "Me! Pick me! Pick me!"

Steve ignored him and went on with our skit as planned. I wondered what would happen if he picked T-Camp. T would probably have destroyed our set or puked on it or something.

"Our first contestant is a carpenter from Nazareth, but His real job is saving your soul. Please welcome Jesus."

Mason ran onto the stage, and people in the audience played along by clapping and cheering. I wonder what the real Jesus thinks when He sees stuff like a church camp skit starring Him as a game show contestant. Is He insulted, or does He think it's funny? Oh, well, there was nothing we could do about it now. We had to finish our skit and worry about what Jesus thought later. I hoped Jesus wouldn't be offended that we picked a kid who ate bugs and worms to play Him.

"Next," Steve announced, "Paul's prized pupil, Timothy."

Chad walked on stage, waved to slightly less applause than "Jesus" had gotten, and stood next to Mason.

Steve announced Teresa (Judas) as the disciple everyone loves to hate and Wade (the devil) as the evil prince of darkness, and they took their spots in the row next to Chad and Mason. I felt a little less nervous now that everyone was on stage and there were more people for the audience to look at. Less eyes should be staring at me now, right?

"The first camp item that you need to guess the value of is a roll of gimp," Steve said, and it was time for my part in the skit.

Kate took a brown roll of gimp off the podium and held it up for everyone to see. I waved my hands all around it, feeling sort of silly, because who models a roll of gimp? The contestants looked at the gimp and pretended to think hard about what they would bid. Kate handed me the roll of gimp, so I could hold it and she could show it off, but I dropped it when she let go, and it rolled towards the front of the stage. I scurried after it. I had to grab it before it rolled down the steps and towards the aisle because I did not want to go running into the audience.

I closed my hand around the brown gimp right before it fell off the stage. I felt like an idiot as I straightened up and went back to Kate. What kind of moron drops a prop? Nobody laughed though, and Carin, with the cardboard microphone she had made in the craft cabin, stepped over to Mason/Jesus and asked him what he thought the gimp was worth.

"I tell you the truth, material items will not get you into the kingdom of heaven," he said.

"I need a number, Jesus," Car said, and Dean Jamie busted up laughing even though that wasn't one of the funny parts of our skit. Maybe it was a delayed reaction to my dropping the gimp.

Mason shrugged and said, "How about three dollars."

Carin stepped to Chad and held the microphone in front of his mouth. "Timothy?"

"Hmm," he said, scratching his chin. "Let me check my last letter from Paul." He pulled a folded-up piece of paper out of his pocket. "Paul says I should guess ten cents."

"And Judas," Car said, swiveling to the left and thrusting the microphone almost up Teresa's nose.

Teresa craned her neck backwards to avoid the microphone and said, "Thirty pieces of silver."

"And last, *the devil*." She said his name very dramatically. "How much do you think that roll of brown gimp is worth?"

"A thousand bucks!" Wade exclaimed, and people in the audience laughed. I don't know if they were laughing at somebody bidding a thousand dollars on a roll of gimp or the devil laugh Wade did after his line.

"The real price of the roll of gimp is..." Car trailed off and waited until everybody was in a lot of suspense. "Five dollars! Jesus wins the roll of gimp."

Carin handed Mason the gimp, and Mason jumped up and down and waved his prize in the air, which I thought was a bit unrealistic because there's no way Jesus would be that excited about some gimp when He had things like healing people and fighting Satan on his mind.

I wondered what Jesus would do with a roll of gimp. Could He make gimp bracelets for every camper in camp with just one roll? Or maybe He would turn brown gimp into sparkling purple gimp.

"The next item you need to guess the price of is something crucial to a week of camp," Steve said.

"A camera?" Dean Jamie asked from the crowd. Good thing he seemed interested in participating in our skit. Maybe this meant he wouldn't be mad when we got to the part about his underwear.

"No," Steve said. "But close. A counselor."

T-Camp stood up again and pointed at Noelle. "Pick her! Pick Noelle!"

"Shut up," Noelle snapped.

I know it's mean, but my next thought was that I would bid negative money on Noelle. I was so glad Kate was my counselor instead of Noelle.

"We don't want any old counselor," Steve said. "We want an extra-special counselor."

Noelle opened her mouth and let out an insulted-sounding noise, but that had been Steve's line even before T-Camp had added to the skit.

"We want my best friend and the most talented potato chip war combatant in this entire camp. Daneford Robert Cunningham, please come to the stage."

Dane jogged on down, turned around, and saluted the audience with a two-handed fist-raising gesture above his head. Smiling, he held his arms out on each side and motioned by flicking his fingers a couple of times.

"Don't I get modeled by Koski's Cuties?"

Kate put on a model smile and went right over to him, spreading her arms out. The Koski's Cutie reference made me want to run out of the chapel. Why did he have to bring it up again? I'm pretty sure everyone had forgotten by now what with Wade's devil laugh, but not anymore. Now it would probably become the joke of skit night. That was way worse than dropping a roll of gimp or forgetting your lines.

Dane waved his arm at me. "C'mon, Squirt, I want both Koski's Cuties." Then he made a goofy face at me, the same face he had made last year when our skit was bombing. I laughed. It was pretty funny when you thought about it.

I walked over to him and waved my arms like Kate was doing.

"Contestants," Steve said, "what is the value of a camp counselor?"

Dane smiled at the audience and flexed his arms in a body builder pose, hamming it up even more than Steve.

"Five million dollars!" Carin screamed.

"You're the host," Steve whispered. "Not a contestant."

"Oh, yeah," Car said. She brushed her bangs out of her eyes and held up her microphone again. "Jesus, you get to guess first again."

"For a human life, I bid infinity."

"Yeah, baby, infinity!" Dane said. He looked at the rest of the contestants and punched his arm towards them. "Beat that."

"Paul says to guess one million dollars," Chad said after another look at his piece of paper. Next year if I have to have a speaking role, I will try to be Timothy because then I could write all my lines on my pretend letters from Paul.

Dane considered Chad's bid of a million dollars with a thoughtful look and nod of his head. "Not bad. Not bad."

"Judas," Car said. She almost hit Teresa in the face with the microphone again, this time because she was watching Dane strike another pose.

Dean Jamie, at this point, was almost falling out of his pew he was laughing so hard. I don't think he had gotten much sleep this week and was getting a little slap-happy. Dean Ron didn't look nearly as amused, so we definitely chose the right dean for the underwear joke.

"What do you think this very awesome counselor is worth?" Car asked Teresa/Judas.

"Thirty pieces of silver."

Dane stopped posing and made a face at Teresa. "Hey now. What kind of bid is that?"

Most of the rest of the audience was laughing by now. Teresa didn't know what to say because we hadn't practiced what would happen if one of the items started talking to the contestants, so she just giggled and shrugged.

Carin put the microphone in front of Wade and said, "Your guess, devil?"

Wade looked at Dane for a long time and finally said, "One dollar, Carin," which set everyone, including Steve, Kate, us campers, the deans, and the audience laughing. Dean Jamie was laughing loudest of all. I wondered if he would still be laughing when we got to his underwear.

"One dollar?" Dane yelled, losing the smug grin. "But you just bet a thousand dollars on a crummy roll of gimp!" Wade grinned and showed no sign of changing his guess. "Brown gimp! You've got to be kidding me."

"I guessed infinity," Mason reminded him, but I don't think he heard because he was still talking about brown gimp.

"The actual price of Dane is infinity," Carin said, "or five million dollars. Whichever is more." That was another line we hadn't practiced, and everybody laughed at it.

Dane went over to Mason and pulled the roll of gimp out of his hand. "What's so special about this?" he asked. Wade just laughed his devil laugh.

"I think we'd better move on to the next item," Steve said, and Dane walked down the aisle back to his group, taking the offensive roll of gimp with him.

The next item was an entire grasshead family. I held up Pierre and Laurette, and Kate managed to find a way to display Marquette, Coritza, and Jean-Luc with just two hands. There wasn't much model waving we could do with our hands full, so we just smiled at the audience. I actually started looking at people like Dean Jamie and Julie and Vanessa to see their reactions.

Teresa ended up winning the grassheads. Apparently, a grasshead family was worth thirty pieces of silver. Nothing too funny happened with that item except when Wade guessed eighteen dollars, and Dane, from the audience, protested, "You can't make a bunch of stupid grassheads worth eighteen dollars and only one dollar for a person! Grassheads are creepy!"

We didn't get any more laughs until Steve held up a pair of underwear and announced that the next item the contestants had to price was Dean Jamie's briefs. We had to wait a long time until the audience stopped laughing because they were so loud nobody would have been able to hear what we were saying.

Steve held the underwear towards us models. This was another thing we hadn't practiced, and neither one of us wanted to hold somebody else's underwear, so we made Steve hold them, and Kate and I just waved our arms around and smiled like we had with Dane.

Timothy/Chad won the underwear for fifty dollars. It was worth that much because it was the dean's underwear, not just any old pair of underwear. Dean Jamie kept protesting that he had never seen the pair of underwear in his life, but nobody believed him. I don't really know if it was Dean Jamie's (like if Steve and Kate had snuck into his cabin and gotten a real pair of his underwear) or if Steve had used his own.

It was funny no matter what, especially when the laughter had finally died down and Dane said, "Even underwear beat me."

Then everybody laughed again, except Steve, who looked irritated and said, "Dude, no, you weren't paying attention. You were infinity."

"Or five million dollars," Carin added.

"Are you guys done?" Dean Jamie asked between chuckles.

"Yep," Kate said. "Let's sit back down, guys."

Everybody clapped really loud for us. T-Camp, Sam, and Hunter stomped their feet on the ground and whistled. On our way back to our pew, Steve dropped the underwear on Dean Jamie like he was giving it back to him, so maybe it really was his.

We watched the last skit. It wasn't as funny as ours, but it wasn't supposed to be because it was a song with motions. Usually, songs with motions are dumb unless it's Bunny Foo Foo, but this one was all right. I guess there was one funny thing about it: a kid in the back row who didn't know any of the motions kept doing the wrong ones.

Dean Jamie announced that skit night was officially over, and we went to the fire pit for our snack and devotion. I ended up walking out with Dane.

"You aren't really mad about Wade guessing a dollar, are you?" I asked just to make sure.

"Nah. It was funny."

"If I was guessing, I would have said the infinity thing."

He smiled at me, but it was a small smile and he shook his head. "You shouldn't. You're the only thing around here worth infinity, Squirt."

CHAPTER TWENTY-FOUR

Homesick

I missed Angela. The funny thing about getting mail from home is that it's supposed to make you feel better about being far away at camp, only I hadn't thought about my parents or sister much at all until I got the letter. Then that was all I could think about, except during our skit when I thought about everybody looking at me.

I don't know why I felt homesick. I was having a blast at camp. I didn't really want to go home. I guess I wanted to be at camp, but I wanted Angela to be here, too. I'm glad she's not going to college this year like Dane. I still have a year left with her at home. She's started applying to colleges though, and some of them are far away like Madison and Platteville.

I've never been an only child before. I think it must be boring and lonely, just you and your mom and dad. What do you talk about at dinner? Your parents' jobs the whole time? The exciting things going on in fifth grade? Angela always has the best things to report about at dinner, things like homecoming floats and stories about kids at school having to go to the office because of the dress code and funny things that happened in the hallway between classes. If it weren't for Angela, we'd all sit there and stare at each other while we ate.

Last year, we had an assignment to write two hundred words about a person we wanted to be like when we grew up. Everybody else picked football stars or actresses. I wrote about my sister. I felt kind of dumb when we had to read them out loud to the class and I realized mine was the only not famous person, but Carin pointed out that I was lucky because the person I wanted to be like when I grew up lived in my house, and I could learn how to be like her every day.

I don't want Angela to go to college, unless she goes to UW-Millers Creek and lives at home.

I lay on my bunk and tried to find the energy to go down to the bathroom with everybody else and get ready for bed, but I felt silly because all that thinking about Angela going to college and the nice letter she had sent me made tears form in my eyes. I tried to hold them in so nobody would notice.

"Are you girls ready to go?" Kate asked from her bunk area.

I wiped at my eyes with the back of my hand. My stomach had a pain in it, the same pain it got the summer Angela and I spent a week with Aunt Teri and then we had to go home and not see her again for five months. I remember having the same ache in my tummy when we waved goodbye to her.

Why do I always have to be like this? So much for my big plans to be tough and cool this summer. I guess I'm just a wimp and can't change that.

"Abby, what's wrong?" Kate asked. She sat down on her bed, crossing her legs as she sat.

"I don't feel good again," I said. It didn't feel like when I had to throw up yesterday at the sleep-out, but I couldn't put into words how it did feel.

"Want me to be your buddy to go to the nurse?" Carin asked. I looked at her, standing by the heater, slipping a pair of pink pajama pants on. You'd never know it by the way she stood tall, tapping her fingers on the heater, but I knew that was a tough offer to make. She was just as scared of The Scary Nurse as I was.

"Not really," I said, and I think I heard a relieved exhale that didn't come from the heater. "It's not that kind of sick. I miss my sister."

The tears got so big that they popped out of my eyes and ran down my cheeks. Kate shifted on her bunk. I couldn't look at her. She must have thought I was the biggest baby in our cabin. All of Brenda's campers had gone to the bathroom already to brush their teeth and take showers and all that, and Kate was stuck in the cabin with a crybaby. She was probably supposed to meet Dane for something again, and here I was slowing down the whole get-ready-for-bed process.

"Um, well, that's a bummer," she said.

She didn't even know what to say to someone who was homesick on Thursday. That's because nobody except the mini-campers, who only go to camp for three days, get homesick...and sometimes first year elementary campers. The more I thought about it, the more things I missed about home: Mom's grilled cheese sandwiches, Dad kissing me good night on the forehead and turning my light out every night, Angela coming home from a date Friday night and waking me up to sit on my bed, our pinkie fingers intertwined as she told me all the juicy details.

I think that's the thing I love most about Angela. She could have woken Mom up to tell her all about her dates or called a friend on her private phone in her room, but it was me she told everything to first, her little sister, someone she could have written off as a dumb little kid and not told anything to, first or last.

I only had one more year with her. This time next year, she would be getting ready to move out. None of my Friday night sleep would be interrupted by stories of holding hands with boys at the movies or winning touchdown passes in overtime. She would be gone, gone away to college with a roommate who she'd tell everything to instead of me.

"Um, well…are you sure you don't want to go to the nurse?" Kate asked.

Just the thought of The Scary Nurse made me actually want to go home. I needed to make sure Angela was still there, that she hadn't gone to college early or disappeared. I knew it was crazy, but home seemed more than a few hours away. I always feel like that at camp, like home is another world, a distant dimension like in science fiction movies, and I was off on my own exploring somewhere separate from the rest of the world. That's never been scary before because my family was with me. It's hard to get homesick at junior high camp sharing a bedroom with my sister, my parents on the other side of a wall so thin that I could hear my dad snoring.

I felt the bed sag on the side as Kate moved from her bed to mine. She put her hand on my forehead and brushed my hair back. I think she was checking to see if I had a fever. I don't think I did though because her hand felt warm on my head and not cool like Steve's had yesterday.

Is this how Steve felt all the time? I missed Angela, but deep down I knew I'd see her in a couple of days. But what happened when your sister or brother died? Did that pain in your stomach ever go away?

"Ab, I don't know what to say," Kate said, smoothing my hair some more. It made me feel sleepy and like I could close my eyes right now and wake up to the bell in the morning. "It's Thursday night though." She had a nice, soft voice, even and soothing, like somebody's mom would have after a bad dream. I wondered if Kate had any little sisters who would miss her when she went to college. "Only one more full day of camp, and then it'll be Saturday and your parents will come and pick you up." The steadiness of her voice cracked, and I moved my eyes to see the tears in hers. "And then you'll get to see your sister."

She pulled her hand away from my hair and stood up, leaning against her own bed.

I wiped my face again and sat up, feeling not as dumb now that a counselor was crying, too. Maybe she was homesick. It wouldn't be so bad to be homesick if your counselor was also.

"Why are *you* crying?"

Kate smiled at me a little. I don't know why but the way she looked at me reminded me of Dane last year standing over me while we compared bee stings on a nature hike that got a tad painful.

"I'm sad because you're sad," she told me.

"You are?"

"Yeah." She held her hand out for me to take, and I started to scoot off the bed. "I don't want any of my campers to be sad."

It didn't seem like she cared about getting us to go to bed quickly, which I thought was very nice of her because she could have just said, "Go to bed now so I can leave the cabin and hang out with my friends." But it was like we were more important than Dane and Steve and Julie. It's nice to have a counselor who takes care of you. Poor Rachel had Noelle who I don't think would care if one of her campers was homesick. She also had Julie though, and I think Julie would help a homesick camper.

I hugged Kate and told her I felt better, so we walked to the bathroom with Car and Teresa. Teresa even told me that she was homesick on the first night of camp but hadn't said anything about it. We had to go to the boys' side of the bathroom since we were practically the last people to get ready, but that was okay because Car and I got to show Teresa all about urinals. I think that's something every girl learns about her first week of camp.

After devotions and lights out, when we were supposed to take turns telling everyone what we were thankful for, I said I was thankful for my counselors. Carin, of course, had to be goofy and rattle off a list of about half a dozen things including Pierre the Grasshead, the color hot pink, and cute boys. Lindsay said camp friends, and that made me really happy that I was at camp and not at home.

I didn't feel homesick anymore. At least homesickness only lasts a little while. Camp sickness sits on you month after month, especially when you flip television channels and see one of those nature shows with trees and little paths. When you're homesick, your counselor can say something like, "Well, it's Thursday, so that means you're going home in just two days."

When you're camp sick, all your mom can do is shrug and say, "Well, it's February, so that means you're going to camp in five or six months."

I lay there smiling into the darkness, thinking about those things, when the door squeaked open and shut again.

Carin leaned down, shaking our bunk. I'm glad I don't get motion sickness, otherwise I wouldn't be able to share with her. "What do you think the counselors do at night?" she whispered.

"I think they play cards and eat potato chips," I said. My parents always hang out at the dining hall after lights out with the counselors at junior high camp, and that's what they do.

"No way," Car said. "It has to be something better than that. I think they have parties and go swimming at midnight and go to, what's that town named? Marquette? I think they go there and eat fast food and go to the mall."

"At eleven o'clock?" I asked.

"Well, maybe not." She paused for a minute, keeping still. Then she leaned down even farther, so far that I thought she was going to slither off the bunk and land in a heap on the wooden floor. "I bet when we're asleep, the counselors have camp romances."

CHAPTER TWENTY-FIVE

Friday Blues

We had a tragedy during our last arts and crafts hour, but it was a funny one. Steve wrote a pretend police report all about it, which pretty much summed up what happened:

Date: Friday morning of elementary camp
Crime scene: The craft cabin
Reporting officer: Lt. Steven J. Koski
Victims: Pierre, Laurette, Marquette, Coritza, and Jean-Luc Grasshead
Perpetrator: Cunningham, Daneford, criminal number 49861
Witnesses: Katherine Alexis Chandler, Julianne Hayes, Abby Leah Riley, Carin Alexandra Morgan, Chad Darrin Bayard, Cammie L. Hill—craft director
Recorded Events:
Abby, Carin, and Chad discovered the victims' house empty and became alarmed. Upon further investigation, a note was found which included a map to the victims' whereabouts. The witnesses followed the map to the restricted upstairs area. The first brave camper to arrive on the scene was Abby, who reported the sight of grass and dirt everywhere and the perpetrator (Cunningham) attempting to jump out the window. The perpetrator was apprehended without the need of force, and the victims were attended to. By the time the investigating officer (me—Lt. Koski) arrived on the scene, four of the victims were pronounced destroyed. CPR and emergency medicine were attempted on Pierre, but both were unsuccessful, despite the use of super glue. The final victim was pronounced destroyed when part of his head fell off the balcony, narrowly missing an onlooker, Noelle Donnely, who screamed and called all involved "idiots." Craft Director Cammie L. Hill, in an attempt to secure the perimeter, made everybody go downstairs and continue with their craft projects.

As this was a hate crime against grassheads, cubbyholes were investigated to check on the well-being of other grassheads, but all were accounted for. The jury of the perpetrator's peers (K. Chandler, J. Hayes, and Officer S. Koski) determined his sentence, which he complied to, and part of which is attached to this document. Besides the attached letter of apology and the promise to buy everybody's canteen today, a restraining order has been placed on the perpetrator. He may not physically place himself within five feet of any other grasshead or he will be sentenced to life without parole in the deans' cabin. Detailed graffiti was put on one wall explaining the situation so that future grassheads will know to keep their distance from the perpetrator.

The situation is under control. Respectfully submitted, SJK.

Steve used a lot of words I didn't know in his report because he was trying to make it sound like a real police report, but I could still understand it because I knew what had happened. Carin and I fought over who got to keep Steve's report and Dane's apology letter until Kate said she would take both of them with her and photocopy them in the office at lunch. We pretended that we were devastated that Dane had crumbled up Pierre's dirt head, but really it was sort of funny.

***

Nobody was tired during rest hour. You would think that by the end of the week, everybody would want to rest, but it seemed like we got more and more hyper as the week went on. We did not want to waste any of our precious time left at camp by sleeping. We could sleep all day when we got home tomorrow. Now was the time to write each other secret notes and deliver them by folding up the pieces of paper, attaching them to long strings of gimp, and flinging them across the cabin to the people they were for.

We had made up this method of note delivery during rest hour last year. Our counselors, Eva and Allie, had gotten a little annoyed at the amount of noise we made doing this, but I didn't think Kate and Brenda would mind.

I wrote a note to Carin first.

Dear Car,

I can't believe that tomorrow we have to go back to Millers Creek. I told my parents not to come right away to pick us up. I don't want to be the first person to have to leave. Did you have fun this year? I did. And I have a big secret to tell you, but not until we are in the car where nobody else can hear us. You will like it. It's about a boy.

Love,
Abby

Then I wrote to Lindsay.

Dear Lindsay,

I just realized that we have known each other for a whole year already! Isn't that weird? And even though we've only seen each other for two weeks out of that year, you are one of my very best friends. Isn't camp great? The only bad thing about this week was that you didn't get to be in our day group. I have a plan for next year already though. There's a spot on the camp registration form where you can write a person's name to be in your group. Well, we can write each other's names, like I would write Carin, Carin would write you, and you would write me. Then we would get to be together all the time instead of just during rest hour and cabin clean-up. What do you think of that plan?

I'm glad we got to at least be in the same cabin. I have to go now so I can write more letters.

Your best camp friend,
Abby

It was fairly easy to send my first two pieces of gimp mail because Carin was on the bunk on top of mine, and Lindsay was directly across the aisle on the bottom bunk. I knew that my third note, to Teresa, was going to be a more difficult delivery. She was the next bunk over on the top.

It was harder to come up with a letter for Teresa than it was for Carin and Lindsay. With Car and Linds, I just picked up my pen and wrote the first thing that I thought of. For Teresa's I had to think about it and chew on the cap of the pen for a minute.

A piece of gimp mail flew between the bars of my bunk and landed by my feet. It had come from Lindsay's direction, so I knew she had sent it. I wanted to open it right away, but I made myself finish Teresa's letter first. If I read Lindsay's, I would want to write back right away, and I might never send Teresa's. I didn't want her to feel left out.

Dear Teresa,

I hope you had fun at camp. It's always hard when it's your first year. It was a lot of fun to win that game at the water Olympics, wasn't it? And just wait for the big banquet tonight! You will love the chocolate cake. Maybe we can write to each other when we have to go home. Lindsay and I wrote a lot last year. Well, then Christmas came and we didn't write so much, but we still did sometimes. Anyway, I hope you had a good week.

Your new friend,
Abby

As soon as I had tossed Teresa's letter up onto her bunk, I pulled the gimp off of the one Lindsay sent me and unfolded it.

Dear Abby,

That sounds like a great plan you have for geting us in the same cabin and group. I missed you guys. Jenny and Autum are nice but you are my best camp friend. Does your family ever visit Marquette? I thought you said once your dad was from there. Well I live about twenty miles away. So if you ever go to Marquette you have to visit me okay? Can you hardly wait for choclate cake tonight?

Love, Lindsay

***

Rest hour always goes by faster when gimp mail is involved than it does when you have to sleep or read a book. It seemed like we had only been in the cabin for ten minutes, and I still had lots more notes I wanted to send, when the bell rang.

Nobody was happy to hear the bell. Usually, it's a good sound because it means it's time for canteen. But today it was sad because it meant we only had one afternoon, one evening, and one morning left to be at camp. The last day of camp is always fun but sad at the same time because you know you have to leave soon.

Kate and Brenda tried to get us to forget that it was the last day of camp and have fun, but it didn't work. Nobody ran to canteen. We all stuck together and shuffled down the path, as if moving slowly would make the day go slower.

I sat at our picnic table near the canteen with Carin, Lindsay, Teresa, and Rachel. We had all gotten taffy candy, the kind with jokes written on the outside of every wrapper and the punch lines on the inside.

"What did one monkey say to the other monkey?" Carin asked, as she peeled the wrapper off of a square, yellow candy. "I'm bananas for you." We laughed as she put the candy into her mouth. "Hey, it's banana flavored."

"Yuck," I said. "If I get a banana one, you can have it, Car."

Rachel said something I couldn't understand because her mouth was full of taffy.

"What?" Lindsay asked, giggling. Rachel's garbled question was funnier than the actual jokes.

Rach chewed some more and then swallowed. "Where does a monster sit at the movie theater? Anywhere he wants."

We all laughed like it was the funniest thing we had heard. Lindsay ended her laugh with a sigh and said, "That really wasn't a very funny joke."

"I know," I agreed. "But it's funny at camp."

"I don't think these jokes would be so funny at home," Car said, looking at the printing on another piece of candy. "Why are fish so smart? Because they travel in schools."

That joke was more corny than funny, but as soon as I heard Rachel snickering, I laughed, too.

"I think there are a lot of things at camp that aren't as good at home," Lindsay said.

"Like s'mores," Teresa said. "Every year we have a bonfire at our youth group leader's farm, and we have s'mores. I always thought s'mores were just okay until I came to camp." She smiled. "But camp s'mores are awesome."

"And nature," I said. "Our house has a big backyard with lots of flowers and nice trees, but they seem ordinary compared to everything we have at camp."

I wanted to add that underwear was much funnier at camp than it was at home, but I didn't want to bring it up again. My camp friends were going to start to think I was obsessed with underwear if I talked about it too much.

"My brother's a lot better at camp than he is at home," Rachel said. "At home he yells at me a lot and we fight about everything. Even dumb things like who gets the last ice cream sandwich and which door he drops me off at when he drives me to school. But at camp, he's still annoying—"

Car interrupted with, "And cute."

Rachel rolled her eyes but kept talking like Carin hadn't said anything. "But we get along better here than we do anywhere else. It's like he's different. He doesn't worry about stuff here."

"Dane?" I asked. "He never worries about anything."

"We could stand on the dining hall roof and jump up and down, and he wouldn't get worried," Lindsay said.

"At home he gets mad about stuff all the time."

"I'm not as shy at camp as I am at home," I said. "I think camp makes you feel different."

"I felt a lot older this week," Teresa said. "It's neat to know that you have to remember to brush your teeth by yourself. Nobody's going to remind you if you forget. I like being responsible."

The bell rang and Carin, Teresa, and I had to leave Rachel and Lindsay and go rock hopping.

CHAPTER TWENTY-SIX

A Banquet, a Communion, and a Funeral

The banquet was a big bummer. I mean, we had yummy food like roast beef and mashed potatoes with gravy, but there weren't any awards. The awards are the best part of the banquet. At junior high camp all the campers who are graduating to high school camp get awards. Last year at elementary camp everybody got an award. But this year—nobody. The graduating kids got their names announced, but they didn't get any pieces of paper or anything.

Plus I didn't get to sit by Lindsay. I sat by her last year at the banquet, and we bonded. Then again, Carin sat by me this year because she couldn't sit by Dane. I wished we could all sit together like at junior high camp where you can sit anywhere you want at the meals no matter who is in your group.

"They didn't have chocolate cake last year," Car said when the counselors brought out dessert.

"Yes, they did," I said.

Car took a big bite of cake and said, with her mouth still partly full, "I would have remembered this cake."

"They had it. Remember, Eva put the leftovers in plastic bags, and we got to eat cake back at the cabin."

"Are you sure? I don't remember that."

She had probably been too busy looking at cute boys and cute counselors to pay attention to unimportant things like the best chocolate cake in the world. I might be starting to like boys and think that a counselor or two is cute, but I will never be so boy-crazy that it interferes with good camp dessert. No way.

"Ask Lindsay," I insisted. "Eva didn't even make us brush our teeth again after we had the cake."

"You didn't brush your teeth after you ate chocolate?" She looked horrified. "You're going to get cavities." Dr. Morgan had trained her well.

"I haven't yet. I've gone to your dad twice since then, and no cavities."

Carin went back to her chocolate cake, and I tackled my huge piece. I had been smarter about how much food I ate for my main meal this year, so I had enough room for cake and ice cream.

I don't know if it was because camp was almost over and everybody was dreading saying goodbye in the morning or if we were all tired from rock hopping that afternoon, but everyone in our group ate almost in silence except for what Carin and I said about the cake and another time when Mason asked if the lumps in the mashed potatoes could be flies, and Steve said, "No."

"Aw, shucks," Mason muttered before taking a big bite.

It wasn't hard for T-Camp to get my attention from the table behind us. "Chocolate cake. Me want chocolate cake. Yum. Yum."

I turned around to see what he was doing. He had a plate of chocolate cake in front of him. Well, he had a plate with a few crumbs and a brown frosting smear on it. Each hand squished a piece of cake, and he had so much cake on his face that if I didn't know better, I would think the enormous mixer in the camp kitchen had exploded all the batter onto his face.

I probably wouldn't have noticed what Hunter said next, but since I was turned around looking at T-Camp, and Hunter was sitting next to him, I saw him push his piece of cake across the table to Dane.

"I saw a mosquito land on it," Hunter said.

"That's okay," Dane said. "It's camp. I bet mosquitoes land on lots of the food."

"But mosquitoes carry diseases," Hunter said. "I'm not eating that."

"I'll eat it!" T-Camp yelled, leaning forward from his spot at the end of the table and grabbing the cake off Hunter's plate.

"But a mosquito landed on it."

T shrugged and shoved a bunch of it into his mouth. "So what?"

"It might have pooped on it," Hunter said.

"Gross!" Noelle shouted, glaring at him. "You are a gross little kid!"

Hunter looked down at his plate and slid part of the way under the table. I could tell Noelle had made him feel bad.

"Knock it off, Noelle," Dane said. "I wouldn't want to eat something that had mosquito poop on it either."

"Who's eating mosquito poop?" Mason asked from our table, sitting up straight in his chair and looking at the other group's table.

I turned back to finish my own piece of cake. The people at my table were now having a normal conversation about skit night and which skits they had liked the best yesterday. How did Carin and I get a normal group while Rachel ended up with such an odd one? I wondered what Lindsay's group was like. Autumn and Jennie from our cabin seemed pretty normal, but you can never tell with boys. Really the only weird thing about our group was how Mason ate strange things, but that was more funny than weird and not even close to T-Camp and all the weird things he had done that week.

***

I sat in my pew, soaking in the serious mood of chapel.

Communion reminded me of Scott's funeral for some reason. I think it was because of the serious mood. I listened to Dean Ron talk about Jesus dying on the cross. I had heard it a million times before, and I had Jesus in my heart, but heaven never meant as much to me as it did that night.

"If you ask Jesus to be Lord of your life," Dean Ron said, "not only will He be with you guiding your choices and helping you on earth, but when you die, you will go to be with Him in heaven. That's why it's so important that you share what you learn here about Christ with your family and friends back home, even though it might be hard. Jesus is the way to heaven. The only way."

I had always thought of heaven as Jesus' home. Now I knew that it was Scott's home, too, and no matter how many years I had to wait, I would get to see him again someday, just because both of us had said and believed at one point in our lives, "Jesus, I believe in You and want You to be in my heart."

I don't know why people don't do it. I mean, if nobody ever told you about Jesus, you wouldn't know what you had to do. But I don't get why some people don't want to go to heaven and have Jesus as a friend they can pray to. Jesus is never too busy to listen to me like Carin is sometimes. He doesn't answer me back with words, but I know He's listening.

I said a different prayer than I usually do after I dunked my piece of bread into the grape juice and ate it. I knelt down at the altar next to Car and looked up into the kind, brown eyes of Jesus in the picture that hung on the wall.

Dear God, I am so glad You made heaven and gave us Jesus so that we can someday be with people we love who die. I don't know what the rules are about You giving people in heaven messages, but if that's allowed, can You please tell Scott that I miss him this summer and that I couldn't make any good craft projects without him and that I hope he is having a good time in heaven playing a harp or whatever else people do up there.

Car got up and went back to our pew a long time before I did. Thinking of Scott made me feel like I was going to cry, but I don't know why because he was in heaven, and you shouldn't feel bad because someone's in heaven. Every time somebody in a movie dies and the other characters talk about how he's in a better place now, they all get happy again. I was glad Scott was in heaven, and it made it feel less awful knowing that I would see him again someday, but someday seemed so very far away that it was hard to be happy about it.

***

Pierre needed a funeral. I think I had funerals on the brain, having just gone to my first one two months ago. We had a little free time at the campfire after we ate our s'mores, so I went over to Steve. He was talking to Ben about a movie. When there was a pause, I reached up and touched Steve's arm.

"What can I do for you, Abby? You want another s'more?"

I shook my head. "We should have a funeral for Pierre."

"A funeral for Pierre?" he repeated, and I couldn't tell if he thought my idea was silly or if I had just surprised him with the request.

"Yes," I reasoned. "Even though he was a grasshead, he was our craft cabin friend, and now he's gone."

"Well, I don't think there's ever been a grasshead funeral in the history of camp, but if you want one, we can do it, as long as it's within the next few minutes because I think Dean Ron is about to send everybody to bed."

"Okay," I said. "Meet us on the craft cabin porch in five minutes."

I went as fast as I could (without running) back to where Carin, Kate, and Teresa sat together on the bench, eating s'mores and laughing about something.

"We're having a funeral for Pierre."

Carin's eyes got as big as I've ever seen them. "That is the best idea. It'll be so much fun!"

I don't think anybody has ever called a funeral fun before besides Car, but I also don't think anybody has ever heard of a funeral for a grasshead.

"It's in five minutes," I told everybody. Then I looked at Carin and Teresa. "C'mon, you guys, we have to go get stuff ready."

"I think I'll just go back with Brenda and them," Teresa said. She had kind of been a party pooper about the whole grasshead thing all along. Teresa and Dane could start an "I hate grassheads" club together.

Kate promised to tell Chad and Julie about the funeral, and Carin and I went to the dark craft cabin. The door squeaked louder than usual in the dark, and it took a while to find the lights. I walked to the cubbyholes, hearing each of our steps thump on the wooden floor.

There was poor, old Pierre, smiling away at us. I touched his button nose and tried to straighten out his tie. He looked the same as he always had, except that part of his head lay in a crumbly clump next to the rest of him.

Carin came over to me with a shoebox in her hand. It said "size ten" on the side of it. "This can be the casket. I found it under the gimp counter."

I put Pierre in the box and started to put the top on, but Car pulled the box top out of my hand.

"No. You're supposed to leave it open for the funeral, and then put the top on when you bury the person."

I reached for the box top. "Uh, uh. It stays closed the whole time."

"No," Car said in that tone she gets when she thinks she's right and everybody else is dumb. "At my grandma's funeral, it was open, and we could see her."

"I don't think you remember right because at Scott's funeral, it was shut the whole time."

I had to tug really hard to get the top out of her hand. When she finally let go, I stepped backwards, and Pierre jiggled in his casket.

"They must have done it wrong then," Car snapped, like my dad and Scott's parents wouldn't know what to do at a funeral. "All the funerals on TV have it open, and you can see the actor pretending to be dead."

"Well, TV is make-believe," I said. "I think my dad should know how to have a funeral because he has to do them all the time."

"Give me the box top, Abby. You can't have a funeral with the box shut."

"You *can* have a funeral with the casket shut because I just went to one like that."

The door to the craft cabin opened, and Steve leaned in. "Ready? We're supposed to go to bed now, so we'd better make this quick."

Carin took advantage of my focus on Steve and grabbed the box and the top and ran out the door. I followed her outside to where Steve, Kate, and Julie stood. We all walked in a line around the big rock to the back of the craft cabin. I don't know why Carin got to carry Pierre. Actually, yes, I did know: because she was bossy, that's why. Sometimes I think she's the bossiest person I know.

"We are here to commemorate the life of Pierre the Grasshead," Steve said when we all stood in a circle around Pierre's open casket. "Pierre was a good grasshead, the best I knew. I'd like to open the floor to comments by all of you."

"I have a comment," Car said. She clasped her hands together and looked mournfully at the grasshead. "The thing I loved most about Pierre was his sense of humor." She made her voice crack like we were at a real funeral. I played along by sniffing like I was crying. Car looked up and smiled at me for a second before she went back to her speech. "That time he rolled into a puddle of glue and got his head all gooey was hilarious."

I patted Car on the back like I was comforting her, and she hugged me. I knew we wouldn't talk about our fight over the box top. We never do. Whenever we disagree, we just finish the argument and never bring it up again. We probably should talk about our fights, but it hasn't hurt our friendship yet. Carin isn't someone you can reason with easily. We'd probably have more fights if we tried to talk about things.

Julie told the story of how Pierre almost hit Noelle when a piece of his head fell off the balcony, and Kate started laughing. That made me laugh, and my snickers made Carin giggle.

"Quiet, people!" Steve scolded us, his dark eyebrows coming together as he made a stern face. "This is a funeral. It's supposed to be serious."

At first I thought maybe we had upset him with the whole funeral thing, but then he cracked a smile and laughed with us.

Kate put an arm around Car and one around me. "Come on, girls. We have to get to bed now."

"Wait!" Car dropped to the ground and started digging with a big stick. "We need to bury him." She dug a little hole, and Steve turned the shoebox over so the two clumps of Pierre fell into the hole. That was not very realistic, but I think he didn't want to wait until Car had dug a hole big enough for a size ten shoebox.

I knelt down and put the dirt back over Pierre, patting it down, and Kate picked up a popsicle stick that somebody evidently hadn't thrown away from crafts or canteen and stuck it on the mound of dirt.

We started back to our cabin up the pebbly path.

"Hey, Kate," I asked, "do real funerals have opened or closed caskets?"

"I think usually they leave them open, at least for the visitation," she said. "A lot of people need to look at the person they've lost for closure."

Carin leaned forward so I could see her pointed look of, "See," around Kate.

"But at Scott 's funeral, they didn't have it open, not even at that visitation thing."

"Oh, hon," Kate said, sounding sad, "sometimes..." But then she stopped like she wasn't going to finish her sentence.

"Sometimes what?" I asked.

We passed the bathroom and the big streetlight behind it, so I could see her swallow and blink her eyes hard.

"When somebody dies, there's a person at the funeral home whose job it is to put make-up on them to make them look like they did when they were living, but sometimes when people have very bad accidents, the make-up person can't fix it. So they leave the casket closed."

"Oh," I said. That thought must have bothered Carin, too, because she didn't even say, "Told you so," about most funerals having open caskets.

We got to our cabin, but Kate didn't open the door. She looked at me, her big, pretty, green eyes becoming shiny under the yellow porch light and the spider web woven around it.

"What's serenity mean?" I asked.

"Serenity? It's like something that's calm or peaceful. Why?"

"I just wondered is all," I said.

Carin pushed the door handle down and opened the door. Everybody else must've gone to the bathroom already because the cabin was empty. I wanted to be alone and look at my card again, so I putzed around as Kate and Carin grabbed their bathroom kits.

"You guys go ahead," I said.

"I'm not going to leave you alone," Kate said.

"I'll be down in just a minute," I promised. "Please?"

She looked at me for a long time but finally gave in. "Okay." I think she understood I had something important to do.

Car and Kate left, and I opened my Bible and read the whole phrase off the card again. "God grant me the serenity to accept the things I cannot change, courage to change the things I can, and wisdom to know the difference." Now that I knew what serenity meant, it made a lot more sense.

I heard a bunch of giggling, and the door opened. Brenda, her campers, and Teresa were back from the bathroom. I knew I had to hurry up now, so I put the card back, shut my Bible, and grabbed my bathroom bag and one of my flashlights. I don't usually bring a flashlight to the bathroom because it's not very far and the path is pretty well lit, but I'd never gone to the bathroom along the path by myself that late at night before.

I passed Carin and Kate walking back on my way down. "Be quick, okay?" Kate requested.

"Yep," I promised.

"We were almost the last ones," Car said.

I picked up my pace a little, focusing on the cement wall of the back of the bathroom that I could barely make out in the dark.

CHAPTER TWENTY-SEVEN

The Shared Gift

I walked into the bathroom and found out that the only people I got to share it with were Alana and Imogen. I suppose I should have expected it; who else would take that long getting ready for bed? The shower was running, so there must've been somebody else in the bathroom, but those two were the only ones in the main section with the stalls and sinks. They stood gazing into the mirror above the sinks, Imogen drying her brown curls with a towel and Alana poking some kind of dental floss on a stick into her mouth.

"Remember that counselor who was here last year who gave you a talk about not wasting glue?" Alana asked.

"Oh, yeah," Imogen said with a laugh that sounded like a snort.

I thought about going around to the boys' side, but that would look dumb since I had already walked three feet into the girls' side of the bathroom, and there weren't any lines or anything, so there was no reason to go to the other side except to avoid Alana and Imogen. They'd love that—bullying someone into the yucky boys' bathroom.

"I'm glad he's not back this year," Imogen said, pausing her hair drying to make a face that reflected back at me in the mirror. "I threw away a tiny scrap of paper yesterday. I wouldn't want to get yelled at about it."

Alana giggled. "Oh, my God. What was his problem anyway?"

I hate when people say, "Oh, my God." It's an awful expression. People say it at school all the time, and nobody seems to care. It should get you a trip to the principal's office, just like swearing does. I think that phrase is worse than swearing because it's mean to God.

They hadn't acted like they even noticed I had walked into the bathroom, which was fine by me. I went into a stall as far away from them as I could get, the one near the shower section of the bathroom. I was getting to know that stall quite well this week. The toilet was partly plugged, but only by toilet paper. I sat down and went as fast as I could. I didn't like the thought of being alone in the bathroom with just those two.

"I know," Imogen said. Even using the last stall couldn't get me away from her loud voice, made even louder than usual by the echo of the almost-empty bathroom. "Remember when Dean Ron said we needed to clean up the canteen area or we wouldn't get any more canteen for the week, that same counselor stood up and gave us a big, long lecture about saving the environment?"

Why did I care what they thought about me when they even made fun of the counselors? I tried to ignore them and focus on the etching of the word, "Lock," on the stall door and the arrow that pointed to the real lock. What original graffiti.

"That was him, too," Alana said. "Mr. Goody-Two-Shoes Counselor Man."

"What was his name again?"

"I dunno," Alana said, her words muffled, probably by that flossing thing. She must have taken it out of her mouth then because her next sentence came out loud and clear and made me almost fall right off that toilet seat. "I just always called him Steve's brother."

Scott? Scott was Mr. Goody-Two-Shoes Counselor Man?

I sat there and listened to them even though I didn't have to go any more.

"I'm glad that guy's not here this year," Imogen said. "I can't believe he made us pour the glue from our cups back into the bottles."

"There are a billion glue bottles in the craft cabin. I don't think anybody would have missed that little bit," Alana agreed.

"What was his name?" Imogen asked again.

"Why do you care?"

"I was just wondering. I wonder where he is this year."

"Maybe saving the planet or the African rain forests," Alana said. The only thing that didn't make her giggle as annoying as Imogen's was that she didn't snort when she inhaled.

I wished I could tell her that. I wished I was the kind of person who could walk right up to the two of them and tell them they sounded like a bunch of hyenas and that they were nasty girls who didn't deserve to have fun at church camp. I should have said something when they made fun of the grassheads, but I didn't. I should have said something when they were saying mean things about Kate at lunch the other day, but I didn't.

The coolest thing would be if Dane would walk in right then and hear what they were saying. He'd knock their blocks off if he had any idea they were saying such mean things about Scott. "Knock their block off" is what my dad says whenever he watches football and someone tackles someone really hard. That would be great, but it would never happen though because Dane is not allowed in the girls' bathroom.

"I bet Mr. Goody-Two-Shoes Counselor Man isn't back this year because the deans were annoyed by his, 'Don't waste that,' lectures, too," Imogen said.

I stood up to leave, but my knees felt like I had climbed Mount Spirit twice, and I stumbled into the door and the "Lock," graffiti.

"I'm glad we don't have perfect little nerdy counselors," Alana said. "Noelle is cool."

I pushed the stall door open and walked into the main area of the bathroom with Alana and Imogen. I saw them right in front of me, but I felt like they were on a movie screen and not really in the same room as I was. They both stopped talking and looked at me in the mirror. Instead of running out of the bathroom, I stood there and stared back, partly because I was furious that they had bashed Scott and partly because I didn't know how well my Mount Spirit legs were working yet.

"Scott," I said.

"Scott what?" Alana asked.

"That was Steve's brother's name," I said in a voice loud enough to bounce off the tiled walls and echo out the open window. The volume was more like Carin's and the strength like Rachel's, but the sound was my voice, somehow. "He was a good counselor, probably the best ever, and if he said you shouldn't waste glue, then you shouldn't waste glue."

I don't know who was more surprised, those bully girls who had just been told something by a shy, quiet kid who I'm sure they thought of as a nobody, or that shy, quiet kid (AKA me) whose flashlight shook right out of her hand and cracked open on the bathroom floor, sending one of the batteries rolling towards the muddy drain. (And that, by the way, is why you should always bring two flashlights to camp.)

Alana recovered first and tossed her hair over her shoulder. Carin does that, too, but when Car shakes her hair, it's cute. When Alana did it, it just looked snotty.

"Are you his mom or something?"

"No," I said. "He was my friend. And the only reason he told everybody about the candy wrappers in the canteen is because it's bad for the environment and some campers are too lazy to pick up after themselves."

"Hey, Alana," Imogen said, smirking. She pointed at me. "She's a goody-goody, too. Like Mr. Goody-Two-Shoes Counselor Man, only she's a camper instead of a counselor."

The shower stopped. I had never heard the bathroom so silent before. Then came the scraping of a chair and rustling of somebody putting on clothes in the shower area.

Alana turned around so I looked into her actual face instead of her mirrored image. "You're just like Steve's brother. A big goody-goody loser who does exactly what the counselors say."

I smiled as wide as I could. I thought about Eva's sparkling white grin from last year for inspiration.

"Thanks."

"No," Alana said in a tone of voice as if she thought I were really stupid, "it's not a *good* thing when somebody calls you a goody-goody."

I shrugged and stepped towards the door with legs that felt like they had only run up Mount Spirit once now instead of twice.

"Maybe, but you also said I was just like Scott, and that's the nicest thing I can think of."

"You girls ready to go back to the cabin?" It had been Julie in the shower, and she now came out in pajamas and flip-flops. "Oh, hey, Abby."

Her hello barely registered because I was too busy smiling my Eva smile at Julie's campers. I had one last thing to say to Alana and Imogen. "I'm proud that somebody thinks I'm like Scott Koski. And guess what? You guys are like your counselor Noelle." I pushed the heavy door that actually didn't seem so heavy at that moment and walked back to my cabin, leaving the broken flashlight in the middle of the bathroom floor.

On the way back to the cabin, away from those girls and the infuriating feelings they gave me, I thought about Scott and me. My gut reaction to Alana's statement that I was just like Scott was that she was wrong. She had meant it in a bad way because she thought we were both "goody-goodies," but as glad as I was to be compared to him, I knew it wasn't true. Scott was everybody's friend, outgoing, artistic, things that I will never be even when I'm twenty like he was.

But what was the one thing I loved about him the most? That he was popular? That he had started up a conversation with me without even knowing me? That he had made a brilliant rainbow on the craft cabin windows?

No. What had drawn me to Scott and made him one of my favorite counselors and even a hero was how he had been so nice to me. He had realized that I was upset and had put his own beautiful craft project aside to help me with my messed up one. He had included me in his window painting to make me feel better and become my friend because he cared about me and felt badly that I was having a crummy week.

The gift of compassion. Scott had that, the same thing my dad always said about me. God had given Scott and me one of the same gifts. It didn't mean I was a baby or a wimp. It didn't mean that thinking about bad things that happened to other people made me weird. It *was* a gift, like my dad always claimed.

It meant that someday I would be the counselor who cured a kid's homesickness. I probably wouldn't help anybody with their craft project because that would be a disaster and the kid would probably want to go home even more. But I would do something different to help.

I was like Scott. He had helped me again. I hadn't seen him for a year, and wouldn't see him again until I died and got to go to heaven, but Scott had shown me two things that changed my life: that elementary camp could be really fun if I gave it a chance and that being a compassionate person was something to hold on to, not something to try to change about myself.

Thank You, God, for Scott. And thank You for the gift of compassion. I think I know what it is now. Thank You that I got Kate and Steve for counselors instead of Noelle. And can You please tell Scott that I miss him and if the people in heaven can look at things on Earth, he should look at the craft cabin windows and think about me.

If they had that funeral now, I could have stood up in front of everyone and told them why I loved Scott and how we became friends. I could have *totally* done it now.

CHAPTER TWENTY-EIGHT

Favorite Camper

Most of the kids in our group got picked up to go home right away. Lindsay's mom came even before we had a chance to bring all of our suitcases and sleeping bags to the fire pit, which I was not ready for at all. I didn't think I would have to say goodbye to her so soon. We put our arms around each other and hugged for a long time. Then she hugged Car and said goodbye to Brenda and the other girls from her group.

"Don't forget," I said, as Lindsay turned around on her way out the cabin door and waved to us, her face looking like she was going to start crying as soon as she got into her car. "I've got a plan for next year. We'll be together all week long."

Lindsay smiled just a little with the very corners of her mouth and followed her mom out the door. The rest of us finished packing our things and carried them down to the fire pit. There's no way I could have gotten all of my things, but Kate helped me. She helped Teresa, too. Car said she didn't need help and then ended up dropping her sleeping bag and kicking it all the way down the hill.

The counselors were pretty busy for a while as parents came to pick up their kids and sign pieces of paper. The pieces of paper were very important. They have the same ones at junior high camp. Nobody can leave camp unless their parents sign the piece of paper. It's yellow and has a list of people the camper is allowed to leave with on it. If your parent doesn't sign it, the dean has to stay at camp and wait until you get home, and then he has to call your parents to make sure nobody kidnapped you. When this happens, the dean gets really mad. I know that from personal experience two summers ago at junior high camp when Holly Peterson forgot to get her form signed before she left, and we had to wait until she got all the way to Newberry and her parents answered the phone. That was not the best afternoon at camp.

Teresa left, and I saw Mason and Wade and their parents signing their yellow forms with Steve. The boys didn't come over to us to say goodbye. I wasn't especially broken up about that though. No offense, but I wouldn't really miss them a whole lot.

Things started to slow down after the first half hour or so, and the stream of traffic was much less crazy. Alana and Imogen got picked up by somebody in a blue mini-van. I watched them walk over to the van because I wanted to see what kind of parents would raise such snobby girls, and who do you think got out of the back of that blue van but Holly Peterson, the form-forgetter, herself. She hugged Imogen. I think they were sisters. Maybe Imogen would forget to have her forms signed, and Noelle would have to sit here until they got to Newberry.

More campers left, and Carin started brushing her hair with her fingers.

"What are you doing? We're just going to sit in the car for four hours," I reminded her.

"I'm going to give Dane my phone number," Car said. "That's what you do when you like a guy, and then he calls you and asks you out on a date."

"I don't think that's going to work."

"Watch."

First she went over to Kate and asked her for the pen she had been using for parents to sign their yellow sheets with. Then she trotted towards Dane and Steve, who were sitting on the bench by the campfire. Kate walked over to me and sat down in the grass.

"I have something to give you," she said, watching Carin. "But it's just for you. They didn't give out awards at the banquet, but some of us counselors got together and wrote this for you." She took something out from between her yellow papers and handed me a folded up note.

A special award just for me! I started to open the paper, but Kate put her hand over mine.

"We only did one for you, so don't open that until you're alone. I don't want anybody else to feel left out."

I think "anybody else" meant Car. I folded the note back up and put it in my pocket, but I didn't know how I was going to be able to wait four whole hours to look at it.

Kate was still watching Carin. "What's she doing?"

"Giving Dane her phone number."

"That's so cute," Kate said with a laugh.

"I think it's silly," I said. There's nobody else at camp I could say that to because Kate was the only one I trusted enough to never, ever, ever as long as she lived tell Car what I said. "I can't believe she thinks he will call her up for a date."

"Ab, every girl camper has a crush on a counselor or camp staff member." She gave me a sneaky look. "Don't you think any of these guys are cute?"

"Sure." I could feel my face turning red just at the thought of Steve's smile. "But I don't think they're going to want to date me or anything. I'm ten."

"You are a very practical kid. But most of us aren't."

I watched Car talk to Dane. She did a lot of moving her head around and flipping her hair and probably the eye batting that always makes her look like someone threw a handful of dirt in her face. He held his hand out, and she put her left hand under it and started writing something on his palm with Kate's pen.

"Did you have a crush on a counselor when you were our age?" I asked.

She raised her eyebrows at me. "If I tell you, it has to be a secret."

"Okay. I wouldn't tell anybody." I love, love, love secrets.

"When I was in elementary camp," she began, leaning close to me, "I wanted to marry Ben when I grew up."

"Oh, you should!" I exclaimed, forgetting about the secret part. "He's really nice."

"Hon, he's twenty-four, and I'm sixteen. That's not going to happen. And someday, Carin will realize the impracticality of her crush and rethink the potential of different romantic relationships."

"Huh?" That was a lot of big words for one sentence about Carin and boys.

"Sorry. She'll realize he's too old for her and find some boys her own age to flirt with."

"Oh."

But I don't think a week was long enough for Kate to get to know Carin enough to know that once Car got an idea in her head, it was impossible to change her mind.

We all hung out for a while, waiting for the rest of the parents to come. Steve and Julie and almost everybody else left. Car and I sat with Kate and Dane until Rachel came over to us and said she wanted to go home. Dane went to get the car out of the parking lot, and Rachel sat on the grass right between us.

"Don't go home until our parents get here," Car said.

Rachel shook her head. "I don't like long, sappy, yucky goodbyes with lots of hugs and crying." She made a face. "Yuck. It's better to just go."

That was weird. Everybody at camp ends the week with long, sappy, yucky goodbyes and lots of hugs and crying. Then again, Rachel isn't really the long-sappy- yucky-goodbye type of person.

"Next year we'll have to request to be in each other's cabins," I said.

"That would be awesome."

"You have to write to us," Carin said.

"And every time you drive by camp, you have to say hi to it for us," I said.

"I'm not doing that," Rachel said. "If I said hello to a camp, everybody in the car with me would think I was crazy."

I heard the crackling of tires on pebbles and looked up to see if it was my parents' van. It was a car, not a mini-van. Rachel stood up and grabbed her green and white duffle bag, and I realized it was Dane back with their car from the parking lot. They squeezed her things into the back seat that was already filled with Dane's stuff. Rachel got into the car and waved at us. That was it. No sappy, crying hug.

Dane was much better at saying goodbye. He hugged us and talked to us and promised again to come to camp forever. He hugged Kate a lot, too, and put his hands in her hair again. If she couldn't marry Ben someday, maybe she could marry Dane. They could have a big camp wedding like my mom and dad or Eva and Jason.

Part of Carin's phone number had already rubbed off of his hand, but I don't think Car noticed because if she had, I'm sure she would have written it on there again, probably with permanent marker. I had a feeling he wasn't going to call her. I think guys have better things to do at college than call their campers.

Dane got into his car and waved out the open window at us. Rachel sat there looking straight ahead. I guess she didn't want to look back and get sad or something. He honked the horn really loudly on his way out. It wasn't like a little "beep beep." This honk was more like, "Hooooooooo-nnnnnnnnnnnnnk!" It was funny and made us laugh.

Car and I sat on either side of Kate on the bench and watched for a while as more and more people left. All three of us cried. I was kind of glad Kate cried. Last year when I was sad about leaving, Eva had said, "It's okay. Nobody wants to leave camp." But she had smiled when she said it, so I didn't know if she was really sad about leaving or not. I knew Kate was.

There was nothing to do now but wait to go home. I wanted our van to never come up the hill because I wanted to stay at camp forever, but a smaller part of me was excited to see Angela, and the sooner we left camp, the sooner we'd get home, and then I could look at whatever was on that piece of paper Kate had given me.

Finally, the mini-van appeared, kicking out a cloud of dust from the pebbles and dirt on the path. Car and I looked at each other. It was time to go home.

***

Carin fell asleep shortly after our fast food lunch in The Big Town. I had already read my entire newsletter, so I unzipped the front flap of my duffle bag and took out the paper Kate had given to me. It was the first time that day I had had the chance to be alone. Well, I was with my parents, Angela, Carin's mom, Joey, and Car. But nobody was paying attention to what I was doing in the very back of the van.

I looked over at Car to make sure she was still asleep. Then I very carefully unfolded the piece of paper.

<u>Favorite Camper Award</u>

We hereby give the top-secret Favorite Camper Award to Abby Riley in honor of her sweet nature and the fact that she never gives any of the counselors any trouble and is just the <u>best kid we know</u>.

Dear Abby,

Thanks for being such a great camper. I was nervous about my first time counseling, but you made it easy. You are a sweet girl, and I'm glad you were my camper, one of my first campers ever. I will miss you very, very much.

Love,

Kate

Abby,

I wish I could tell you how much your thoughtfulness and prayers mean to me. You helped me a lot this week. Scott told me how cool you were last summer, and now I know for myself.

In Christ,

SJK

Dear Abby,

You are a fun kid! I'm glad I got to know you this week. My own campers were kinda lame, so I liked hanging out with you.

Kisses and lots of hugs,

Julie Hayes

Hey Squirt!

You're awesome! You're the best! We survived two years of elementary camp together and no bee stings for either of us this year. I'll have an even better ghost story for next year.

Love,

Dane

cunningd@warner.nh.edu Write me or else.

I read that piece of paper over and over. Favorite camper? Out of every single kid at camp, *I* was the favorite camper? That was pretty cool.

ABOUT THE AUTHOR

Jenifer Brady is an elementary camp expert, having been a camper, counselor, and even a dean. Some of her favorite things about camp include seeing old friends, watching (but not being in) skit night, and sitting around the campfire. She has even participated in campers verses counselors water balloon fights (although that was at junior high camp, of course!). She and her husband love camp so much that they got married in the chapel in August of 2000.

Jenifer is a 1997 graduate of Iron Mountain High School in Michigan's Upper Peninsula and a 2001 summa cum laude graduate of the University of Wisconsin—Green Bay. *Favorite Camper* is the second book in her series *Abby's Camp Days*. She has published two young adult novels also set at Camp Spirit, *Buddy Check* and *Super Counselors*. Visit www.jeniferbrady. com to read passages from future books in the *Abby's Camp Days* series, find out more about Jenifer Brady, learn how to order her other books, and have some camp fun.

About the Artist

June Westgate grew up in Monroe, Michigan. June graduated from Eastern Michigan University in 1973 with a degree in Art Education. She taught art and elementary education for five years. Following her teaching experience, she continued with her education at the Methodist School of Theology in Ohio, graduating with a Masters of Divinity degree in 1982. For the next twenty-five years she served as pastor at five local churches. She has now retired and lives in Howell, Michigan. This is her first book cover art. Although she enjoys drawing, her main interests are in pottery and fiber arts.

HERE'S A SNEAK PREVIEW FROM ABBY'S CAMP DAYS VOLUME 3: BOY-CRAZY CAMPERS

Carin broke the news to me in the van five miles out of Millers Creek. She held up an open magazine in front of our faces and spoke quietly to me from behind it so my parents couldn't hear what she was saying.

"This week at camp, I think we should go on an important mission."

"What do you mean?" I asked. You can't really leave camp except to go to Mount Spirit, and that's with the counselors. I don't know what kind of mission Car thought we could go on.

She looked over the magazine at my mom and dad. My parents had taken a couple of days vacation to bring us to camp and to visit Aunt Teri, who lives about a half an hour away from camp. Mom already had the summer off because she's a teacher, but Dad is a pastor, so he had to take a special vacation since it was Sunday and all.

Dad was singing off-key and tapping on the steering wheel in time to the Steven Curtis Chapman song that played on the radio. Mom was reading a book. I don't know how she could concentrate on what she was reading with my dad singing so badly next to her.

Car ducked back behind the magazine. "We need to find out about boys this week."

"What?" I exclaimed.

Dad looked at us in the mirror.

"Shh," Carin hissed.

"But, Car," I whispered. "I don't want to know about boys. I just started liking them last year."

"We are going to be in sixth grade in a few months," she said. "In sixth grade there are dances. I think we need to know about boys before we go to any dances."

"How are we supposed to find out about boys at camp?" I asked. "It's church camp, not dating camp."

"You know," she said, rolling her eyes. "Camp romances? Camp has lots of those. We can watch all the people who have camp romances."

"But there aren't very many camp romances at elementary camp," I pointed out. "Just the counselors sometimes."

Carin sighed and stopped smiling. I think I was ruining her excitement about camp and boys.

"Then we'll ask the counselors about boys," she said.

"Why don't we just ask my sister?" I asked. "Or Robin?"

Robin was Carin's baby-sitter. Car just this year stopped having to have a baby-sitter. I never had a baby-sitter before because my sister is so much older than me, so Angela was always in charge when Mom and Dad weren't home. Car had to have a baby-sitter for so long because she has a younger brother who had to be watched.

"We can't ask them!" Car whisper-shouted.

"Why not?"

"We don't want anybody we *know* to know we are finding out about boys. It's embarrassing."

"But we know the people at camp," I said.

"It's not the same. It's different knowing someone at camp and knowing someone at home. We might need to practice what we learn on the boys at camp. Like one thing I think we should learn about this week is how to flirt, and then we should practice flirting with the boys at camp. I think that would be easier than learning how to flirt with the boys at school."

I don't know why, but I agreed with her. I guess if we had to find out about boys, I'd rather do it at camp than at home. At home, there was always a chance that someone from your class at school could see or hear you.

At least at camp if we made fools out of ourselves learning about boys, nobody from Millers Creek would know about it unless someone from camp moved to Millers Creek, but that would never happen because our town is in Wisconsin and camp is in Michigan. It's very rare to see someone from camp in the real world. Once we saw Blane Adams at a fast food restaurant in Escanaba, and at first I didn't even recognize him. I'd only ever known him as a counselor at junior high camp. It was weird to see him ordering a burger and fries.

"Okay. I guess that's an okay idea."

"Okay?" she asked. "*Okay?* It's a fabulous, wonderful, perfect idea!"

I didn't know about that. Car is outgoing, but I'm usually shy. The idea of flirting with boys did not sound so good to me. But Car had a point. It would be a lot easier to flirt with boys at camp than at school. If I had to learn about boys sometime, I guess this was the best week to do that.

The rest of the ride to camp, I felt queasy. I've never been carsick before, so it couldn't have been that. Camp is a safe, fun place. But not if you have to flirt with boys there. That made me nervous.

Last year, I worried on the ride to camp because I thought I wouldn't know anybody, like maybe all my friends wouldn't come back. I knew that Lindsay was going to be there this year because we wrote to each other about it all the time, and my counselor Kate had written to me saying she was going to be there and Steve probably, too, if he could get time off from his summer job.

I hadn't heard from Dane since January when he sent me a late Christmas card, but I knew he'd be there. Last summer he promised me that he would always come to camp as long as it was fun. That's kind of a joke because camp is *always* fun, so that means he'll always be at camp. He promised me that because I was upset about our other counselor, Eva, not coming back.

Nope. I wasn't worried about not knowing anybody this year. I felt like I was going to puke because I was scared of having to learn about boys.